Praise for *The D*

"Claire Kilroy is brave—and taler
stab at portraying the kind of Irela
Celtic Tiger. . . . Put[s] one in minc
edies. . . . *The Devil I Know* is well written and fun."

—*Vincent Boland, Financial Times (UK)*

"A perversely entertaining show of how easily men are corrupted by wealth . . . [Kilroy's] prose flows irresistibly from page to page . . . A pleasure to read."

—Nick Brodie, *Time Out* (UK)

"Kilroy takes delight in literary allusions and diabolical puns, but despite the humor there's real fury in her portrayal of the casual greed, corruption, and willful delusion that pervaded society 'like the pox, creating a belief in a kind of modern alchemy.'"

—Amber Pearson, *Daily Mail* (UK)

"*The Devil I Know* is about as black a depiction of Ireland in its crazed Celtic Tiger heyday as you could imagine. Feelingly, elegantly written, it exerts the ever-tightening grip of a thriller. . . . An elegy to an Ireland despoiled and betrayed by those who led it into financial ruin, it is also a cautionary tale of the depths to which unbridled greed can take you . . . [with] the frisson and magnetic force of a compelling and dangerously unreliable narrator. . . . [A] searing, savage novel. Kilroy . . . is flinty sharp in her observations about her country and those who sold it short."

—Rosemary Goring, *Herald Scotland* (UK)

"One of Ireland's best young novelists . . . Ambitious, satirical, and Gothic."

—Sue Leonard, *Irish Examiner* (UK)

"*The Devil I Know* focuses on the Irish property boom (and bust) and is, therefore, a tale of our time: a story of lavish greed and selfishness; soullessness and economic devastation. . . . It would be deeply depressing without Claire Kilroy's joyously mad prose. Her writing hops over the darkness in lively, lyrical, sometimes vitriolic leaps."

—Lucy Atkins, *Sunday Times* (UK)

"A well-paced and well told cautionary tale, a page-turner with lots of droll moments as the author skewers the moral mindset that both created the Celtic Tiger and then brought it to its knees."

—John Boland, *Irish Independent* (UK)

"Kilroy's almost exclusively male cast is well etched, and she has a dead eye for shriveling detail and truth-telling."

—Christina Hunt Mahony, *Irish Times* (UK)

"*The Devil I Know* is a public novel, even a political novel, about how Ireland went from hyperventilating affluence to agog beggary . . . Kilroy provides some of the most stunningly sly and wry writing being offered at the moment. One moment she is lyrical . . . The next she is brilliantly satirical."

—Stuart Kelly, *Scotland on Sunday* (UK)

"*The Devil I Know* may be the best book you have ever read about Ireland's property bubble . . . whip-smart, funny, and angry, this is a triumph."

—*Hot Press* (UK)

"Kilroy's strength lies in evoking emotional states. . . . linguistic inventiveness . . . [she reveals] a simple but profound truth."

—Lilian Pizzichini, author of *The Blue Hour*

"A riveting and brilliantly unnerving book. To read it is to be plunged right into the madness and obscenity of what has been done to Ireland—or what Ireland has done to itself. People wanted the boom-to-bust novel; well, here it is."

—Belinda McKeon, author of *Solace*

"A riot of energy and enjoyment . . . I must confess to a sense of dread when I see that a book breaks the 350-page barrier, but this one went down like—well, like the Irish economy."

—John Self, *The Asylum* (UK)

"*The Devil I Know* perfectly captures the madness and chaos that gripped Ireland during the boom years. Indeed, that madness and chaos becomes Beckett-like towards the end of the novel, which descends into a kind of crazy magic realism. . . . Rife with puns, wordplay, and Irish literary references—great fun."

—Kim Bofo, *Reading Matters*

THE DEVIL I KNOW

by the same author

All Summer
Tenderwire
All Names Have Been Changed

THE DEVIL I KNOW

A NOVEL

CLAIRE KILROY

Black Cat
New York

This edition first published in Great Britain in 2012 by Faber and Faber Limited

Printed in the United States of America
Published simultaneously in Canada

ISBN 978-0-8021-2237-7
eISBN 978-0-8021-9269-1

Black Cat
an imprint of Grove Atlantic
154 West 14th Street
New York, NY 10011

Distributed by Publishers Group West

groveatlantic.com

In memory of John Long, 1944–2010

riverrun, past Eve and Adam's, from swerve of shore to bend of bay, brings us by a commodius vicus of recirculation back to Howth Castle and Environs.

Sir Tristram, violer d'amores, fr'over the short sea, had passencore rearrived from North Armorica on this side the scraggy isthmus of Europe Minor to wielderfight his penisolate war:

James Joyce, *Finnegans Wake*

First day of evidence

10 MARCH 2016

‘Please state your name for the record.’

Don't be coy, Fergus. You've known me since I was yay high. I beg your pardon? Oh. It's like that, is it? I see. Very well. As you wish. This is going to take longer than expected, but then, you lot are running on a pricey meter. Two and a half grand a day, I hear. Well, Fergus – I mean Justice O'Reilly – my name, for the record, is Tristram St Lawrence. Tristram Amory St Lawrence, the thirteenth Earl of Howth, *Binn Eadair*, hill of sweetness. I was – I am – the only son your old pal, the twelfth Earl of Howth, managed to sire, and not from lack of trying. People have been saying a lot of bad things about me in the press. I am here to say a few more.

What brought me back to Ireland? Good question. An act of God, or maybe the other fella. That was back in 2006. I had not set foot on this green isle for twelve years. I agree, Fergus: it is a long time in the lifespan of a comparatively young man, particularly one with such ties to the locality. Personal reasons kept me away. Personal, personal, unspeakably personal. This is neither the time nor the place.

I was en route from a conference in Birmingham to one in Florida. That is how I used to spend my life, travelling from one point on the globe to another, keeping my nose clean. As you are probably aware, I am by profession an interpreter. I was engaged in that capacity by large international institutions such as the IMF, the EU and the ECB. The Troika. I do all the major European languages.

No, I cannot tell you what the Birmingham conference was about and not because the subject matter was commercially sensitive, but since I am unable to recall a word of what has been said once the sessions are called to a close, such is the level of concentration translation demands of me. The interpreter is the medium through which other people's thoughts and arguments pass. The key is not to engage with those thoughts and arguments. If you allow them to capture your curiosity for even a fraction of a second, you will lose the next sentence. And then you're in trouble. The whole thing backs up. One must hollow oneself out. One must make of oneself the perfect conduit. This is a trick I have mastered.

It used to drive Hickey mental when M. Deauville and I conversed in what he called foreign – it was second nature to me to respond to M. Deauville in his language *du jour*, which depended on what part of the world he was calling from, for he travelled constantly too. Hickey thought I was concealing something from him and generally I was, just as generally he was concealing something from me. In short, I was recognised as the best at what I do, and had I spent the rest of my life on the international conference circuit, I would not be before you giving evidence today. They said my gift was uncanny. That was the word my clients used in their various mother tongues. *Étrange*, *unheimlich*, uncanny. Sometimes I thought they intended it as a compliment, but other times I wasn't so sure.

M. Deauville? No, he wasn't my employer, as such. And no, I wouldn't describe him as a colleague either. He was more what you'd call a consultant. And we all know who Hickey is.

The plane was not long in the sky after take-off from Birmingham. The cabin crew had commenced their in-flight service, that is to say, an air hostess was reversing a leaden trolley down the aisle. 'A drink, sir?' she enquired when she reached me.

I smiled sadly. 'No, thanks. I'll have a cup of tea, please.' I released the catch of my tray table and lowered it into position.

I was sitting in the window seat. The flight was full. A mother and son occupied the two seats next to me, the mother in the middle seat and the boy on the aisle. He kicked the back of the chair in front of him as he played his computer game, just as someone was kicking the back of mine. The stewardess leaned across to pass me tea in a plastic cup. I added two capsules of hydrogenated milk and looked at it. The water hadn't been boiled. There are moments when I lose heart in the whole endeavour. That was one of them. Strapped into a bucking chair for the next seven hours, contemplating that cup of grey tea. A limescale scum was forming on the surface. I put the cup down and set my watch to Eastern Standard Time.

Then the tea blew up. It erupted out of the cup into my face. A scream of fright from the other passengers – the plane had taken a hit.

I gripped both armrests. The impact was followed by a blast of freezing air. I turned to glimpse a fracture in the plastic casing of the ceiling. A shard of metal had punctured the cabin. The gash was spurting electrical cables and frills of silver foil.

The plane began to shake violently. Several of the overhead bins sprang open, disgorging cabin luggage onto the aisle. The oxygen masks dropped, a dangling yellow crop of them, swinging and jerking in synchronisation. Hands reached up to pluck them like fruit, so I plucked mine and strapped it onto my face. Through the window, I saw that the engine was on fire. The pain in my ears was excruciating.

The plane entered a nose dive, juddering with such force that I thought our seats would come unbolted. It kicked to the side and the drinks trolley went lunging in the direction of the cockpit. The stewardess went lunging after it, swinging from headrest to headrest to keep herself upright. Beneath the flaming engine, the lights of a city had appeared in the darkness.

The captain said something on the intercom but we couldn't hear him over the noise. I pulled my mobile phone out of my pocket. It was switched off and I couldn't remember which button switched it on. I literally could not begin to make sense of the digits. The city beneath us was rapidly approaching. I made out the grid of roads. This is it, I thought. To hell with it. I peeled the rubber mask off my face and released the seat belt. I squeezed past the mother and son and went lurching down the aisle, tripping over the fallen hand luggage.

'Get into your seat, sir!' a stewardess shouted at me when I made it to the front. 'Get back into your seat immediately, sir!' Then the cabin lights went out.

I followed the emergency strip lighting and located the trolley. It had been locked down. The first drawer was crammed with miniature cans of soft drinks. I had to shove it shut to get at the contents of the next one down. 'Sir, get into your seat,' the flight attendant shouted from the jump seat. 'We are preparing for an emergency landing. Get into your *motherfucking seat now.*' It was an American carrier.

The nose of the plane lifted. We were horizontal once more. 'Brace for impact,' the captain shouted, loud enough that we could hear him this time. The third drawer down contained the hard stuff, tiny bottles of spirits, a casket of priceless jewels. I grabbed an amber one. My hands were shaking so hard that I could barely break the foil seal.

The collision with the ground catapulted me clear of the trolley. The groan of brakes was catastrophically loud and then the thrust reversers kicked in. It seemed the earth itself was grinding to a halt, such was the force of the resistance. The cells in my blood vibrated, the teeth chattered in my head.

The plane finally came to rest. Somebody applauded but no one joined in. The bottle of precious amber had shot out of my sweaty palm. I rolled onto my belly and groped around on the floor but in my heart I knew it was already too late.

'Leave the aircraft, leave the aircraft,' the captain was chanting.

We were evacuated via emergency slides. A fleet of fire trucks had assembled on the runway to hose down the burning engine. Firemen hoisted us off the base of the slide and sent us reeling towards the flashing lights and coaches waiting beyond. 'Keep moving, keep moving,' they ordered us as we were hustled along. A sign over the terminal building shone yellow in the distance. *Dublin Airport*, it said.

'Are you hurt?' M. Deauville wanted to know as soon as I got the phone up and running. It rang literally the instant it located a network. He must have had my number on redial. I could barely hold the phone to my ear with the shake in my hand. Our emergency landing had made it onto the news – the television screens in the terminal were broadcasting images of the flaming aircraft. They said it was an emergency landing but it felt like a crash. Journalists were interviewing passengers behind me. 'No,' I assured M. Deauville, 'I amn't hurt, but I . . .'

'Yes?'

I thought about the amber bottle. I couldn't stop thinking about the amber bottle. The cool heft of it in my hand, the tiny pocket of sanctuary it promised. If I could just squeeze myself into the amber bottle and screw the lid back on, seal myself off. 'I think I'm in shock,' I told M. Deauville, 'but it's nothing physical.' Actually, I'd broken a rib and deserved as much. There was no need to fuss.

Several passengers were taken to hospital with minor injuries and the rest of us were transferred to an airport hotel. It was a miracle, people remarked to each other over and over on the coach; a flock of worried sheep. A miracle, an absolute miracle, they bleated, until soon I was bleating it myself. Then I was on my own again, separated from the herd. The elevator bell *dinged* and I limped out onto a hushed hotel corridor hugging my aching side. I stared at the arrows on the wall. Bedrooms 600 to 621 were this way, and bedrooms 622 to 666 were that. I read the number on my key but for the life of me, I did not know which way to turn.

'Mr St Lawrence, you claim your stopover in Dublin was unscheduled, yet the next day you attended a business meeting in the airport Hilton with the property developer Desmond Hickey?'

It is true that I ran into Desmond Hickey the following day in the Darndale Hilton, as he asserts, but to call it a meeting is to grossly overstate the occasion. It was a wholly chance encounter. I came down late the following afternoon to enquire after the whereabouts of my luggage when this total stranger accosted me.

'I thought you were dead,' he said.

I didn't recognise him, but then, how would I? He could have been anyone under that balaclava of facial hair. 'None of the passengers were seriously injured,' I assured him.

'Wha?'

'I know. Absolute miracle.'

'You were on that plane last night? The one that shat itself?'

'Ahm.' I checked my watch. 'Why else would I be dead?'

The receptionist put down her phone. 'I'm sorry, Mr St Lawrence. The airline still hasn't located your luggage.'

'You *are* him,' said the hairy man.

'I see,' I said to the receptionist and thanked her.

'You're Tristram St Lawrence,' he said as if outing a thief.

'I'm sorry, can I help you?'

The man frowned. 'But you're dead?'

'That was another Tristram St Lawrence.'

He looked at me askance. How could there be two of us? Two men with a name as uncommon as that? 'Another Tristram St Lawrence,' he repeated dubiously, unconvinced by this explanation of a death-evading trick.

'I don't quite seem to have caught your name, Mr . . . ?'

He winked. 'Ah, you know me.' I looked at him blankly. He winked again. 'Ah, you do.'

I took out my phone and frowned at the screen. Force of habit. When in doubt, I consulted M. Deauville. No new calls. Even M. Deauville had to sleep, whatever time zone he was in. I replaced the phone in my pocket and returned my attention to the stocky man. 'I'm afraid I don't seem to—'

'Don't tell me you've forgotten your oul pal.'

'Well, I . . .'

Then he laughed and it was the laugh that did it. Watching him laugh at me triggered a memory of him laughing at me many moons ago. It was the act of ridicule that I recognised, the utter freedom he felt in expressing it, and my utter powerlessness in having to listen to it. This man was never my oul pal.

He put his hands on his hips when he was finished. 'Are you seriously telling me, Tristram, that you don't recognise me? Because I sure as hell recognise you.'

'I remember you now. We were in primary school together.'

'That's it! You have me. The little school.' He thrust out his hand and gripped mine. 'Jaysus, your hands are freezing. Dessie Hickey.' Gick. Gicky Hickey. He looked fiercely into my eyes – we might have been making history. He had dispensed those same intense handshakes even back in the playground. Trying to be everything his unemployed father was not, I suppose, and who could blame him? 'You were me best customer before you, eh, disappeared . . .'

I released his hand. 'I beg your pardon?'

'Ah, relax. I don't deal any more.'

'I have no idea what you're referring to.' I checked my phone. Nothing.

'Here, I'm on me way out to the hill. Come on out an celebrate.' He produced a set of car keys and tossed them up and down in the palm of his hand, a purse of gold with which to tempt me.

'Celebrate what?'

'That you're not dead.'

'I've to fly to the States tonight.'

'Tonight is ages away. What are you doing between now an then?'

'—'

'Too slow. I'll drive you to the airport meself. I'll show you the hill an then drop you off at Departures. Can't say fairer than that. There are a few people who'd love to see you. Come on.'

I looked at my watch and made a production of sighing to illustrate that the bargain he drove was a hard one, although the truth of it was that I had nothing better to do. I had lost my luggage and missed the Florida conference. 'Go on,' I said ruefully, as if acting against my better judgement, which I suppose I was, but I am a weak man. That is why I needed M. Deauville.

Hickey loaded me into his labourer's truck along with the rest of the junk he'd accumulated – Coke cans and crisp packets, chocolate wrappers and Lotto tickets, rolled-up *Daily Stars*. He cleared the passenger seat of debris with a swipe of his hand. I climbed in and looked over my shoulder through a filthy pane of glass. The truck's flatbed was stocked with tools – a spade, a ladder, a wheelbarrow, a variety of hammers and planks. A sack of grit slumped in the corner like a dozing drunk. I reached for my seat belt. Glued to the dashboard was a plastic figurine of St Christopher.

Hickey maintained a taxi-driver patter for the duration of the journey through the early evening traffic. Howaya getting on abroad, Tristram? You keeping well? An your da? How's your da? Desperate business about your ma, poor woman. Ah, we were all very sorry down the town to see her go. She was well liked, so she was. Thought we might see you at the funeral but they said you were too busy . . . ? Then a course we all heard you were dead. Must be some job to keep you away from your own ma's funeral . . . ? I heard you were high up in the world of international finance . . . ?

At this, I turned my head. 'Who told you that?'

Hickey smirked. 'A little bird.'

I rolled down the window to get some air. I hated little birds.

'Almost there,' he reassured me in case I hadn't been born in Howth. In case my father's father's father's father's, etc., hadn't been born in Howth. Who did he think I was? Some blow-in?

The truck ascended past ponied meadows and heathered slopes until the road crested and Dublin Bay appeared below, broad and smooth and greyish blue, patrolled by the Baily lighthouse. The whitethorn was in full blossom and the ferns were pushing through. Better to have been born somewhere dismal, I sometimes think. Better to have grown up shielded from striking natural beauty, to have never caught that glimpse of Paradise in the first place only to find yourself sentenced to spending the rest of your life pining for it, a tenderised hole right in the heart of you, a hole so big that it seems at times you're no more than the flesh defining it. I rolled the window up to seal the beauty out.

The road got steeper. I swallowed and my ears popped. He's taking me to the Summit Inn, I realised, and the fact of his taking me, of my being brought, a passenger in another man's car, lessened the degree of my culpability in the enterprise. I touched the mobile phone in my pocket. M. Deauville would not approve. But M. Deauville need not know.

'Here we are,' Hickey announced as the road levelled out. Here we certainly were. The picnic tables outside the pub were packed with sunglassed drinkers – bare-shouldered girls with ponytails and boys in rugby shirts. Silky spaniels and retrievers lay at their feet panting along with the jokes. A younger crowd had come up, but apart from that it was all the same, right down to the sparrows flitting for crumbs across the sun-baked flagstones, going about their business as if nothing had changed. And for a moment, nothing had. The sun and the sea, the harbour and the islands, the horses and the gorses, the beer and the fear of the beer. Not a precious thing had changed.

Hickey cruised past while I observed the drinkers through the window, creatures in a different element, an aquarium. For a full year, I had lived my life on the covert side of a two-way mirror, screened from the ordinary souls, quarantined from their reality, studying the line-up on the other side, the blessed, unaware that they were blessed. They made life look so very easy when it was so very hard.

Hickey parked on double yellow lines and wrenched up the handbrake. I sat tight. He pocketed his mobile phone and extracted the keys from the ignition. I didn't budge. He reached for the handle of the door. 'Don't,' I urged him.

He retracted his hand. 'What's the problem?'

'Sorry. Just give me a moment.'

But Hickey never gave me anything. 'For wha?'

I lowered my head. I didn't know.

Hickey pulled the lever and broke the hermetic seal. The glorious smell of stout came flooding into the cabin, pricking my tear ducts and nostrils. If adventure has a smell, if promise has a smell, if youth has a smell, it is that of beer in the sun.

Hickey got out and stood on the road. 'Are you coming or wha?' I consulted my watch, from habit as opposed to checking the time – it is one of the many gestures I have developed or, rather, adopted, that make me question whether I know myself, or whether I even *am* myself, and not some studied automaton copied from some other studied automaton, ad infinitum with nothing at the centre. I consulted my watch and it said that the time was early summer and that I was a boy of eighteen again, no damage done.

'Just the one,' I heard myself saying.

I climbed out of the truck and let the sunlight wash over me. Irish light in May, the magic month. The whitewashed façade of the Summit blazed in the evening sun and the stone walls radiated waves of heat. I should have been looking down on the peninsula from a height, gazing at its nubbled coastline from the window seat of a plane, but I wasn't. I was standing right in the thick of it. It was up to my neck.

'Just the one, though,' I warned Hickey, and my lips could all but taste that pint. I licked them and gulped down air with the thirst – these are not mannerisms I picked up from others, but ones that are so inherently, ineluctably mine that it is my life's work to break their hold on me. 'Just the one, though, Dessie, just the one,' I protested as I stumped along, though Hickey never paid my misgivings the slightest heed. Let's get that on the record now.

Gaffney's was cool and dark after the sunny esplanade of picnic tables, like going below deck on a ship. I stood there blinking as my eyes adjusted to the light. Polished wood, glinting optics, gleaming brass, the captain's table. It was exactly how I remembered it. My past life had been razed so comprehensively that I had presumed to find its components razed too. I checked my phone to get my bearings. It was all getting a bit much.

Hickey took up position at the bar, anchoring himself against it by an elbow. 'What are you drinking?' he called over his shoulder, fishing a roll of notes out of his trousers.

'I'll have a sparkling mineral water, thanks.'

'A drink, man, a drink.' He peeled off a twenty and slapped it on the bar, then returned the money roll to his pocket, adjusting its position in his trousers as if it were his penis, which in a way it was.

'That is a drink,' I told him coldly.

Hickey removed his elbow from the counter and stood to attention. A grey-haired man had entered through the door behind the bar and was taking stock of the premises in a proprietorial fashion. He drew up sharply when his eyes alighted on me. I should never have come here, I realised then. I should never have darkened this door.

'Look who I found,' said Hickey.

Christy Gaffney stood frozen rigid, a man who had seen a ghost. Hickey faltered. 'It's Tristram,' he clarified, though Christy knew perfectly well who I was. 'Tristram from the castle,' Hickey prompted him, though there could hardly have been two of us on the hill with that name. Christy took hold of his polished wooden countertop and leaned across the bar to inspect me. His eyes roamed over my features for a good thirty seconds, an expression of the utmost gravity on his face.

'Is that who I think it is?' he finally asked and I nodded. He assessed me a moment longer, then the hand was extended across the bar. I grasped it and we shook solemnly, man to man. 'Christ, son, your hands are freezing.'

He shook his head in disbelief at the fact of my presence, as confounded by the sight of me as I had been by the sight of the pub. How was it all still standing? How were we all still here? Where did damage register, if not in people and in places? 'I thought you were dead, Tristram,' Christy confided, and looked around the lounge to see if his amazement was shared, but no one else had noticed yet that something was amiss. 'Everyone thinks you're dead, son, I may as well tell you now.'

The three of us laughed as if this were a punchline. Nerves, I suppose. For a moment, I felt tearful. Tearful that Christy should have been sufficiently affected by the news of my death to remember it a full year on. I had presumed that my so-called passing had gone unnoticed by everyone. Other than my mother, that is. 'Tristram,' she had gasped down the line, 'the Guards told me you were dead!' 'That was another Tristram St Lawrence,' I reassured her, and said it again when she didn't respond – there was just the white noise of a long-distance call travelling across a mobile network with a broken connection. I was talking into the void.

'A pint,' Christy declared, and selected a glass which he held to the light streaming through the stained-glass window for a benediction before tilting it under the tap.

'Ah no,' I declined, and Christy made a swatting gesture to indicate that he would brook no refusal. Christy knew what the spirit ached for and how to minister to its needs. All men stood equal before him in their thirst, from the heir to the estate to the layabout's son. Hickey pushed his twenty across the counter. 'Put your money away,' Christy instructed him, and set a second pint on the go with his name on it, followed by a third for himself.

'They're all coming back to us, the wandering souls,' he observed as he returned to my pint and eased more stout into the glass. Two-thirds full now – the tension. 'From New York, London, Saudi Arabia, what have you. The wives go there on shopping holidays now. Isn't that right, Tristram?' He raised an eyebrow in my direction without removing his attention from the task at hand, a pro. I nodded avidly: that's right, Christy. Shopping holidays. I'd have agreed with anything by then.

'Buy the fucken places up these days, don't we?' said Hickey.

'True enough,' Christy conceded. 'But you won't find a good pint in Dubai. You won't find the like of that.' He selected a beer mat and set my pint upon it with the pride of a master craftsman. 'Now,' he said with satisfaction. We fell quiet to consider the voluptuous curve of the glass.

Christy reached for a second beer mat and placed Hickey's pint beside mine. 'You're looking well all the same, Tristram,' he said as he topped up the final glass.

'For a dead man,' said Hickey.

Christy knocked off the tap. 'Don't mind that fella.' Another beer mat; Christy's pint completed the trio, racked in a triangle like snooker balls. The game was about to begin.

We waited for the tumult within the glasses to settle, the chaos that miraculously resolves itself into a well of black topped by a head of cream – a trick, a cruel trick – it never resolves, but lapses back into chaos the second you swallow it. A chaos so calamitous that you don't know where to turn to escape it, but by then it is too late. The chaos is inside you. That is the nature of a pint.

I reached out to lay claim to the one nearest me. I rotated it on the beer mat, admiring its splendour from every angle. That pint was immaculate. Christy had outdone himself. I nodded my appreciation.

Christy raised his glass. 'To the returned son.' Hickey raised his glass and I lifted mine. A shake in my hand betrayed me. The two men glanced at each other. This was how they found me. Exactly as they had left me. A trembling wreck.

We clinked the bellies of our charges together. The stout was dense and the clunk was dull. A swell of cream spilled over the lip and coated my knuckles. It took every fibre of my being not to stoop to lick that cream away. I hadn't fallen yet.

The other two sank their pints a third down in one go but I remained contemplating mine with an outstretched arm. My universe at that point in time had contracted to myself and that pint. We were a closed energy system.

'I've been away a long time,' I told the pint.

'You have indeed,' Christy agreed.

'No wonder we thought you were dead,' said Hickey.

The pint was cool and pure, tranquil as the moon. How patiently she had waited for me, knowing all along that I would come back to her, that sooner or later I would return. It was only a question of time.

Hickey was trying to get me to recount for Christy's amusement the part he maintained I'd played in setting a Cortina on fire. I didn't know what he was talking about. You *do* know, you *do* know, he kept insisting, pulling exasperated faces at Christy, and it occurred to me that if Christy wasn't there, if the pub were empty and Hickey had me to himself, he'd have taken hold of the collar of my shirt and belted a confession out of me, for that is how D. Hickey did business. That is how he did business with me.

'Ah, would you let the man enjoy his pint in peace, for the love of God,' Christy interceded. 'Sure look: he hasn't even touched it yet.'

We all looked at my untouched pint and I brought it closer to my lips. I had never felt so pared down before, stripped so keenly to my basest elements. My darkest depths were contained in that vessel, a chalice I had crossed the earth to evade, pinballing from one hemisphere to the other, from one continent to the next, in the hope that if I kept moving it would not catch up with me, but now here it was, pressed like a coin into my hand by those who knew me, those who had known me as a child. This was it. This was what I was. A cubic pint of deepest black. I was holding my soul, distilled into liquid and aching to be reunited with my body, howling to be poured back in. I brought the glass closer again. I knew this would happen. I wanted this to happen. I still want it to happen. I always will.

My mobile phone rang. I put down the pint. *Unknown* read the screen.

'Yes, M. Deauville?' I called him Monsieur and he pronounced the Saint in my name as San, though generally he just called me Tristram. Hickey flicked the tip of his eager tongue over his moustache of foam and tried to earwig. I turned my back and retreated to a quiet corner.

'No, M. Deauville. I'm, ahm ... I'm still in Dublin. I'm waiting for, ahm ... for my luggage.' I checked my watch again – habit, habit. I didn't give a damn about the time.

'You mean, this minute?' I looked around the pub. 'This minute, I'm in the Summit.'

I lowered my head. 'Yes,' I admitted, 'that is the name of a bar.'

I listened to him touch-typing on his keyboard, *tocka tocka, tocka tocka*. He was seated at his control panel watching his monitors, firing off instructions from his executive chair. That is how I pictured M. Deauville. A face illuminated blue by a bank of computer screens.

Tocka tocka. 'The Church of Ireland hall? Yes, I think I know which one that is.' So many churches on our little peninsula. So many shots in the dark at salvation.

'Do, please, yes,' I said to his offer to book me a taxi.

Tocka tocka. 'Five minutes?' I checked my watch and only then registered that it was still set to Eastern Standard Time. 'Perfect. I'll be waiting outside.' 'Thank you,' I added as the sheer gravity of the episode began to sink in. I had almost fallen and there was so very far to fall. M. Deauville had plucked me from the jaws of Hell. Again. Relief was followed by euphoria. 'Thank you, M. Deauville. Thank you so—' but he had already hung up.

I turned back to Hickey. He was alone now and perched sullenly on a bar stool. I returned the phone to my jacket pocket and offered him my hand. 'Good seeing you again, Mr Hickey, but I'm afraid I must leave immediately. I have to take an important conference call.'

Hickey looked at my hand without accepting it. 'It's five to eight on a Friday evening,' he pointed out flatly.

I withdrew my hand. 'Not in New York, it isn't.' I raised a palm in farewell to Christy and headed for the exit. Hickey sighed and laboured off the bar stool. I pushed the door open onto rose sunlight. A yacht race was disappearing around the back of Ireland's Eye and fishing boats were setting out for the night catch. Hickey joined me on the top step, a fresh pint in his paw, no doubt the one I'd put back on the counter. He kept his eyes on the view as he spoke.

'I have something to show you,' he muttered out of the side of his mouth. That was Hickey's idea of discretion: act as suspiciously as possible. 'A business proposition,' he added when I didn't bite.

I smiled perfunctorily. 'Next time, Dessie.' He made eye contact then. Both of us knew there would be no next time.

A taxi drew up at the gate piers. Every order issued by M. Deauville was carried out to the letter. That's what money does. I picked my way across the sprawled dogs and opened the door to the back seat. 'St Lawrence?' The driver nodded.

I sat in and turned to reach for the handle. A hand held the door rigid. I looked up. Hickey was standing on the kerb.

'Tristram, you're a fucken dry shite,' he said before slamming the door shut. That's me, I agreed grimly as the taxi pulled away. I fixed my eyes on the road ahead and did not look back at the Summit. That's me, yes, that's who I am now and let no one forget it, least of all myself. I am Tristram the Fucken Dry Shite, Thirteenth Earl of Howth.

The taxi smelled not of youth and beer and summer, but artificial pine. I was sealed into the sterile safety of a moving body once more – M. Deauville had seen to it. I jammed my fist into my mouth and tasted the pint. I suckled the knuckle the stout had doused, the taxi driver eyeing me in the rear-view mirror all the while as we retreated back down to the bottom.

*

A brief note on how that episode ended, if I may. It ended as my episodes all end. As they all must end if I am to keep body and soul together. It ended in the circle.

The bottom of the hill was already in shadow. I had been banished from the realm of the gods. I kept my eyes averted as we passed the entrance to the grounds of the castle and continued on to the church hall.

We are drawn to churches. All those passions and redemptions and casting out of demons – you can see the attraction. The taxi dropped me off at the gates, the fare, as ever, taken care of by M. Deauville. I never carry cash. I never have to. I barely interact with this world. I am barely here. The driver departed, leaving me standing alone by the pillar. A breeze was blowing in from Claremont Beach, evocative beyond description, not air but the essence of my past, the medium in which it is preserved.

The church gates were open but no lights burned. I checked my watch. Five past three, which meant it was five past eight. Had I the right hall? The car park was empty. Nothing unusual per se about that. We like to keep our gatherings discreet, and who can blame us? So we park down side streets or around corners and slip out individually after the meetings to go our separate ways, feigning that we don't know each other although we know one another intimately. At least one of our number is here.

The hall porch was in darkness. I tried the door. It was locked. This did not unduly discourage me. There are generally a few precautions in place to prevent strangers from accidentally wandering in. I listened for voices and heard them, muffled and subdued. I walked around the side and sure enough, light was glowing through the fanlight over the back door. I'd found them.

I raised the latch and pushed open the door. The people huddled in the circle sat up at my intrusion. I approached to show myself, to reassure them that I was okay, that I was one of them and not some straying parishioner. I made the meek face, smiled the apologetic smile, and the meek apologetic smile was returned in kind, distinct as a Masonic handshake. We are all the same. Wherever you go, no matter what country or class or creed you belong to – or don't belong to – we are all the same.

The man chairing the meeting stood up and unhitched an extra seat from the stack in the corner. 'We were just about to begin,' he said, carrying the chair into the circle. It was a small meeting. Six men and one woman. One damaged woman. Young and attractive but no good to us. By virtue of her presence there, we could never have been interested in her. Nor she in us. Let's not kid ourselves, lads.

The exchange of meek smiles continued, the nods of welcome and recognition – I had never been to that place in my life, never met those people, yet they recognised me as piercingly as I recognised them. We recognised each other's nature. You as well? their eyes asked, and I did the sheepish smile, the afraid-so shrug. Yes, me as well.

Down at the back on a trestle table, the tin of plain biscuits and the Burco boiler presided, the bag of white sugar congested into boulders by spilled droplets of tea, the mismatched mugs that smelled of Milton fluid, the stained teaspoons and carton of milk. Those items were our guardian angels, offering whatever homely consolation could be hoped for under the circumstances. They would never hit the spot. The Burco geared up to boiling point and simmered down, geared up to boiling point again and simmered down, dreary as windscreen wipers.

'Any anniversaries?' the chairman enquired after the prayer.

I stood up. 'Hi, my name's Tristram and I'm an alcoholic.'

'Hi Tristram,' they said in unison. Hi Tristram, fellow prisoner, fellow lifer, you're an alcoholic.

The blood was raging inside my skull, crashing like waves against rocks. My mobile phone was in my breast pocket, next to my heart. I touched it briefly for reassurance before clearing my throat to speak. 'It is one year since my last drink.'

The circle clapped as I stood there in disgrace. An act of supreme paradox, applauding my shame. My face burned and I sat back down.

*

Night had fallen by the time the meeting was called to a close. I stood on the kerb and waited for a taxi. None arrived. I checked my phone. No missed calls. No instructions from M. Deauville. I had missed the late flight.

I gave it another twenty minutes before making my way to the ribbed stone columns of the castle entrance for the first time in twelve years. The street lights ended at the public road and the avenue beyond lay in darkness. It was not how I had envisaged my return.

An outbreak of barking erupted from the gate lodge. A small white form came barrelling out of the shrubbery and lunged at my ankles. I kicked out and it veered past, all scrabbling claws on the tarmac. 'Toddy!' called a voice from the past and I caught my breath.

The dog beat a retreat. A figure was limping straight off the storybook pages of my childhood, a crooked man who walked a crooked mile. He edged up to see what had tripped his trap, pausing about six feet shy of me to peer into my face. I couldn't quite make out his. My eyes had yet to adjust to the dark.

'Is it the young master?'

'Larney?' I said in amazement. 'You're still alive?' I had to keep from blurting, gauging that he must be over a hundred by now, for Larney had been an old man when I was a boy, and a young man when Father was a boy, having served our family since he himself was a boy.

He ventured another step towards me, sidling crablike as ever, his body as twisted as an old vine. I had watched him once when he thought himself unobserved. I was on my way home from school when I came upon him in the woods. No limp. He looked almost normal, a working man from the village. 'Ha!' I had cried, plunging out from the trees, 'caught you!' Larney had reverted into his hobble and raised his hands to shield his head from a beating. The panic on his face had sent me backing off uncertainly, for I was just a child, and so, I realised, was he.

He drew up alongside me, head cocked like a bird, his upper body thrust forward and bobbing slightly. 'You're home, so, are you?'

Though I could make out his white teeth, the rest of his features remained dim. He was smiling wildly. I knew better than to mistake this for joy at my return. Larney always smiled wildly. It was an act of ingratiation, a plea not to inflict pain.

'Yes, ahm . . . That would appear to be the case.'

The voltage of the smile did not waver. Indeed, he registered no surprise whatsoever at my appearing out of the blue, as if it were the most natural thing in the world that I should pitch up unannounced in the night like this. As if nothing had changed in the intervening years. As if there had been no intervening years.

'All is well with himself up above,' he offered, although I had not enquired after my father's health. He had not enquired after mine.

'Right.'

The smile guttered at my tone but it quickly lit up again. 'I have a riddle for you, Master Tristram. What begins and has no end, and what is the ending of all that begins?'

'I don't know, Larney. What begins and has no end, and what is the ending of all that begins?'

'Death.'

'Death,' I repeated.

His smile hovered in the seething darkness, just his smile, as if his skin were black around it. 'Yes, death,' he said. 'Everyone thinks you are dead.'

'That was another Tristram St Lawrence,' I informed him, and hurried away with a curt goodnight.

The avenue was longer than I recalled, and steeper too. Graveyard ivy clotted the orchard walls in grotesque guises – cut-throats, hanged corpses, ghouls. I am a troubled man. I have a troubled mind. I see things in the dark. For a panicked moment I thought I had lost my phone and clapped a hand to my heart, but no, there it was in my pocket. Finally, the avenue opened out onto a familiar expanse of gravel. The pebbles formed a pale moonlit square at the foot of the castle steps. It was a long stretch to cross, a long and exposed stretch past all those looming windows.

I doubled back down the avenue and ducked around the old tower to Mrs Reid's apartments. Through the gap in her curtains I saw her sitting at her kitchen table with a magazine, feeding chocolate digestives into the slot of her mouth like documents into a shredder. Larney had claimed her as a distant cousin, an allegation she denied, although everyone from the village was related to everyone else. You weren't a real local unless your mother was from your father's side of the family.

I tapped on the windowpane. Mrs Reid spilled her tea in fright. 'It's only me, Mrs Reid,' I called to reassure her. A pause as she processed my voice.

The porch light came on and she opened the door a fraction, the safety chain tautened above her top lip like a brass moustache.

'Hello, Mrs Reid.'

She blinked in astonishment then shut the door in my face. I took an affronted step back. Then I heard the chain sliding across. Mrs Reid flung open the door and gathered me to her, just like in the old days. She was a good woman, a kind one, and most certainly a forgiving one. I am sorry to have dragged her name into this.

'My poor pet,' she crooned, 'your hands are freezing.'

'You didn't think I was dead, did you?'

'Tristram! What a question.'

'But you didn't, Mrs Reid, did you?'

'No, of course not. Your mother told us before she passed away that it was another Tristram St Lawrence.'

'Nobody told me she was dying.'

Mrs Reid wasn't willing to drag that whole ugly business up again, so she ushered me in to the warmth of her kitchen and set about producing dishes of food, trying as she had always tried to fill some hole she perceived in me, but I wasn't hungry. The red door loured beside us, connecting her quarters to the castle proper. She glanced at it from time to time, wary of rousing the big bad ogre who lived on the other side. Surely the old bastard was deaf by now? What was he, after all – ninety?

When the teapot was empty and our cups drained, Mrs Reid nodded at the clock over the stove. 'You really should go in before he retires for the night,' she advised me, standing up to clear away the plates. 'He heads upstairs around midnight. I'd show my face before then if I were you. If he hears you stealing around in the night, he'll take you for an intruder and shoot you on sight. You know what he's like.'

I did. I knew what he was like. Both of us knew what Father was like.

*

The connecting stone passage was littered with cigarette butts. He was still rolling his own. Mrs Reid was no longer able to bend down to pick them up, or perhaps she was no longer willing to bend down to pick them up, in the hope that Father might get the message and stop generating extra work, for he was a man who had never had to clean up after himself, being the last in a long line of patriarchs. He had sired me, his only child, at an advanced age with a considerably younger wife. His initial joy at fathering a son was short-lived. His disappointment in me, on the other hand, knew no limits.

I knocked before entering the dining hall, and pushed open the door when I received no reply. The hall was dark and empty. I crossed over to warm myself by the fire. Even with it burning, even in May, that room was cold. I ran my fingers over the engraving on the architrave of the mantelpiece. *Qui Panse*; 'Which Heals'. The family motto.

A commotion broke out as two setters exploded through the far door. They skidded to an aghast halt at the sight of me, then crouched and growled.

'Get out of that!' I commanded them, and although they were young dogs and had never laid eyes on me before, instinctively they understood that they should submit, and they flattened their long bellies against the floor. They recognised me as their breed, just as I recognised them as my breed, since there have always been Irish setters in the castle. Several were depicted at their masters' feet in the family portraits lining the hall. But I'm not here to give a history lesson.

I got down on my hunkers to caress their long ears. These two were beauties, the breed at its best – alert and agile, muscular and sleek, a map of liver-brown continents on the white sea of their backs. They kept their handsome heads on the floor and swallowed contritely. 'That's better,' I told them.

They heard him first. Their bodies tensed. I looked up.

A tall lean figure of military bearing was watching us from the doorway. Arnhem 1944, rank of colonel. I got to my feet. Father lowered the rifle.

'Heel,' he said coolly in his own good time, and the two dogs scrambled over and prostrated themselves at his feet. He propped the rifle against the frame of the door and clasped his hands behind his back. I raised my chin and aimed a thousand-yard stare at the wall.

'Why have you returned here?'

'This is my home.'

'This most certainly is not your home.'

'I am your son.'

'Only when it suits you.'

This was how we spoke, Father and I. If we spoke at all. I rested my eyes briefly on his face. Ninety-odd years of age and still possessed of his silver helmet of hair. He was already grey by the time I was born although old photographs reveal him to have been blond. It was about the only feature I had inherited from him. The fair hair and the height.

He circled me slowly, examining my person. The inspection had commenced. I directed my gaze at the wall again, or at a point just beyond it.

'Have you come to apologise?'

'I have not.'

'Then this conversation is over.'

With that he left, collecting the rifle upon his exit. 'Heel,' he instructed the setters once more and they fell in line behind him. I remained standing to attention for some time in the wake of his departure, listening to the embers settle in the grate as the fire faded beside me, as I faded beside the fire. I don't know why I'm talking about all of this in the past tense. Nothing is past. Everything is tense. You'll forgive me, Fergus, if I leave it there for the moment.

Second day of evidence

11 MARCH 2016

'Mr St Lawrence, returning to the brief conversation you conducted with Mr Hickey on the steps of the Summit Inn on 26 May 2006 in which he mentioned that he had a business proposition for you: at what point did you enter into a partnership with him?'

Not for a number of weeks, and when I did enter into a formal business arrangement with Mr Hickey, I did so at M. Deauville's instigation. He called me the following morning wanting to know how I had come to find myself in one of my old haunts. 'It was late,' I said, 'where else was I supposed to go?' presuming he meant the castle, but no, he meant the Summit Inn. How had I come to find myself in the Summit Inn? I had no answer to that.

Didn't I realise how foolhardy that was? he persisted. Didn't I grasp that I was treading on thin ice? There were danger zones, areas of unusual turbulence, like sunspots on the sun, M. Deauville explained, and they were to be avoided at all costs. The Summit Inn was one such zone. The old man – if he was an old man: it was difficult to gauge M. Deauville's age, but he was my old man in a way – the old man had kept me sequestered in airport hotels and conference centres. But I had strayed from the path.

'I am sorry, M. Deauville.' I was such a sorry soul that it was hard to quantify. Crossing Christy's threshold had been reckless in the extreme. I blamed the shock of the crash, or the emergency landing, and I blamed D. Hickey. I still do.

'D. Hickey?' The name piqued M. Deauville's interest.

'Yes. Desmond Hickey.'

Tocka tocka on the keyboard as M. Deauville ran a check. 'The property developer Desmond Hickey?'

I thought of the bag of grit sleeping it off in the back of his truck, arm in arm with the shovel. 'Well, he's more what you'd call a builder.'

'And why did you agree to enter licensed premises with this individual?'

'He said he had a proposition.' Clearly, this was a disingenuous representation of the previous evening's sequence of events. I had entered the licensed premises because I was gasping for a drink. Hickey only mentioned his proposition as I was leaving.

'A business proposition, did Mr Hickey say?'

'Yes.'

Tocka tocka. 'See what he wants.'

'Well, it's obvious. He wants to make money.'

'And what is so wrong with that?'

He had me there. You could say that M. Deauville brought Hickey and me together. Yes, I think it would be fair to say that.

*

Hickey was back that afternoon, tugging on the bell pull on the front door and not pushing the buzzer by the tradesman's entrance. I looked out the window and saw his truck parked below on the gravel.

The tails of the setters thumped the floor in welcome when I appeared downstairs, then they remembered themselves and angled worried eyes at Father, who was standing at the window looking out at Hickey's truck. I had hoped that the castle might be large enough that we should not have to rub up against each other in this fashion. 'Do you know that . . . ?' Father groped for a suitable word as he contemplated the hairy spectacle of Hickey. '*Character*,' he eventually managed.

'Yes.'

'Kindly go out and inform him that we've nothing left to steal.'

Hickey had already cased the joint in the time it took me to get down to him. 'Gutters need replacing,' he pointed out. 'Chimley's bollixed. Rotten windows. State a them slanty walls. An here, have you seen this?' The cracks under the sills. 'Subsidence.' He sucked air through his teeth. 'You're talking big money there, big money.'

I opened the passenger door of his truck and got in. 'I believe you have something to show me, yes?'

Hickey drove as a dog might, with some part of his anatomy – his elbow or sometimes his head – shoved out the window. The apple on the dashboard rolled to my side when he swung a right onto Harbour Road. 'See that?' He indicated a chipper facing the marina. 'Built that in '04. Do you remember what was there before?'

Nope, I admitted, I didn't.

'That's because there was nothing there!'

'Gosh.' You would think he had invented matter. I never met a man with a higher opinion of his abilities.

The tour-guide commentary persisted up the hill as my attention was drawn to this converted shopfront and that new townhouse. 'Small fry,' he protested with false modesty, as if such an assortment of odd jobs could be interpreted as anything other than small fry, but then, I suppose they were big fry to a man like Hickey. 'Wait'll you see what I'm up to next, Tristram.' He flashed me a wolfish smile.

At the church in the village where the road forked, Hickey blessed himself and took a right, speaking with great animation about his next project. A posh old pile, he said over the engine, which was struggling with the gradient. The apple toppled off the dashboard. I caught it and placed it in the handbrake well. He dropped down to second gear, and then first, telling me he hoped to get it off the owner at a fair price. It had been vacant for some years now and was a bit the worse for wear. Not in the same state as the castle, obviously. I mean, it wasn't totally banjaxed. Huge gardens though, he added, nodding to himself. A good eight acres at least, though he hadn't had the land surveyed since the property hadn't come to the market yet. The zoning in the area was one dwelling per eighth of an acre, so he estimated he'd get permission for a small luxury development on the eastern boundary. Large family dwellings, five bedrooms, a jacks for each arse sort of thing. Retain the mature trees, obviously, or a few of them at least. Mature trees sold a development. Pain in the hole building around them but there it is.

Windgate Road still retained the leafy air of a country lane. A country lane punctuated by ten-foot-high electronic security gates, but a country lane nonetheless. Verges of cow parsley, honeysuckle, buttercups. Anyway, Hickey continued, the house itself was probably a protected structure since it was Victorian, or Georgian, or Edwardian, or something, but he reckoned he could still squeeze twelve or so luxury apartments behind the façade.

He slowed down when we reached the highest point of Windgate Road, the blind bend before it began its descent over Dublin Bay. I hoped he wasn't bringing me where I thought he was. And then he did.

Hickey pulled in at the old stone gate pillars. The name of the house was barely legible. 'Hilltop' it read beneath the clusters of lichen. The house itself was screened from view by the woodland garden. The bluebells were still in blossom, thousands of them lining the forest floor.

Hickey jumped out of the truck and grabbed the rusty padlock on the gate. He selected a key from his key ring and unlocked it. I rolled down the window.

'Where did you get that key?'

He pretended that he couldn't hear me over the huffing and puffing and grunting and belching required to lever open the gates, which had sagged over the years into the tarmac. He glanced at the rust staining his palms before climbing back into the cabin, a slick of sweat across his forehead.

'Where did you get that key?' I repeated.

'You could a helped,' was all I got out of him.

We proceeded up the driveway – he'd chosen the shorter one; there were two – and emerged from the trees to encounter the elevated prospect of the house. Hilltop was mounted on a plinth and divided into two wings to capitalise on the view, one of the finest on the hill, if not the city. Ships sailing across the glittering water, Bray Head a cresting whale in the distance. The harbour and islands on the other side. Forgive me if I sound like an estate agent. I have nothing left to sell. The lawn had reverted to a wildflower meadow, alive with butterflies and the hum of bees.

Hickey sighed. 'Told you it was special. Come on an I'll give you the tour.'

Why wasn't I surprised when he produced the key to the front door also? Like the gate, it was sagging on its hinges, as if the departure of the family from the family home had caused Hilltop to slump in dejection. Hickey prodded the scuffed kickboard with his toe. 'Whole door'll have to be replaced. An these windows will have to go. Jaysus, have you ever seen so many cobwebs?'

We continued through to the hall. He flicked a few light switches but the electricity had been cut off. It was an internal hall with a deep red carpet and the doors leading off it were shut. We shuffled along in darkness.

'The main reception's down here,' he said, although it was not. The main reception was upstairs where the view was best. 'An this is the dining room,' he continued, indicating the study. 'An in here . . .' the two of us wandered into the music room, 'we have the lounge.'

I looked around. Remarkably little had changed since the house had last been occupied. Same furniture, same carpets, same books on the shelves – the same photographs, even, displayed in the same photograph frames. The place still even smelled the same, for the love of God. It was as if the owners had just popped out and might return at any moment. Or as if we might happen upon them in another part of the house, two interlopers barging in on top of them as they read the morning papers. Hickey was back out on the corridor blundering through the darkness, throwing open doors, a man working his way through the carriages of a train in search of an empty seat. He went at everything in that manner: bullishly, and in haste, and he was heading, by the sounds of it, for the French doors.

'Watch out for the—' I called, but too late. He'd gone on his ear where the level of the house dropped. He picked himself up and dusted himself down. No harm done. A man that short hadn't far to fall.

Back out on the terrace, Hickey examined the set of keys on his palm before turning to the mews. 'There's a sort a granny flat that comes with it.'

'Yes, the party room.'

'Ha,' he said, thinking this a joke.

We followed the path to the portico and Hickey tried a number of keys before hitting on the right one. The pair of us wandered in. Maple dance floor stippled by stilettos immemorial, balcony for the band, ornate plasterwork. I glanced at the ceiling. The Waterford Crystal chandelier was missing. I turned to Hickey.

'Where's the chandelier?'

He assumed the wilfully blank expression that had seen him through school. I indicated the ceiling.

'The chandelier, Dessie. The Waterford Crystal chandelier that was commissioned to hang in this room. Where is it?'

'You seem very familiar with the spec.'

'My mother was born here.'

'How was I supposed to know that?' he countered angrily, meaning: I wouldn't have nicked the chandelier had I known it belonged to you. Actually, who knows what he meant.

I walked out of the party room and he faffed about with the keys behind me. 'Don't bother locking it,' I muttered. The valuables had already been plundered. I dug my nails into my palms. Accept the things you cannot change, I silently coached myself. He joined me at the top of the driveway.

'Anyway,' he said, looking on the bright side, 'if it's your ma's gaff, you'll know where the boundaries are.'

'I never found them.'

He was delighted with that. You could see him regaling the lads with it down the Cock. *He never found the boundaries!* 'Yeah,' he nodded, scratching his armpit, 'we had that problem with the back gardens in Grace-O too.' The local corpo estate. 'Seriously though, where does the garden stop an the West Mountain start?'

'I told you. I never encountered a fence or a wall. It was a jungle, even back then. You'd need to hack your way through.'

'This is not a problem.' Hickey reached into the flatbed of the truck and produced a pickaxe and a hatchet. He gave me the hatchet. 'Hammertime.'

'What about gloves?' There were briars and nettles down there.

'Gloves,' he snorted. 'Don't be such a puff,' and then, 'Oh sorry man, no offence.'

It grew shady to the point of cavernous as we progressed

down the long driveway. The trees had not been cut back in years, and at intervals their branches enmeshed overhead to form a tunnel lanced by shafts of sunlight. The dappled surface of the driveway was mossy and crumbling away.

Hickey and I split up and set off in different directions. He hacked a path parallel to the road and I headed uphill towards the West Mountain. The rhododendron bushes had bolted to the size of caravans, and what had once been the lower lawn was now a drift of ferns. I came upon a pair of rusting barrels in the centre, the remnants of one of the jumps I'd built for the pony. The pony! How could I have forgotten the pony? Girls came out of nowhere to pop him over the jumps. They plaited his mane and oiled his hooves, clipped his coat and spent their pocket money on fancy brow bands. I, the lovelorn boy, looked on as he joggled them about, wondering what he had that I didn't. The girls called him Prince and he was. He was their monarch.

I lifted one of the showjumping poles and panicked woodlice scurried down its length. The grass underneath was moulded into a curd-white channel speckled with slugs. I could have broken the pole in two over my knee, it was so rotten. Most of the paint had flaked away but it was still possible to tell that it had once been striped white and blue. I had painted those stripes on myself, setting out my little trap to lure the jodhpured girls. Life was simpler then.

My phone rang. *Unknown*. I dropped the pole back in the grass and glanced around before answering. No sign of Hickey. Which did not mean he wasn't lurking.

'Hello, M. Deauville.'

I listened for a protracted period as M. Deauville outlined an unexpected proposal. It came at me out of the blue. 'I see,' I said every so often to reassure M. Deauville that I was still there, still within coverage, but mindful not to allow my responses to betray the content of the conversation, what with Hickey sniffing around. Instinctively, I relinquished the open ground of the drift of ferns for the cover of the trees.

M. Deauville's proposal necessitated that I live in Ireland. Domiciled, was the word he used. Was I willing to remain domiciled in the Republic of Ireland? he enquired, explaining that a position had come up in a company that was seeking to open an office in a low-taxation jurisdiction with benevolent regulation policies. I looked at my hatchet.

M. Deauville sensed the waves of reluctance radiating from me as I contemplated the prospect of returning to the sunspot, the danger zone, the area of unusual turbulence where the trouble had kicked off in the first place, and although I did not express these misgivings to M. Deauville, I did not have to. He sighed. 'Sometimes you need to go backwards to go forwards, Tristram,' he stated in the firm, coaxing tones of the early days, the scraping-by days, the talking-me-down-from-the-ledge days. His voice on the other end of the line had guided me through the darkest episodes imaginable. I will not trouble you with that period of my life here. Suffice it to say that M. Deauville had held my hand through it, and that I quite literally owed him my life.

I said I needed some time to think about it.

M. Deauville pointed out that it was a figurehead position. The responsibilities it entailed were few and need hardly take up more than twenty hours of my year. The post came with a significant salary attached. 'In summary,' he concluded, 'there is nothing to think about,' but there was.

When M. Deauville rang off, I looked up to find that during our conversation I had strayed into a pocket of the garden so deep, so dark and so choked by creepers that I was unable to discern a way out.

'*Arrrgh!*'

A blood-curdling cry. I gripped my hatchet.

'*Whaaagh!*' came the cry again. It was Hickey.

'Where are you?' I roared, thrashing through the undergrowth in the direction of his voice.

'Here!' he roared back. His voice had moved. I changed course.

'Where?'

'Here!'

I switched direction yet again and the two of us practically landed into opposite ends of the same clearing. Hickey pointed at the trees.

'There's a massive fucken animal in there!' Then: '*Hwauuuugh*, it's coming out!' He raised his pickaxe. I readied my hatchet.

Nothing for a moment as we crouched in preparation, and then the sound of a footstep. Then nothing again. Then another footstep. A pause, and then a third. We glanced at each other as the creature advanced through the foliage. Then the animal's hopeful face emerged from the leaves.

Oh no. I lowered my hatchet. The damage. Here it was.

The animal looked at Hickey, then at me, and then back at Hickey, who lowered his pickaxe and laughed. 'It's only a moth-eaten oul pony,' he said, and turned to leave.

'Don't you laugh at him.' The hapless old pony pushing his eager face through the leaves only to have it laughed at by an oaf like Hickey. 'Don't you dare laugh at him.'

Hickey told me to fucken relax and stalked off in a snot. For a man who attracted so much criticism, he handled it very badly. The pony whickered to me, a deep *huh-huh-huh*, hoping for attention but no longer expecting it, no longer presuming upon it as his due, for he knew those days were gone. I went to his side and stroked his nose. Prince snorted warm gusts of welcome into my hands. 'How long have you been in here on your own, you poor old fellow? That's the boy.' I didn't remember him being so small.

I encouraged him out into the clearing to look him over. He came willingly but with lowered head and unsure footing, as if crossing a sheet of ice. It was a terrible thing to see him that way, his joints all seized up. I scratched the patch behind his ear, the patch that was always itchy no matter how much you scratched it, and it had not been scratched in some time. Years, by the looks of it.

He angled the itchy patch towards me with half-closed eyes. Tufts of his coat floated onto the grass in drifts. It was early summer and he was moulting. 'Ah the poor boy.' When Prince had first arrived, I had thought that a pony was a baby horse and that he would get bigger as we did but, as with a lot of things, it turned out that I was wrong. By the time they were fourteen, the girls had outgrown him. Soon the girls were no longer girls but he wasn't to know that, and so he'd been waiting for them to return ever since, wondering, if ponies can wonder, and I fear that they can – I fear that every blessed thing on this earth is cursed with the capacity to wonder at its predicament – Prince was left wondering what he'd done wrong. His offence must have been egregious to be abandoned like this. It had started out so well. Meanwhile around him the trees grew higher, the bushes grew denser, and his world grew smaller. The house became vacant and the gates rusted up. Hilltop was sealed off with him trapped in the heart of it. The fruits of doing your best.

His steel-grey dapples had faded to white and the skin around his eyes had balded pink. I flicked a bluebottle from his trickling haw but the insect immediately reattached itself, all sticky tongue and wringing hands. His back was a knuckled ridge of spine and his hips propped up his hindquarters like tent poles. If I could have picked Prince up and cradled him in my arms like a lamb, I'd have carried him out of there. As matters stood, he couldn't walk to the driveway. Animals must know when they are finished. They may not understand death, as such, only that the world has left them behind, that it is time to lie down. He was still so good-natured though, so delighted to see me, standing there with his trembling knees. 'Girls are fickle,' I explained to him. 'They turn into women.' 'And then they run away,' I added. I put my hand to my face in surprise. A tear was rolling down my cheek.

Prince lifted his head and whickered once more. I wiped my cheek and turned around. Hickey was standing in the clearing. 'Load of bleedin grass here,' he pointed out. 'If the animal's too fussy to eat grass, I mean . . .' He shook his head in disapproval.

'Grass? How can he eat grass? The animal barely has a tooth left in his head. Look at him, for pity's sake!'

I hadn't meant to raise my voice. Prince's ears flicked back and forth in alarm. I told him to pay no attention to the bad man.

'Here,' said the bad man. 'Give him that.'

I looked around again. Hickey was holding out an apple. It was the one from the dashboard. He'd gone back to the truck to retrieve it. That was the maddening thing about D. Hickey: he always managed to cheat you of your anger. 'Peel the sticker off,' I told him.

He removed the sticker and passed me the apple. Prince speculatively gummed it about in his mouth, trying to puncture it with what remained of his teeth, his jaws skewed wide apart like a braying donkey. We willed him on but he failed to find purchase, and in the end the apple popped out and landed in the grass. Prince lowered his head to sniff it. I picked it up. It was slathered in slobber. I turned to Hickey.

‘Give me the hatchet.’

‘Eh,’ he said. ‘The tools are back in me truck.’

‘Jesus.’

I kicked around in the long grass until I located a rock, then I placed the apple on a tree stump and brought the rock down. There was a moist crunch. Hickey smirked at my handiwork. The apple hadn’t split crisply into the two neatly severed halves I’d envisaged, but instead had burst like a tomato. A trickle of juice oozed across the rings in the wood. It looked so thwarted.

Prince whickered and hazarded another step towards us, worried that he’d been forgotten again. His eyes and ears were trained on the sorry seeping spectacle on the stump, the apple that we’d wreaked our human havoc on. I prised it apart and fed him a piece. He sucked on it then nudged me for more. When all that remained was the twiggy stalk, he licked my palms.

The world then flinched as if I’d blinked though I had not. Prince flattened his ears. A dry crack of thunder warped the air followed by a second flash of lightning. The seagulls cranked up their war cries – the first drop of rain was so plump and warm on my scalp that I thought I’d been shat on. Another thunderclap buckled the atmosphere and Hickey and I made a run for it.

We were soaked by the time we made it back to the truck. My trousers were stuck to my legs. I waited for Hickey to start the engine but he did not. Instead we sat contemplating the house through the rain runnelling down the windscreen. There was something of the caveman about this arrangement, the two of us sheltering in that nook.

‘So,’ he eventually said, ‘what d’ya reckon?’ He had to raise his voice to make it heard over the drumming rain, which was hopping off the bonnet and roof like a plague of locusts.

'What do I reckon about what?'

'About the house. The grounds.'

I peeled the sodden fabric of my trousers away from my knees. They were scattered with hairs from Prince's coat. The water in my shoes was warming up. 'It's a fine house.'

'I'm going to buy it.'

'I wasn't aware that the house was for sale.'

'Yeah, well, it's not. I'd have to approach the owner.'

'Indeed you would.' I strapped on my seat belt to indicate that I was ready to leave. He didn't take the hint.

'Get in on the bottom level, know what I'm saying?'

'Ground level.'

'Exactly.' As if it were a proposal I'd made, and not a correction.

The navies and whites of Hilltop trickled down the windscreen. 'And what shall you do if the owner isn't selling?'

'Between you an me,' he confided, 'the owner could use a few readies.'

I raised an eyebrow at him, or at the back of his head, rather, since that's what he had presented me with, the back of his big thatched head, staring out the driver's seat window as if he wasn't speaking to me at all, that my information did not come from him. But it did. All my information came from him.

'Is that so, Dessie?'

'It is, Tristram. From what I hear.'

'And where did you hear this, Dessie? From one of your little birds?'

Hickey smirked. 'No, Tristram. It's common knowledge.'

'Common knowledge,' I repeated in wonderment. The things that came out of his mouth.

It was steadily growing gloomier inside the truck. The windows were steaming up. Hickey kept his face averted for fear of being photographed in conversation with me by the surveillance man with the telescopic lens who appeared on the rooftops of his mind gathering evidence against him whenever he was up to no good, i.e. more often than not, though the point of this particular charade escaped me. No one could see us through the fogged-up glass.

He examined the dials on the dashboard and reset the mile counter, adjusted the minute hand of the clock, calibrating his universe, the man in control, sighing gravely for my benefit as he made a production of weighing up how much to tell me. 'Speak to your oul fella,' he finally remarked in a pointed tone.

'And why would I want to do that?'

'I'll make him a good offer. Enough to fix up the castle. An there'll be something in it for you.'

I returned my attention to the blurred mass of Hilltop. 'And what business is this of my father?'

Hickey met my eye at last. 'It's his house now, isn't it?'

I looked down to smile a small smile before facing Hickey once more. I inspected him in silence. This was a trick I had learned from Father. I knew how it worked. The secret was to do it slowly. Hickey's shirt had turned semi-translucent in the rain. The thin cotton fabric did not cling to his skin the way my shirt clung to mine but was instead draped over his matted black whorls of chest hair like a picnic blanket spread over tussocks of grass.

I sighed as Father sighed when an inspection was complete, in order to express my disappointment, for inspections inevitably culminated in disappointment. That was the point of them. 'Father doesn't own Hilltop.'

Hickey's eyes darted wildly around the floor of the truck, as if fragments of his shattered plans might be salvaged there.

'So who owns it?' he demanded, and then, before I got a chance to answer: 'The Viking. I fucken knew it.'

'The who?'

'The fucker got there first, didn't he? That bollocks is buying up Howth. Right.' He turned the key in the ignition.

'Watch out for the lawn,' I warned him as we shot blindly forward. He hit the brakes and switched the heater up to max, directing twin blasts of air at the windscreen. Two clear saucers appeared in the condensation as if snorted from the nostrils of a bull.

'Fucken place never went up for sale. It wasn't on the open market. Did you know that? I bet he got it off youse for a song.'

'Stop!' I protested as he mounted the lawn, the truck bucking under us like a pony. 'Jesus Christ' – he dialled full lock onto the steering wheel and mashed the accelerator into the floor – 'what the hell do you think you're doing?' The truck slewed sideways across the sodden lawn, spraying mud like a slurry spreader.

I tried to wrest the steering wheel from his grip but those muttony arms held it firm. So I groped blindly amongst indicator stems and bonnet-release levers and his knees until I located the keys. A twist and the parched blare of the exhaust cut out. The truck slid to a halt. For a moment it felt epic, as if I'd disabled a bomb.

I sat up. The windows were spattered with mud. Hickey's skin was mottled by the grubby light. He put out his hand. 'Give us me keys.'

I rolled down my window. What had been a meadow of butterflies and wildflowers was now a ploughed field. I turned to Hickey. 'What did you do that for?'

'Give us me keys,' he said again.

'You've destroyed my lawn.'

'Correction: I've destroyed the Viking's lawn.'

'Hilltop doesn't belong to the Viking.'

'Your oul lad still owns it then?'

'No, the house does not belong to my father.'

'So whose is it?'

I turned my attention to his set of keys and went through them one by one, deliberating over the features of each in turn as if they were suspects on an identity parade. There were thirty or so keys threaded onto a large ring and none of them looked familiar. It was going to take a while to find the right one.

'*I said*,' Hickey said, 'whose is it?'

I sighed to indicate that he had broken my concentration and I returned to the beginning of the set.

The keys didn't get any more familiar the second time around. I lowered them and looked up to find the weather quite altered, as if a new theatre set had been wheeled onstage for the next act or, rather, the old backdrop returned. The mackerel clouds had yielded to the clear blue sky of before and the sea was a glittering sheet of brilliance. A wood pigeon started up its warm coo-cooing, at which sound a small trapdoor of recognition sprang open in my chest, injecting a spicy shot into my bloodstream. 'It's mine,' I said when I was good and ready.

'What is?'

'Hilltop. My mother left it in her will to me.' A pain in my soft tissue at the mention of her, and all my tissue is soft, all of it pains. 'You've destroyed my lawn.'

'I'll get you a new one.'

I handed him the keys. 'Kindly return my keys and then drive me home. You're trespassing.'

He didn't look at the keys but grinned at me. 'Tristram,' he declared, 'I'm about to make you a rich man.'

'Hilltop is not for sale.'

After a brief hesitation, during which Hickey gauged whether or not to push his luck and for once decided against it, he selected the Toyota key from the ring and inserted it into the ignition.

*

I knew him. I knew him the second I saw him. I recognised him from his moniker. Tall, fair-haired, blue-eyed, buff and in rude – no, obnoxious – good health. An invader to this island if ever I saw one. Not an indigenous short-arse like Hickey or a gaunt Anglo-Norman like me, but a Viking right down to his marrow.

We came upon him on Harbour Road. Hickey was driving me back in silence when there he was. You couldn't miss him. Everything about his bearing announced itself. I am here, his strut proclaimed as he strode up and down the frontage of a new giant green wine bottle of a bar, patrolling his strip while taking a call. A black Range Rover Sport with twenty-inch alloys was parked in his loading bay. He eyed it every time he passed. Or maybe he was eyeing his reflection in it.

His face was tanned and his collar-length hair tossed back in a salty tangle, as if he'd just come ashore after scudding the waves on his speedboat or longboat or yacht. He was rigged out in deck shoes and no socks. Wide-legged trousers in an off-white fabric, like linen only finer, as if fashioned from the fabric of sails. Whatever it took to advertise his nautical status was nailed to his mast.

People were seated at silver bistro tables on the pavement, installed like his personal audience. 'That's him, isn't it?' I said.

Hickey did not respond, other than to bristle and bridle in

the seat next to me. He slowed the truck down to get a better look, for there is something almost pleasurable in being riled to that extent.

The Viking clocked Hickey's approaching truck and nodded a greeting, or not so much a greeting as an acknowledgement: I see you, I know that you are there. Then he returned his attention to the phone. Hickey and his passenger were of little interest to him. 'What a cock,' Hickey remarked and I nodded. For once, we agreed on something.

*

'Here we are now,' he announced heartily as we pulled up outside the castle. Hickey was a great man for the hollow cheer when trying to end things on a positive note. Here we are now, is it yourself, you'll be having another, ah ya will! He thought it made him charming, a bit of a character, a lovable rogue, but although he was fooling no one, it was still somehow endearing in its sheer ham-fistedness. His fists of ham and my feet of clay. How did we get so far?

'Here we are now,' he repeated, and inserted an expectant pause to prompt me to respond. I knew that I was forgetting something, but it wasn't my lines.

'Yes, well,' I said, fussing over the catch of my seat belt. What was it I'd been meaning to do?

Hickey nodded at the castle. 'Bet it's deadly in there.'

That was one word for it. The castle was crawling with the deadly members of my deceased family – the ancestors on whose chairs I sat, in whose bed I slept, at whose table I dined. They say the place has a ghost now and I have every reason to believe them.

'Tapestries an stuff . . . ?' he nudged me.

Hickey didn't strike me as the type who might harbour an interest in tapestries, still less know what one was.

'I'd say they're mad yokes,' he speculated. 'I never seen a real one . . .'

Mad yokes, yes, like the stolen Waterford chandelier. 'I'm afraid we don't have any genuine tapestries left,' I said carefully. 'The original hangings are long gone, replaced by replicas. Same with the paintings. Copies, the lot of them. The valuable stuff was sold off years ago. But keep that under your hat.' This was not in fact the case. Hickey may have treated me like a blow-in, but I treated him like a thief.

'Have youse a dungeon?'

I laughed as I climbed out. 'Thanks for the lift, Dessie.' I swung the door shut and patted the muddy roof. Off you pop now, like a good chap.

He leaned into the passenger seat and rolled down the window. 'Ah, you're grand,' he said, 'you're very good but I won't.' I blinked at him in incomprehension. 'I won't come in for the cup a tea cause I'm up to me teeth, but I appreciate the offer, so I do. You're a gent. I always said that about you. Always stood up for you, no matter what they accused you of. Mental psychopathic things. Dodgy satanic shit. Ah, not at all, I'd say: you have him all wrong. Bit up his own hole, I grant you that, but he wouldn't hurt a fly. An as for his lovely manners! His dead mammy would of been proud.'

He hauled himself back into the driver's seat and stepped on the accelerator. The keys. I had forgotten to retrieve the keys. 'Hey!' I shouted after him but he didn't hear me. The setters did. They came belting around the corner in response, pebbles flying in their wake, ears tossed to the wind, for the fact of there being two of them seemed to egg the other on, turning every endeavour into a competition.

Halfway across the courtyard, the pair simultaneously

about-turned and scrambled back to the arch at the same frenetic pace, having been summoned to heel by Father. I stood to attention when he appeared, awaiting one of his caustic remarks – *Is that the company you keep now, I see you've found your level at last* – but he simply walked past me as if I were dead to him, pausing briefly to note the skid marks that Hickey had carved in the gravel.

‘What happened to the pony?’

Stop. Poor Prince. The damage.

At the time, I did not envisage that I would remain in the country for more than a day or two, so I did what I believed was best for him under the circumstances, seeking to remove a fraction of pain from the world, to relieve an iota of suffering. I went inside and rang the vet and arranged to have him destroyed the following morning.

Third day of evidence

14 MARCH 2016

'Mr St Lawrence, when did your directorship of Castle Holdings commence?'

The date is on the paperwork in front of you. Was it the following week perhaps? I am poor with numbers and getting worse with time but the good news is I left a paper trail. About a week after the expedition to Hilltop with Hickey, I pulled open the front door to encounter a blond man in blue overalls on his knees, a hammer in his hand. I had been wondering what the noise was. A toolbox was set out by his side, its tiers fully extended.

I stepped outside to see what he was up to. He was mounting a brass plaque to the door surround. 'What do you think you are doing?'

The man nodded at the plaque to indicate that he was mounting a brass plaque to the door surround – yes yes, I could see that, I wasn't blind. Father, by some small mercy, was out. A smart blue minivan was parked in his spot, *Transylvanian Tradesmen* printed on the side in livery matching the man's overalls. I gestured at the plaque. 'Who authorised this?'

The man returned to his work. *Tap tap* with his hammer, *whir whir* with his drill as if I weren't there, an exemplar of the implacability of the Eastern European that confounds the Irish psyche to such a degree. Instead of embarking on long-drawn-out descriptions of the task at hand, followed by a rundown of potential pitfalls to unnerve the customer, concluding with a few horror stories to illustrate that the competition are cowboys and that the cost of labour is not as extortionate as it may at first have seemed, all the while angling for a cup of tea as any self-respecting Irish workman might, this man simply got on with it.

Castle Holdings read the italic lettering on the plaque, which was the name M. Deauville had chosen for the Irish branch of his company. Sorry, Fergus? Yes, apologies, my mistake. You are quite right: Castle Holdings was not a branch but a separate financial entity.

When the workman was gone I inspected the plaque. It was dappled with his fingerprints, fingerprints which I neglected to polish off, instead leaving them to set into the protective lacquer coating the metal, although it wasn't the Romanian workman's dirty fingerprints that were smeared all over that operation from the start.

The sound of another vehicle reached my ears. It was not the tinny rattle of Father's old Polo, nor was it the return of the smart little van. A powerful engine was ascending the avenue. I turned to face the courtyard.

The vehicle seemed on the brink of appearing for a protracted period, but instead of rounding the corner it continued to grow louder. Louder and ever louder while I stood waiting to receive it. Finally, a motorbike appeared through the trees, the reflections of the leaves flickering upon its obsidian flank. The front fairing was bulky and clenched, the shoulders of a charging bull, but the tail was sleek and tapered, the sting of a wasp. The motorcycle made straight for me across the gravel as if this meeting were scheduled. I checked my watch. It was precisely three o'clock.

The biker dismounted, stiff and bowed in his creaking leathers, a warrior in armour, a medieval knight, one who had ridden for days to reach this place. He removed his gauntlet of a glove but not the helmet. The original Sir Tristram might have looked like this, I remember thinking. The original Sir Tristram, the real Sir Tristram, might have stood where this man stood now, regarding me as this man regarded me now, his black destrier panting behind him, ticking as its cylinders cooled. I wanted to see his face.

From the pannier, he produced a small device, the screen of which glowed elixir green. There was a stylus attached and I signed my name. The motorcyclist then offered an envelope and I looked at him, but his glossy black visor returned only my reflection in miniature, a crooked and contorted man. I did not like what I saw there. I accepted the envelope and thanked him.

He nodded by way of acknowledgement before mounting his motorcycle. I retreated inside and leaned against the door, anxious for him to be gone. The silence of the transaction had unnerved me. The silence of this transaction, and of subsequent transactions, because yes, it was the first of many. As you well know. That is why I have been summoned here. Isn't it?

When the sound of the motorcycle had faded from the avenue, I brought the envelope to the dining table and sat down. A document of great consequence was contained inside – I see you have it in your possession. Exhibit A, or a portion of it. Yes, I can confirm that that is my signature.

That document possessed a distinct magnetic pull. It had its own field of gravity. The fact that it is presently being passed around the room in silence corroborates that it is no ordinary piece of paper. Exhibit A, you will find, is a remittance advice, a salary slip. The staggering figure of €100,000 is printed in the *Payable* box. And the staggering name in the *Payee* box is mine.

I stood up from the dining table.

I sat down again.

I stood up.

I sat down again.

I tried to concentrate.

It was very hard.

My eyes shuttled compulsively between those two electric points on the page: Tristram St Lawrence – €100,000.00 – Tristram St Lawrence – €100,000.00, until it felt like incipient epilepsy. At the bottom of the page, divided by a row of perforations, was a tear-off cheque drawn on a bank account in the Cayman Islands. The cheque portion, as you can see, was subsequently detached. By me.

The cheque was made out to Tristram St Lawrence and the amount was the same. Two new points of seismic activity for my eyes – they started their compulsive shuttling again. Then an irregularity leapt out. A key portion of the cheque was blank. The authorised signature was missing. The cheque was invalid.

Then I spotted my name again. Beneath the dotted line where the signature should be: Tristram St Lawrence, Director, Castle Holdings. *I* was the authorised signatory. I had to sign the dotted line to get the money. I turned the document over in search of further instructions. The reverse was blank.

My name, the zeros, my name, the zeros – my eyes cranked up their shuttling. Money disrupts the cognitive process. It gums electrodes to your skull and scrambles your brain. That document was a test, I see now, of my character. A test I failed. *Tristram St Lawrence* I wrote at the bottom of the page. Everyone has a price.

That's when I became the Director of Castle Holdings. The sixth of June 2006, it says here. In accepting the money, I was accepting the position.

Yes, that is correct: Castle Holdings was a shell company. It bought nothing, sold nothing, manufactured nothing, did nothing, and yet, as your piece of paper states there, it returned a profit of €66 million that first year. Huge sums of untaxed money were channelled through it out to the shareholders of its parent companies, which is perfectly legal under Irish tax law, as you know. I did not make the laws. You made the laws. You are the lawmakers and must shoulder some blame. Me? I was merely the conduit. My appointment struck me as appropriate on a mordant level. Who better to direct a shell company than a shell of a human being? M. Deauville could not have chosen a more fitting candidate. Uncanny. That was the word they used.

I went straight to the bank, as their records will confirm, and lodged the cheque into my account. Yes, into my personal account. I have no other type. At least I had a bank account, which is more than the Minister for Finance could say. I wrote out a second cheque while still at the counter. This one was made out to Father for €15,000. That sum represented his commission – no, commission is the wrong word – I take it back. Father had no hand, act or part in Castle Holdings. He never took a penny from them. His money came from me. Father's cheque was drawn on my account, not theirs. I put it in an envelope and placed it on the console table outside his study. Guilt money, you could call it. This offering was accepted, or, at least, when I came down in the morning the envelope was gone. The €15,000 was lodged by him, as you can see. I noted when leafing through the subpoenaed records that he deliberated for a number of weeks before cashing it.

The same procedure was followed with every cheque M. Deauville's courier delivered. I signed them, lodged them into my personal account, and made out a second cheque to Father, which I left in a sealed envelope outside his study. The way I'd heard it, the owner could use a few readies.

The envelopes were removed, the cheques were cashed, and no mention was made of the matter. Money was not a topic Father was equipped with the vocabulary to discuss, yet I suspect it was all he ever thought about. I suspect it ate him up. How could he but think about money, or the want of it, when the roof was leaking and the plaster was mouldering and the floorboards were caving in beneath his feet? Watching it all fall around him and knowing that when he passed away it would be entrusted to his fallen son. It is a mercy that he did not live to see this day.

I soon learned to take up sentry duty in front of the brass plaque at 3 p.m. on the first Tuesday of every month, waiting for that envelope like a junkie for his fix. The cheques M. Deauville's courier delivered were generally as substantial as that first one, yet the hit was never as intense. Always, I was left craving more. I became addicted to waiting for the man because that is my nature. M. Deauville had me exactly where he wanted me. Hi, my name is Tristram and I'm an alcoholic. And an addict and a diabolical gambler.

‘Mr St Lawrence, what precisely is the nature of your relationship with the financier Mr Deauville?’

Ha! What a question!

‘Just answer it, please, Mr St Lawrence.’

I'm not sure I can, Fergus. To try to do so, I'll have to go back to the beginning. I'll tell you everything I know about M. Deauville, which isn't all that much for a variety of reasons, one being that the gentleman in question is an extremely private individual, and another that our relationship was focused from the outset exclusively on me and my sobriety, seeing as I was in dire need of saving when he found me. I did all the talking and he did all the listening – pretty much the same set-up as here, I've just noticed. What does that say about me? Nothing positive.

I need hardly point out that M. Deauville would be most displeased at finding himself under such scrutiny, the chief witness being a former . . . how shall I describe myself? A former protégé. I am not of his church now. Our relationship had not always been a business one, you will have gathered. It ran far closer to the bone than that. M. Deauville was my sponsor. Everyone in the fellowship has a sponsor, someone you can talk to in your hour of need.

I joined Alcoholics Anonymous – or first attended it, rather, since it is not a movement you can really join as such, just as it is not a movement you can really leave as such – in May 2005, three or four days after missing a flight home to attend to my mother who had been hospitalised. Nobody told me she was dying. I missed the flight because I was too drunk to board the plane. M. Deauville was the man who saved me. From what? Lord, do you really need to ask? From myself.

The morning after I missed the flight, I did not wake up.

The cleaning staff admitted themselves to my room when I failed to check out on time. I was in a Brussels airport hotel, though to put it bluntly I did not know where I was. Did not know who I was either. I had methodically popped a full month's supply of sleeping tablets out of their blister packs and knocked them back with the contents of the minibar.

The cleaners found me comatose and called 999, but the phone must have been upside down and 666 dialled in the panic because it was Hell that I was despatched to, and not hospital, make no mistake. Sheer hell. I had hit what is known in the trade as rock bottom.

They loaded me into the back of an ambulance, it was explained to me later by the registrar manning the ward when I came around and demanded to know where the hell I was and how the hell I'd gotten there and who the hell had stolen my clothes. Hell, hell, hell. I couldn't stop saying that word. Still can't. The registrar informed me that my heart had stopped beating. The cardiac team had worked to get it going for a full half hour. Time of death was called by the duty surgeon at one minute past midnight. My body was growing cold in the harsh glare of the emergency room when the monitor detected a pulse. The instruments transmitted news of this development to the nurses' station and the team was recalled. They had never seen anything like it before, the registrar said. Uncanny. That was the word he used.

I checked my chart when he left the room. *Temps de mort: 00.01h.*

I am somewhat hazy on the passage of time following my emergency admission. It lasted for eternity, as is the way with Hell. Days bled into nights, faces morphed into other faces and then back to the original face, monitors beat time. My back ached from the burden of lying on it, my stomach was a knot of acid. That period felt like a thousand-hour flight.

The electronic atmosphere, the toxic static, the unremitting cramp. Around and around the globe we orbited, conflating time zones, cruising airspace, never touching down to get out and stretch for there is no rest for the wicked. I had woken in a foreign country with a tube in my arm, confused and gasping for a drink. I wanted my mother. She was my first thought. I needed her to comfort me. And then I remembered that she was in hospital too and needed me to comfort her. My body clenched with shame. 'Nurse,' I cried, '*Infirmière! Verpleegster!*'

I attended my first meeting in the hospital itself. A porter propped me into a wheelchair and transferred me to a room upstairs in which sat a group of people who were blatantly not part of the medical corps. 'What the fuck is this?' I wanted to know, because I used to curse a lot back then. I used to do a great many bad things back then. I am paying for it now. The nurses had kitted me out in a pair of geriatric pyjamas and a maroon dressing gown since my luggage hadn't accompanied me to the hospital. I wouldn't accompany me either, given the option. The porter rolled my wheelchair into the circle and made a song and dance of applying the brake, letting me know in no uncertain terms that I was parked.

The group turned to me and smiled the meek, apologetic smile. I scowled, wondering what their game was. They would have registered that I was a hard case. You soon learn to recognise the signs. I wasn't there of my own volition and they knew it. All I knew was that I could murder a pint.

The meeting was conducted in French. *Salut, je m'appelle Marcel. Je suis un alcoolique. Salut Marcel,* let's hear it for Marcel, a big hand for Marcel. I stared at him with open hostility. What had he ever done that was so great? Then Marcel started speaking. The meek smiling stopped and the earnest listening began.

The woman beside me leaned in and took to translating Marcel's story into English, making a fair fist of it too. Marcel knew it was time to knock his drinking on the head when he woke up in the North Sea one freezing November dawn clinging to a rock. He rolled up his sleeves to show us the scars of the wounds he had sustained, and the stump where his ring finger used to be, at which sight I looked away and stared at my feet. They were clad in another man's slippers, old brown things that smelled a little ripe. Then one of them slid off and landed with a slap on the linoleum floor. Marcel broke off his narration to glare at the slipper as if I'd laid a turd. No one stooped to pick it up and replace it on my bare foot. And me in a wheelchair. Marcel re-embarked on his story. When he was finished, he wiped away a tear and everyone clapped except me. Then they chanted some class of prayer.

The meeting ended, but there was no sign of the porter coming to rescue me. The lot of them tramped out, leaving me alone in an empty circle of seats with my back to the door. There is nothing so atmospheric as a recently vacated room. I extended my foot to the floor and hooked the slipper with my big toe, flipped it back onto my foot. Why the staff had installed me in a wheelchair, I could not say. I still had the use of my legs. Fuck this, I thought, and got up and headed out for a smoke.

That was my first meeting. It was a beginning.

*

They discharged me a few days later, and I was standing on the hospital steps looking up and down the street in search of the nearest bar when my mobile phone rang. I took it out and frowned. Last I'd looked, the battery had been dead. *Unknown*, read the screen.

'Hello, Tristram.' The voice was a cultured one, grave and authoritative. 'My name is Monsieur Deauville,' the caller continued. 'I realise that you are dying for a drink, and I am ringing to inform you that if you pursue this course of action, you most certainly *will* die for it.'

For a lurid moment, I saw my death certificate. *Temps de mort, 00.01h.* I reached for the handrail to steady myself, blinking to drive out the sight of those words, but the pulsing letters had seared my retina and were superimposed on the street, and the hospital and the sky, and anywhere else that I cared to look.

'Do you wish to die?' M. Deauville asked.

I was having trouble breathing. A man came up offering assistance but I waved him away because what help could he possibly have given me? My heart had stopped and I had been pronounced dead, during which time a signal had been triggered and my death certificate retrieved from whatever vault it had been stored in. It had been loaded onto a trolley just as my body had been loaded onto a trolley, and wheeled to some senior functionary's desk, where it was stacked with the certificates of the other souls awaiting the authorisation to be dispatched. I was dying for a drink.

When I did not answer, M. Deauville repeated his question. 'Do you wish to die?'

'No,' I wheezed down the line. 'No, I don't wish to die.'

Tocka tocka in the background – what was that strange noise? 'Good. Go back to your hotel room,' he instructed me. 'I have called you a car. You will find it waiting by the hospital entrance.'

I wheeled around. A man in a suit was standing by a black Mercedes, holding a sign which bore my name.

‘I will call back when you have checked in.’

‘Wait.’ I didn’t have M. Deauville’s number, but he had already hung up.

*

I have been here before. That was my first thought when I entered the hotel room. I took off my jacket and shoes and lay on my back on the bed. Was this the room? I couldn’t tell if it was the same room in which I had almost killed myself because they are all the same room. They are all hell. You cannot imagine the depth of the hole into which I had dug myself. At least, I hope you can’t. I leapt up and sprang across the room and wrenched open the minibar. It was empty. Everything was empty. I looked at the ceiling and moaned. And then M. Deauville called.

*

We were like lovers. We were holed up in that one room together for days on end like lovers, talking the long hours away. We shut the rest of the world out since the equilibrium we had chanced upon was so very fragile. At least, it was so very fragile to me. I was terrified of upsetting the balance, having spent my life upsetting the balance. But M. Deauville assured me that there was no such thing as a pattern that could not be broken.

I had my meals sent up and I deposited the emptied trays out in the corridor. Housekeeping exchanged old towels for new at the door and replenished my stock of sparkling water. I did crunches and press-ups in front of the window and kept to my fourteen-by-twelve cell. For the first time since hitting his teens, Tristram St Lawrence was sober. I had broken my mother's heart. With a racing pulse I picked up the phone. 'Tristram,' she gasped, 'the Guards told me you were dead!' I had not heard her voice in years. Too ashamed to call or show my face. 'It's okay, Mummy, I'm still alive!' I was crying. So was she. I promised to come home but the connection went dead and my pledges vanished into the ether. I later discovered that she passed away the following day. It was probably for the best that I did not know this at the time. The news would have finished me.

Did I go to her? Why ask me that question, Fergus? Here, in front of all of these people? You were at my mother's funeral and you know well that I wasn't.

M. Deauville rang at the moments when I felt weak, and there were no moments when I felt strong. He had to check in with me day and night. I could not be left to my own devices for long. When I felt I couldn't cope a second longer and had reached for the hotel phone to dial room service to order up a drink, on cue, my mobile would ring. It was as if he could read my mind. It takes one to know one, I suppose. I'd put down one phone to answer the other, overcome with gratitude tinged with resentment and the inevitable and apparently endless flood of shame.

Once I started talking to M. Deauville, I found I couldn't stop. It all came pouring out. I bared my soul to the man, revealed its shrivelled dimensions, allowed him to gauge its clotted heft, or what was left of it. He appeared genuinely concerned for its fate, wretch slab of offal that it was, as pitted and honeycombed as a consumptive lung. He accepted the sorry state of it and did not condemn me, but instead listened patiently as I droned on. I owed him my life. It was as simple as that. I cannot overstate the degree of my indebtedness. Without M. Deauville, I would be long in my grave. Of that there is no doubt.

'You're a saint,' I told him after one particularly gruelling session which had racked my body with tears, wrung it out like an old rag. I nodded vigorously to persuade him of my sincerity, as if he were there in the room. I felt him there. I felt him with me. 'A saint,' I averred, 'a walking saint!'

It was the only time I ever heard M. Deauville laugh.

*

No, I'm afraid I cannot disclose M. Deauville's full name to the Commission, primarily because I don't know it. He never mentioned a Christian name. Alcoholics *Anonymous* it is called. That first phone call on the hospital steps was the only time he had occasion to use his name, which led to the confusion that later ensued. We'll come to that.

Naturally, I waited for him to invite me to use his forename – *please, just call me X* – particularly since he never addressed me as Mr St Lawrence. Or Lord Howth, if you wish to get pedantic. Always it was Tristram, but this familiarity did not extend both ways.

His nationality? Again, this is something of a grey area. There are no white areas in my tale. His English was elegant although I doubt it was his mother tongue. His use of it was too formal, too academic. I was unable to pinpoint his first language, such was his mastery of them all. When a minion entered his office seeking authorisation on some matter, he would answer in German or French or Russian or on one occasion in what I think was Mandarin, switching from one language to another as if changing stations on a radio. His calls originated from every corner of the globe since he moved about constantly to service his many international business interests. If I apologised for taking up his time at an ungodly hour, he would murmur to think nothing of it, that all hours were ungodly and that it was the working day in his part of the world. Sometimes airport announcements were audible in the background. *The flight for Dubai is now boarding. Please have your passport and boarding card ready for inspection.* And then you'd hear nothing for a few hours, his phone set to flight mode.

Over the years of our association, I came to think of M. Deauville as another Lawrence, pronounced with a Gallic inflection: Laurent. He was my own personal Saint Lawrence, my Higher Power. It is true that M. Deauville did not put his signature to a single document pertaining to Castle Holdings, despite his being the architect of the enterprise. I trawled through every last communication in my possession before submitting the file in its entirety to you. Unfortunately, it is my family name that is scrawled all over the operation, mine and Desmond Hickey's. Therefore, I cannot confirm the spelling. Perhaps I misheard him on the hospital steps. Perhaps he was not Laurent Deauville but Laurent de Ville, Lawrence of the City, the ultimate urbanite, the bottom line in sophistication. Yes, it is fair to say I was in awe of him. He was a man from an old era, you see, from an old family, older than mine. All families are old, it goes without saying, but some – well, they have moulded history. They have exerted a force through time. I would not have been in the least bit surprised had M. Deauville revealed to me that he could trace a direct line to the Medici princes, or to Alexander the Great, or Ivan the Terrible. But he did not reveal any such thing to me. He revealed nothing at all. Monsieur du Veil, he should have called himself, because he always wore one. You will never catch him. There is not a chance of that. There is not a chance in hell.

'Mr St Lawrence, can you clarify the extent of Desmond Hickey's involvement with Mr Deauville?'

No, Fergus, I cannot. That is a matter for Hickey's conscience and Hickey's conscience alone, if he has one. To my knowledge, M. Deauville spoke only to me. To me and through me. I am an interpreter, a perfect conduit, an instrument of others. M. Deauville issued the instructions and I carried them out. At first, I tried to keep Hickey's name out of our conversations on the grounds that M. Deauville would have disapproved of the company I was keeping, or that was keeping me, because I couldn't quite get shot of D. Hickey, I couldn't quite shake him off.

I came out of the bank at Sutton Cross having lodged that initial Castle Holdings cheque. I'd anticipated trouble from the cashier – 'This is not a valid cheque, sir'; 'You cannot write a cheque to yourself for a hundred grand, Mr St Lawrence,' but apparently it was, and you could. Anything was possible in an Irish bank back then. The Cross was dazzlingly vivid, as if I'd stumbled out of the darkness of a cinema into morning light. Each object was remarkable for its industrious wholeness, its bright sovereignty, and I was happy standing there in the afternoon sunshine and being part of it, the cheque for Father in my hand, when the battered red flatbed truck swerved and mounted the kerb. Hickey rolled down the window. 'There ya are,' he shouted at me. 'Hop in.' I'm telling you, that man could smell money.

'Now,' he said as we pulled away, 'I've had a better idea.' I smiled. There were some things you could always count on. Not that Hickey would have a better idea, but that he would think that the idea was a better one. The recent history of this country has been moulded by those without the vision to perceive the flaws in their plans.

He drove in the direction of the castle but pulled in at the old cement factory, which was located a few hundred yards shy of my gateposts and on the other side of the road. Only in Ireland would the acreage flanking a white sand beach be zoned for industrial use.

'We don't own this land any more,' I said, heading him off at the pass.

Hickey threw his hands in the air. 'Did I open me mouth?' He jumped out and unlocked the gate and we trundled around the back of the lot. The factory was derelict. So was the motor company. And the petrol station beyond it.

'So anyway,' he said as we meandered along the perimeter wall, which was festooned with graffiti and edged with weeds, 'this is me next project. I'm developing it for residential an commercial use.' He pointed out through the passenger window. 'There'll be an apartment block here,' we rolled along, 'an another here, an two over there. Eight blocks in total, ranging in height from three to eight storeys. We're looking at the guts of 400 residential units, with about 12,000 square metres of office an commercial space at ground level, to include a hotel.'

'An hotel?'

'Correct. That'll go at the harbour end.'

'Father built an hotel on the estate and it barely ever achieves full occupancy, not even in summer. Not even when there's a wedding. The last thing Howth needs is another empty hotel.'

'This is Ireland.'

'What's that supposed to mean?'

‘You can’t build an apartment complex in Ireland without a hotel.’

‘Don’t be ridiculous. Of course you can.’

‘Ah see,’ he said, ‘you can an you can’t. No investor will touch you unless you qualify for Section 23-type reliefs.’

‘Section 23?’

‘Tax write-offs. So we have to build either a hotel or a multi-storey car park or a hospital or a student residence. None a which are needed, but the way I see it, if you build a hotel, then at least you have a bar.’ He pointed through the windscreen at the western boundary. ‘The leisure centre is going to be over there, an we have to keep the park an public tennis courts or they’ll all be moanin an cribbin, though we’re turning some of it into an all-weather playing pitch, but we may as well not bother if you ask me because no one’s going to be able to use it in anyways seeing as we’re putting it right next to the cream crackers.’

‘The what?’

‘Travellers’ halting site. They have to be given three semi-Ds an a detached four-bed house gratis an for nothing.’ He rolled down the window and hawked out a gullier of spit. ‘The working man up to his bollocks in debt to live in a rabbit hutch an that shower in the proper houses breaking their holes laughing at him.’ He wiped his mouth with the back of his hand.

‘So don’t build rabbit hutches for the working man.’

He shrugged. ‘Logistics. Only way to make it worth me while. An I’ve to push planning permission through before that poncey bill on design standards gets passed, because then it’ll be all dual aspect this an acoustic privacy that. Windows in kitchens an adequate storage, blah blah. There’ll be a few flash penthouses up top, obviously, but the rest a the units will be shoeboxes. I’m going to increase the population of Howth by an eighth overnight.' This stated with pride, as if he personally were to sire each newcomer.

'What about zoning?'

'Don't mind zoning.'

This was what I was dealing with. 'Dessie, the kind of population density you're proposing is appropriate to a city-centre location, not a seaside suburb. You'll never get permission for a series of eight-storey apartment blocks, never mind an hotel.'

Hickey winked. 'I know the very man. Here, open the glovebox.'

'Why?'

'Lamb a God, just open it.'

Inside was the site map. I took it out, and then frowned. 'How can you build three semi-Ds?'

'Wha?'

'You can't, by definition, build an odd number of semi-detached houses. They have to be built in pairs.'

Hickey rolled his eyes, as if this were precisely the class of hair-splitting shite that he'd come to expect of me.

'Besides,' I said, 'I already told you. We no longer own this land.'

'I know that.'

'So what do you want from me?'

'I want you to lend me the money.'

Had he heard about the hundred grand from M. Deauville? Impossible. I'd literally just cashed the cheque. Either way, it wasn't enough. 'You're talking a seven-figure sum there, Dessie.'

'I am.'

I laughed. 'What on earth makes you think I have that kind of money?'

'Not you, ya thick. Your new bank.'

'What new bank?'

'Castle Holdings.'

A clang of alarm down my spinal cord. 'How do you know about Castle Holdings?'

'There's a bleedin sign nailed to your bleedin door.' Hickey wheeled the truck around so that we were facing the length of the site and he switched the engine off. 'An you're the bleedin director. At least, that's what it says in the Register a Companies. Amn't I only after coming from there?' An image of a dusty black ledger of sins, and my name entered into the debtor's column. 'There was a phone number,' he continued, 'a Dublin one, city centre. I rang it an nobody answered. But the ringtone was funny.' He narrowed his eyes at me. 'You know, like, *foreign*. As if me call was being diverted to some other country, like when you dial them computer helplines an end up talking to some gee-bag in Bombay. Something dodgy going on there, I says, seeing as the registered address a Castle Holdings is up the road. So anyway, there I was driving home when I seen you coming out a the bank. An I thought: here, that's dodgy too, His Lordship doing business with the competition, an that's when I copped that Castle Holdings isn't an ordinary bank with local branches an that. No, it's a *commercial lender*.'

'Castle Holdings isn't a bank.'

Hickey shook his head. 'Snot what I heard.' He pulled a photocopy from his back pocket and began to read. 'According to the Register a Companies, Castle Holdings is the treasury-management arm of a transnational corporation. Treasury-management arms of transnational corporations are permitted in Ireland to be licensed as banks. In the case of most group treasury and asset financing operations, the Financial Regulator has disapplied its powers of supervision.'

'Disapplied?'

'Yeah. Disapplied.'

'That's not a word.'

Hickey shrugged. 'That's what it says in the IDA brochure. Quote: "The Financial Regulator has disapplied its powers of supervision." To cut a long story short,' he concluded, 'global corporations can establish unsupervised banks in Ireland. Banks like Castle Holdings. You're routing money through the Irish State to avail a the low corporation tax.' He dealt my arm a fond right hook. 'I didn't think you had it in ya. Personally, I hate the Tax Man. Any enemy a his is a friend a mine.'

I stared at him. What class of racket had I put my family name to? M. Deauville had some questions to answer. At that moment, my mobile rang. *Unknown*. Speak of the devil. I excused myself and climbed out of the truck.

'We need to talk, Monsieur Deauville,' I said. 'I've a man here,' – I glanced back at the truck to make sure that Hickey couldn't hear me – 'who seems to think that I'll loan him money. Capital,' I corrected myself, as seven figures commanded a more imperious title than money. 'This man seems to think that Castle Holdings is some class of bank, and that I'm some class of bank manager.'

I waited for M. Deauville to dismiss Hickey's ludicrous allegation. 'I see,' he said instead. I waited for him to say more. He did not.

'Well?' I prompted him. 'Is this man correct in his assertions?'

'What is his name?'

'It's Hickey again.' The door of the truck slammed. The accused was on his way over.

'Hickey, the property developer?'

'He's a builder.'

Tocka tocka. M. Deauville's fleet fingers flying across the keyboard. The man could type as quickly as he could think. I turned my back on Hickey and put some distance between us.

'And where is the site located?'

I stopped walking. How did he know about the site? 'I never mentioned a site.'

'Mr Hickey is a developer. I assume he requires finance to develop a site. I am endeavouring to establish where this site is located.'

I turned to the perimeter wall and came face to face with Ireland's Eye across the sound – russet against the blue of sea and sky, Lambay Island mauve in the distance. 'It's on the coast,' I told him. 'Along Claremont Beach. Just before you come to Howth Harbour.'

Tocka tocka. 'Indeed,' M. Deauville said. 'Area of high scenic amenity. Beaches and mountains. Yacht club, fishing village. Seafood restaurants, a proliferation of golf courses. Twenty-six minute journey by commuter train to the city centre. A most sought-after location. Castle Holdings is interested in investments of this nature.'

'Is that so?'

A firm 'Yes.'

I looked at Hickey. He was leaning against the truck. Arms folded, head cocked; ever the hard man. Glowering at me as he had glowered across the schoolyard while raising the smoke held pincered between thumb and index finger to his lips, aged what . . . eight? Daring me to rat him out, positively willing me to, so that he could kick my head in after school, the pinched yellow bloodthirsty face of him. And although I did not open my mouth to the teacher, he kicked my head in anyway.

'With all due respect,' I said to M. Deauville, pronouncing my words slowly and with care, seeking to communicate that the subject of our discussion was standing within earshot,

'I don't think Castle Holdings *should* be interested in investments of this nature.'

The *tocka tocka* on the keyboard ceased. 'With all due respect, Tristram,' M. Deauville countered, 'this is business.'

'What kind of business?' I had to ask. 'What exactly is Castle Holdings?'

'Castle Holdings is a specialist lender. We finance exciting business ventures from the ground up. Desmond Hickey has an established track record. How much does he wish to borrow?'

I lowered the phone and met Hickey's eye. 'How much do you need?'

'Ten million,' the clown answered.

'That's eight figures, Dessie. A minute ago, you said you needed seven.' It was the three semi-Ds all over again.

He displayed his palms. 'Prices are rocketing. There's a boom on.'

I raised the phone to my ear. 'He says he needs ten million.'

'And what percentage of that is for the site.'

I lowered the phone again. 'How much of that is for the site?'

'All of it.'

I raised the phone. 'He says the ten million is for the site alone.'

Tocka tocka. M. Deauville had a subscription to every credit-rating agency and private financial database going, his own personal copy of the big black ledger of sins. 'Mr Hickey would need to put at least 390 units on it to return a satisfactory profit. And a hotel or multi-storey car park to secure valuable tax subsidies. Get him to submit a detailed proposal to you by Monday. But yes, Castle Holdings is interested.'

'This is the purest form of speculation,' I objected, relocating to evade Hickey only to find him relocating to tail me like some sort of cosmic detritus entangled in my train. Karma, I suppose you could call it. 'He's talking about purchasing land which hasn't the zoning for the use to which he intends putting it. If he doesn't get a high-rise rezoning – and frankly he hasn't a hope in an area of outstanding natural beauty like this – well, the land is worth a fraction of the ten million he proposes to borrow to pay for it. You won't get your money back.'

Tocka tocka on the other end of the line, followed by silence as M. Deauville considered the results on the screen. It is a regrettable fact that many of us recovering alcoholics become workaholics, replacing one addiction with another. *Tocka tocka, tocka tocka*, and then a wry snort of approval. 'Don't worry,' M. Deauville advised me. 'In light of his recent track record with the various Dublin planning authorities, I think it's safe to say that Mr Hickey knows the very man.'

'What did he say?' Hickey wanted to know after M. Deauville and I had finished up with a quick recitation of the Serenity Prayer.

'He says you know the very man. Submit a detailed proposal to me by Monday.'

Hickey lit up. I thought he was coming over to shake my hand but he walked right past me, gauging his location in relation to the perimeter wall, the road, the railway line. He looked up at the sun and down at his shadow, consulted his site plan and counted out paces, searching for the buried chest of gold with his pirate's treasure map. X marks the spot.

Finally he found it. He lowered the plan and looked about himself, filled his lungs with sea air. 'I'm building me hotel right here,' he proclaimed, throwing his arms wide, a man unlocking the energies of the earth's molten core and channelling them into the universe. Pandora's Box was open for business. 'An it's going to be eleven storeys high!'

Fourth day of evidence

15 MARCH 2016

‘Mr St Lawrence, on the matter of the rezoning of the Claremont site from industrial use to high-density residential, would you elaborate on your statement that Mr Hickey claimed he “knew the very man”.’

Knew him? He had his number on speed dial. He took out his phone and got an appointment there and then, and hung up and winked at me. 'I know the very man,' he reasserted with swagger in a country where knowing the very man meant everything, and it turned out not to be an empty boast.

The meeting was scheduled for the 24th of June at one o'clock in a pub on the busy main street of Blanchardstown, the heartland of the Minister's constituency. I remember that the man was late. The Minister was a full three pints late by the metronomic stroke of Hickey's drinking arm, which lifted and lowered his glass to beat out time.

I can also tell you that it was hot. It was a hot sunny day and for this reason we were the only two customers sitting indoors. That suited me perfectly well. I dislike crowds. At the end of a mahogany-panelled corridor to the rear of the bar the beer garden glowed achingly bright. It was peopled with carefree office staff on their lunch breaks. Hickey and I, pale against the varnished murk of the foreground, were seated like penitents on a wooden pew, our backs turned on the sun as if to God's love itself. I see us so clearly that I could be gazing at us on a gallery wall, a painting commissioned by the Church for the purpose of moral instruction. *The Folly of Greed*, or was it *Hubris*? Or just an all-purpose *Folly of Folly*?

We were facing the door. *Tick tock* went Hickey's drinking arm, with fresh pints appearing to mark the quarter hour. I got lumped with the usual sparkling mineral water, which I order out of pressure to order something. I don't even like sparkling mineral water. I'd rather just sit there with nothing. I gazed at the glass for the duration, turning it this way and that on the beer mat as if it were a diamond of ingenious cut, though I wanted to smash it against the wall for being just water. Water could never slake my thirst.

Hickey drank in silence as there was nothing left to say. The mood had turned sour on the journey over in the truck. I was attending the meeting on M. Deauville's wishes and against my better judgement, and I was adamant that Hickey should know it. I tackled the matter from various angles to drive home my point. 'Get down off the cross,' he said after five miles of this. We hadn't exchanged a word since.

As I've said, the Minister was late. You would think that it was him giving *us* all the money. *Tick tock* went Hickey's pint. I folded my arms and crossed my legs. I was nervous, but then I am always nervous. Look at me. My hands are shaking. Each time the pub door opened to admit a figure silhouetted against the blazing sun, my heart accelerated only to subsequently slump when that figure proved not to be the man in question, whatever he may have looked like, because I did not know him. Hickey knew him, but I did not know the very man from Adam then. Let the record state that I had no dealings with Minister Ray Lawless prior to that day in June.

On the pew was a large crumpled Jiffy pack, propped between Hickey's thighs and mine like a ladies handbag. If witnesses come in here banging on about brown envelopes, I'll tell you right now that they are lying. They are downplaying the sums involved. A large Jiffy pack was required to contain the amount involved in this transaction, a transaction which I am given to understand was fairly typical of the times that were in it, and the amount involved fairly typical too. The fee specified by the Minister would simply not have fitted into one of these infamous brown envelopes. Pardon me?

Yes, *fee* is the word Minister Lawless used. He was hardly going to call it a bribe.

It was this Jiffy pack more than anything else that, to my mind, gave the game away as we sat there scowling in the pub. The dogs in the street could have told you that we were up to no good. That package was as incriminating as a smoking gun, yet there was no place else to stash the bloody thing except right there between us on the pew. You could hardly entrust an amount of that magnitude to the floor. My insides fizzed with the sparkling water and my foot jigged up and down with the stress. I don't have the stomach for dodgy dealings. Unlike Hickey. Hickey had the stomach for them. The stomach and the appetite.

I leaned in to him. 'Will we get a receipt?'

He smirked. 'Will we fuck.'

The door opened for the hundredth time. I checked my watch for the hundredth time. It was twenty to two. Hickey put down his pint and sat up. A tall sullen man had entered the pub, dressed in a belted beige trench coat despite the heat. He had hands like shovels and crêpe-soled shoes on great big splayed-out feet. He spotted Hickey, assessed me with dead eyes, and then clocked the Jiffy pack. Aw Jesus, I remember thinking as he plodded doggedly towards us. This is our man? I threw a glance at Hickey: can't you do better?

A rain-coloured man is how I would describe him. Rain has no colour and nor did he. A rain-coloured man with rain-coloured hair and rain-tinted glasses on his nose. There was an excess of trench coat about his person, not in girth but height, as if there were two of them in there, one standing on the other's shoulders. It occurred to me that he was wiretapped. But were this the case they would surely have done a more discreet job. These days, there's technology.

He smelled wrong, because yes, I could smell him when he

drew up before us. It was the odour of a garment left too long at the back of the wardrobe – mouldy, mildewy, mothballed. I glanced at Hickey again: are you serious? Him? Really? But Hickey was in a state of delight.

I got to my feet and registered that he was my equal in height, a rare enough phenomenon in Ireland. However, instead of shaking my shaking hand, the Minister reached down and pulled a three-legged stool out from under our table. He positioned the stool with both hands as though lining it up for a penalty kick before lowering his sodden weight onto it.

I resumed my seat and found that suddenly I was looking up at him. His height was all in his torso. A fine man, is how party members typically described him, persisting in the peasant trait of equating physical stature with moral fibre. Despite being tall, the truth about Minister Ray Lawless is that he was a short arse.

Lawless was perspiring. His rain-coloured skin was slick and clammy, weeping like the wall of a cave. He produced a balled-up handkerchief and mopped the sweat from his forehead but it immediately reappeared. Still he did not take the obvious measure of removing his raincoat. What was he hiding under there?

He stuffed the soiled rag back into his pocket and folded his arms. The man had not yet so much as grunted. A character entirely bereft of social graces, I concluded, a brute escaped from the zoo, at which assessment Lawless whipped around to glare at me, as if he had overheard me think it. He as quickly whipped his glare away. Uncomfortable with eye contact. That's another thing I remember noting.

'Tanks a million for coming,' said Hickey, and the great big short arse nodded. His arms were folded with such hostility that his fists clenched his elbows. Hickey nodded at the bar. 'What are you drinking?'

'I don't drink,' Lawless said sharply. His first utterance and it was a rebuke. Was he in the fellowship? I didn't think so. He struck me as the sort who had taken the Pioneer's pledge when making his confirmation, then spent the rest of his life looking down his nose at the pathetic wretches dying of thirst around him, a man with no tolerance for human frailty. I knew his type. 'Lookit, Dessie, let's just get down to business, alright?'

Wasn't anybody going to make the introductions? Apparently not. I cleared my throat. 'Minister,' I began.

'Ray,' he said without raising his eyes to meet mine. I followed the line of his gaze. The Jiffy pack. He was staring at the Jiffy pack.

'Ray,' I agreed, and was about to offer my own name when he cut me dead by turning to Hickey.

'Did ye bring the drawings?'

'I did a course,' said Hickey, and presented the plans for outline planning permission across the table like a bunch of flowers, for he was in love with Ray Lawless, I realised then.

We sat in silence studying Ray as Ray sat in silence studying the plans. A police car or ambulance *nee-nawed* past. Hickey flashed me one of his wolfish smiles to indicate that he reckoned we were laughing. A bead of sweat rolled down the Minister's face and landed with a splat on the drawings, followed by another. Ray was raining. He had begun to drizzle.

The wet rag was retrieved from his pocket and swabbed once more across his brow. 'Roastin in here,' Hickey offered to cover up the man's embarrassment, not understanding that Lawless felt none. 'Take off your coat,' I suggested, but when did anybody ever listen to me?

Lawless pushed the outline drawings aside. 'What else do ye have for me, lads?' he wanted to know, returning his attention to the Jiffy pack. 'Oh, sorry,' said Hickey, and reached for the cash. He could not hand that money over fast enough.

I half-expected a third arm to extend from Ray's belted midriff to snatch the package, his little parasitic bag man. You have seen the television footage. The Minister wasn't fat so much as misshapen. And he was misshapen because he grabbed and grabbed, a country spilling over its borders, annexing smaller states, distending with each acquisition.

But no, Ray's two shovel paws clamped the pack. He opened it up and stuck his nose inside, jigged the wads up and down to give them a good toss, a man distributing salt and vinegar through his bag of chips, for Minister Lawless had such an appetite for hard currency that I reckon he wanted to eat it.

He took his pitted nose out of the padded envelope. 'That's grand, boys. I'll get back to ye.'

He rolled up the mouth of the pack and took custody, oblivious to how suspicious this looked, to how suspicious the entire transaction had looked, because Minister Lawless was quite without shame, though it took me a while to get my head around that, shame being one of mankind's founding principles, as depicted in the story of Adam and Eve diving for their fig leaves. To be without shame was, to me, akin to being without thoughts or emotions. I didn't see how a human could be a human without it. And then I met Ray.

He got to his feet and left, no goodbyes, the Jiffy pack wedged under his arm like a hog. When the door swung shut, and the raincloud of Ray had moved on to blight another part of the city, Hickey screwed up his face and rubbed his hands together, fast as he could, as if trying to generate a spark between his palms. 'Sorted,' he said with triumph. 'I told you I knew the very man.'

Ray. I sighed at the irony of a name such as that being given to a man such as him. Who on earth had looked into his cradle, beheld the rain-grey infant inside, and named it after a shaft of light. Ray, a drop of golden sun.

And then I got it. He was not ray as in a sunbeam, but ray as in the fish, that ugly flat fish with its mournful face the colour of a mushroom. Ray, the bottom feeder. Steadily making its way along the ocean bed, ingesting the tiny creatures that strayed across its path, never hungry, never full, never hunting or giving chase, simply consuming methodically until it reached the end of its natural life. I was not one bit sorry when Ray Lawless went down, even though he took the lot of us with him.

‘And further to this “fee” being paid to Minister Ray Lawless, the Claremont site was rezoned?’

Yes, and fairly promptly too – you'll see yourself from the records. Ray had fast-tracked our application. I answered the door one morning about six weeks later to find Hickey standing there, fit to burst with glee. He brandished a letter in my face. 'You get what you pay for!' he informed me before climbing back into his truck and carving a fresh set of skid marks into the gravel. Who knows what pleasure he derived from the skid marks? Some, I hope.

I closed the door and opened the letter.

deeR MiscER hicKy and MiscER Saint LoRenzo

the Minister had scrawled in crayon, or that is my recollection – it was a primitive mind that we were dealing with, scratching primitive marks into the earth. The letter confirmed that the land had been rezoned from industrial use to high-density residential and commercial. We had indeed gotten what we had paid for.

The site had been purchased for €10 million. It was now worth, Hickey rang that afternoon to inform me, six times that. The valuer had just delivered his report and had come up with a figure of sixty. 'That's over a million in profit a week!' Hickey said, ever the class thick – we were up fifty million in the space of a month and a half, a profit of over one million *a day*. Hickey can be forgiven for making this mistake. Even in that economic climate it was difficult to grasp. Besides, he sounded scuttered.

'Come down and see the new site office while you're at it,' he added grandly, as if extending an invitation to a cruise on his private yacht.

*

The site office was a Portakabin with a sign reading Site Office stuck to the door. It was mounted on concrete blocks just inside the old cement factory entrance. Messages were scribbled on its grey flank: *Jenny loves Darren, Kerrie loves Karl,* a cartoon sketch of a nob. I had heard about Hickey's famous Portakabins. He rented them to schools for forty-seven grand each per year, and some schools held on to them for a decade, making D. Hickey a rich man, he boasted. 'Indeed,' I had said, not buying a word of it – why would a school pay €47,000 a year to park a prefab in the playground when proper classrooms could be constructed for that kind of money? But we now know it to be true. The Irish educational system had humiliated Hickey so he had made it his business to expose the real gobshites.

His truck was parked between a fire-engine-red Mercedes SLK and a silver Audi TT, both 06 registration plates. I approached the prefab and knocked. It trembled on its blocks in response to movement within, then Hickey flung open the door. In his hand was a champagne flute, with which he gestured in welcome. 'Come in an for fuck's sake wipe your feet!'

I looked down at the upended beer crate that served as a doorstep. Wipe them on what?

'Ah relax,' he said, 'it's a joke. This is a site office, not a bleedin castle. For builders, not barons, wha! Bet you've never set foot on a building site in your life, am I right?' He looked down at me from his perch and belched. 'Ah, God love ya, you're not the worst. Anyway.' He stepped back from the doorway to reveal an attractive young couple seated at the rear of the cabin. 'Here he is at last. Meet Tristram. He's me business partner!' The man got to his feet and extended his hand.

'Tristram, this is me architect, Morgan. An this' – the woman looked up but Hickey passed over her – 'is the master plan.'

He cleared the architect out of the way and led me to the table. Displayed on a board like a wedding cake was the scale model of a modern urban residential and commercial development typical of and appropriate to, say, a downtown waterside location in an East Coast US city: eight towers of glass clustered in a crystalline formation. The tallest crystal was located at the most easterly point – the hotel, Hickey's Pandora's Box.

Hickey set down his champagne flute and leaned over the table, his nose hovering inches above the model. 'That thing', he said with satisfaction, indicating the hotel, 'could take out your eye.' He breathed heavily over the development, a god admiring his handiwork from the heavens, picking out which bit he might like to toy with next. If you lifted off the top of Hickey's head, you'd find it crammed with plastic models. They characterised his relationship with the world. He had reduced it in scale to a size that was manageable, malleable, an entity he could carve up and sell. He was a very simple man. That's what made him so dangerous.

I could feel the woman's eyes on me. I glanced over at her and was about to introduce myself when Hickey nudged me. 'Here, Tristram,' he said, sensing that he'd lost my attention. He pointed out the encircled H of a helipad. 'That's me parkin spot. H for Hickey.'

'I have the artwork here also, Mr Hickey,' said the architect.

'Go on,' said Hickey. 'Show us the artwork.'

The architect unclasped his portfolio and produced a set of large computer-generated shots illustrating how the proposed development would look at street level. Hickey devoured each one before passing it to me, the glossy photographic paper mottled with his chip-shop fingerprints. He grunted with relish at these images of the world he was on the cusp of bringing into being. Photoshopped women with ponytails and trim bodies toting tennis rackets. Men in shirtsleeves laughing into mobile phones. In one picture a BMW X5 deposited a smiling blonde toddler into the open arms of a smiling blonde childcare worker at the proposed crèche. A Maserati made its exit from the proposed underground car park with a surf board strapped to its roof in the next. Along a glittering limestone avenue with Ireland's Eye in the background a man walked a bichon frise.

'Who's this prick?' said Hickey. 'He looks bent.'

Morgan leaned in to consider the photo. 'With apartment developments in wealthy areas, our firm find it's advantageous to include a representation of at least one member of the gay community. It's a sector of the population with a high disposable income.'

'Keep him so,' Hickey decreed, 'but no lezzers.' He passed me the offending image. It was a man in a pair of calf-length shorts and a polo shirt. The man looked neither gay nor straight, he just looked preposterous. They all looked preposterous. Every last one of them was dressed for a Mediterranean summer. Sunglasses and shorts and sandals. This development promised another climate. Presiding over it all were these green glass towers, the sun glinting off their elevations in every shot. Despite their height, they cast no shadow at street level, as if they themselves were the source of the light, and very possibly of the heat too, a nuclear power station.

Hickey turned to me. 'Whatcha reckon?'

'Smashing,' I told him. 'You've really outdone yourself.' I handed back the photos and the woman covered up a smile. I knew her. I knew that face from somewhere.

*

'So who's the girl?' I asked Hickey when we were back out in the yard, having seen Morgan off in his little silver TT bullet. The red Merc was still parked next to Hickey's truck. I was confused when she hadn't stood up to join the architect as he took his leave but instead poured herself another glass of champagne. I had presumed that she was part of the design team.

'What girl?' said Hickey, and then, tilting his head at the prefab, 'oh, you mean the wife?'

‘Do we understand you correctly, Mr St Lawrence: you are asserting that Mrs Hickey—’

Please don’t call her that.

‘That is her name. Are you claiming that Edel Hickey was involved in the Claremont development from the outset?’

No. She had no interest in construction, or in anything that Hickey did. Looking back, I suspect that she may have come down that afternoon to meet me. That may sound like colossal vanity on my part, but the more I think about it, the more convinced I become that Edel showed up on that occasion for the express purpose of seeing me again.

'Mr St Lawrence, sticking to the particulars of the case: you are stating that Edel Hickey had no involvement in the Claremont development. Is that correct?'

Yes, Fergus, that is correct.

‘Thank you. Now, to get down to the financing of the construction of the Claremont development. Where did you get the money?’

Is that a trick question? I don't understand this game. Where do you think we got the money? Where does anyone get money, after all? We got it from a bank. Not Castle Holdings – M. Deauville only financed the purchase of the site – but from an Irish bank. You remember, Fergus: they were throwing money at people at the time, forcing it down their throats. Hickey said I knew the very man and my heart sank. Here we go. Ray the bottom feeder. 'No, no, no, you muppet,' he said. 'Not Lawless – another head. An *you* know him, not me.'

'What other head?'

'Another head who knows a third head, who knows a whole rack a heads, who between them know every head worth knowing in this country, an once we're in, we'll be laughing, so we will.' And then he reeled off a list of names, Public Enemies numbers one through to six six six. Builders, bankers, financial regulators, county councillors, even the serving Taoiseach.

'Oh,' I said, 'them.' It would have been difficult not to have rubbed up against at least a few of them in a country like this if you were from a family like mine – you know how it is yourself, Fergus. I sighed at Hickey. 'What's it going to cost?' Everything cost. Everything was about money with the class of individual on his list. It was how they measured themselves.

Hickey shook his head. 'That's not how the Golden Circle works.'

The Golden Circle. I had to laugh at that. They had

rebranded. In my day, they had called themselves the Bills, as in, the Billionaires. *Long live the Bills!* they shouted down in Suttonians after matches. They were the sons of wealthy men, but nowhere near as wealthy as they wanted to be. The Mills, technically. Their moniker betrayed the terrible hunger in them, the insatiable drive to acquire.

M. Deauville requested that I supply him in advance of the meeting with a list of the members of this so-called Golden Circle who, according to Hickey, were now running the shop. *Tocka tocka* as he fed their names into his database of base data. Murmurs of approval at the results. The Bills had finally blossomed into billionaires. Excellent, said M. Deauville. *Ausgezeichnet, eccellente.*

Hickey drove us to a district of the city that had not existed when I had fled. The towers were built of the same jade glass as Hickey's crystalline power generator. He had beaten himself into a suit for the occasion, and I don't wish to be unkind, but when I saw him got up in it I couldn't help thinking of . . . ah no, I won't.

The boardroom occupied the penthouse suite of one of the glass towers. A panorama of cranes spanning the horizon was engaged in a courtly dance. One step, two step, swing to your partner, and part. Ten men were seated around the boardroom table and the most senior man stood at the top. 'Ah,' he said upon our entrance. 'Here they are. Do join us.' He was a small man with a brown face and a fleece of white curls. I thought of a Roman senator.

'Dessie,' said Hickey, pumping the senator's hand with both of his. McGee didn't need to introduce himself. We both knew who he was. Hickey jerked a thumb at me. 'This is Tristram St Lawrence,' he told the table. 'He's the brains.'

The men laughed at that and Hickey laughed loudest of all. I lowered my head in admission. Yes, it's true. The brains are stored in this receptacle, me. I provide them so that Hickey doesn't have to.

Only it wasn't true. I wasn't the brains. I was just stupid enough to think that I was.

A man from the far end of the table was on his way over, his arms open in welcome as if I should recognise him. It took me a moment to register that this was O'Dee. He had lost his hair and turned into his old man, a golf-clubbing captain of industry.

O'Dee put his arms around me and clapped my back. 'Welcome home, man,' he said as sincerely as he was able, though no affection or camaraderie had ever existed between us. This display was strictly for the benefit of the others, to demonstrate that we went back, that there was history, that it was kosher. 'Jesus, Trist, I heard you were dead.'

They all laughed again at that, eager to exhibit their approval.

'Eh,' said Hickey. 'That was another Tristram St Lawrence.'

'Marvellous!' said McGee and took his seat to indicate that the topic was now closed. Everyone seemed perfectly satisfied with Hickey's explanation. Nobody wanted to rock the boat. We were here to do business.

Hickey's architectural model of the Claremont development was displayed in the centre of the table. It looked bigger. Had he glued on extra crystals? The skyscraper hotel closely resembled the building we had assembled in, which in turn resembled the building next to it, and the building next to it again, and so on throughout the docklands and across to the opposite bank of the Liffey. Those dollar-green towers were a contagion that had ripped through Dublin.

A knock on the door and a girl entered the boardroom. 'Marvellous!' McGee declared with unfaltering enthusiasm. The girl set a tray of tea and coffee on the console table.

'Anything else I can get you, Mr McGee?'

'This is perfect, Suzie,' said McGee. 'Good job!'

The girl turned to leave. The boardroom table took a moment to assess her pinstriped arse and then it was down to brass tacks.

'Right, gentlemen,' said McGee, 'what have we got here?'

Hickey got up on his hind legs to make his presentation. He threw a load of numbers out there – how much we'd secured, how much we still needed to secure, how many units we intended building – several more than the planning permission granted, I noted, but although the documentation was there in front of them nobody raised a query. Revising planning permissions upwards was not a problem, not in a room like this. He went on to estimate how much profit the development would generate. This figure too had increased, but then, property prices were rising exponentially. We were getting rich by doing nothing. 'An nearest the Dart station and harbour, right at the entrance to the scenic fishing village of Howth,' Hickey concluded, 'we're going to construct a landscape building.'

'Landmark,' I corrected him.

'Yeah,' said Hickey. 'A landmark building for Howth.' He indicated the hotel. 'Eleven storeys high, eighty-eight bedrooms, with bars, restaurant an ancillary areas.' He narrowed his eyes at the horizon. 'Youse'll be able to see it from here.'

'Terrific,' said McGee. He turned to the other ten. 'I like these guys,' he decided, as if the purpose of our presentation had been to make new friends. 'These guys have *balls*.' Assent echoed around the table. *Balls*, these guys have *balls*, and *balls* are what we need.

McGee rose to shake our hands. Our time was up. 'On behalf of everyone, I'd like to thank you both for bringing your proposal to us. Good lord, Lawrence, your hands are freezing.'

'Actually, it's *Saint* Lawrence.'

He clapped my back. 'And I'm Pope Ulick. My colleagues and I will be in touch.'

*

'Here, do you remember the craze for metal detectors in the eighties?' Hickey asked me on the drive home. The meeting had left him in a philosophical mood. They liked us. They liked us guys. We had *balls*. Their validation had filled Hickey with a desire to soliloquise, to survey the great leap he had made in his lifetime, to recall with fondness his humble origins now that they were safely behind him.

The jade city gave way to the hazy blue of the coast road. Hickey blessed himself at the church in Clontarf and inclined his head towards Bull Island. 'Do you remember they'd all be there on Dollymount Strand? Grown men wandering up an down for hours with the buzzin yoke that looked like a strimmer. Fucken eejits, the lot a them. I suppose it was that or the bookies. But when one a them yokes went off, you dropped what you were doing to keep an eye on the digging because for a moment it could of been the next Tara Brooch or Ardagh Chalice that got pulled out a the sand. People were desperate back then. Jaysus, we had nothing. I mean, at the end a the day it was always a supermarket trolley or car axle or some shite like that because you won't find many archaeological artefacts on an island that only silted up a hundred years ago. But you can't help hoping, can you? That's what happens when you rear a nation to chase after leprechauns an crocks a gold. Then the Lotto came in an we all chased after that instead so it was curtains for metal detectors. Anyway.'

The lights changed to red and Hickey took the truck out of gear and let it roll to a halt. He raised his chin to tug at his tie and coils of chest hair sprang from his shirt collar. 'See, the difference with me, Tristram, is that I never stopped trawling the place with me metal detector, do you know what I mean like? I never packed it in. Everyone said this country was a kip, but not me. Everyone left, but I didn't. Because I *knew*.' He prodded the dashboard with his index finger. 'I knew there was treasure buried around here somewhere. I could smell it, so I could. An now I've found it. It was right under me nose all the time. Land. Or what happens to land when a man like me changes it into *property*. I've transformed a heap a muck into gold.'

I looked at him. He believed it. All of them around the boardroom table had believed it too. They believed that the land had changed, and that they, the Golden Circle, were the agents of this change, that somehow, by linking hands around a table, or through the appliance of their *balls*, they had managed to perform alchemy upon Irish soil. Hickey grinned as he contemplated the open road stretching before us. Every light ahead had turned to green.

‘And how long was it before loan approval came through?’

We had it by the time we made it back to Howth.

‘Thank you, Mr St Lawrence. That will be all for today.’

Are you sure?

'Excuse me?'

Are you sure that will be all? Aren't you curious about the identity of the others in the Golden Circle? Forgive me, but isn't the State paying you to conduct a full inquiry? There were eleven men waiting for us in that room, Fergus. McGee has been held personally accountable for the economic implosion. Yes, he was a reckless man, and yes, he was a devious one, but don't you think that blaming him for the downfall of the country is somewhat overstating his hand?

No, that's right, you don't want the list of attendees, do you? And nor do you need it. You already have it. Two of you, after all, were there.

Fifth day of evidence

16 MARCH 2016

‘Mr St Lawrence, you have asserted in previous statements that fractures began to appear in your relationship with Desmond Hickey once work commenced on the Claremont site.’

Yes, Fergus, unfortunately that was the case. When site works began, Hickey grew aggressive and paranoid. He was under a lot of pressure. This was November, possibly December. It was cold and the castle was ice. Hickey's men knocked down the old factory and carted it away in a convoy of trucks like a circus. A bigger circus was coming to town. With the factory razed, Ireland's Eye was visible from the road for the first time in half a century.

Then the digging began. Hulking great turbines boring through the earth, eyeless monsters with obscene nozzles for mouths mindlessly ingesting, mechanical versions of Minister Ray Lawless. We had unleashed something dire upon the land. The weekends brought respite, but the disturbance started up again every Monday. I had extravagant nightmares about subterranean activity – caverns being excavated beneath the castle. The expansion of Hell was under way in these dreams. The demons were at work, or at play, and it was happening directly beneath my sleeping body, or my sleepless body, more often than not, because once work commenced on the Claremont site I was unable to sustain unconsciousness for more than a few hours at a stretch. I had taken to timing these bouts, although I knew that by the very act of timing them I was training myself into the habit.

'It will pass,' M. Deauville assured me.

A rumbling vibration was constant during that period, the *put-put-put* of a fishing trawler setting out for the night, churning the black water into white lace, except that the sound didn't grow fainter with distance travelled but instead louder as the weeks passed. They were getting closer. A flagstone in the cellar might lift at any moment and an army of Hickey's construction workers come charging in to storm the castle.

I rose one morning in the hour before dawn and pulled on the clothes that I had removed just a few hours earlier, for it did not seem to me that a new day had begun but that the old one was being driven mercilessly on, flogged past its limits like a broken-down workhorse, and that since it was yesterday for me still I should be dressed in yesterday's shirt. It had been my worst night yet. I had not even managed one of my two-hour cycles.

The two setters were asleep outside Father's door. They sprang to their feet in hackling defence when I entered the hall and one of them dared to growl, but their long frames yielded to wagging bodily when they saw that it was a friend. I got down on my hunkers and clasped one under each arm. They were so slim. The pair pressed themselves against me, thumping the walls with their tails. 'Good boys,' I whispered, 'good boys, good boys,' and their ardent hearts beat harder. It was so rare to find good boys in this world of bad boys that it seemed crucial to acknowledge and praise it.

The pair loped along after me through the dark passageways, their claws tapping upon the parquetry, their tails swinging in slow arcs, but when I reached the door to the kitchen garden and unhooked the key, they sat down and gazed up at me beseechingly. We had arrived at an impasse. They were creatures of duty. Father was their master. I was asking them to abandon their post. Our adventure had come to an end.

Out on the avenue, the *put-put-put* was louder.

Down at the gate lodge, Larney's Jack Russell shot from

the bushes with the velocity of a kicked ball. 'Toddy!' came the voice from my childhood and the dog trotted back to its owner. Larney came limping out onto the avenue, the usual anguished smile on his face. Didn't the man sleep, or did he lie coiled on his cot through the night, his eyes open and his ears cocked, spending so much time with the nocturnal creatures that he had become one of them? That's if Larney had been in bed. He was fully dressed.

'Would that be the young master?'

'Yes, Larney,' I said, trying not to break my stride – I wasn't able for his nonsense at that hour – but the dog planted itself in my path. I sidestepped but it relocated to block my passage, tackling me like a centre forward.

'It's been around for millions of years, but it's no more than a month old. What is it?'

I looked up from the terrier. 'Excuse me?'

Larney sidled closer, smiled harder. 'It's been around for millions of years, but it's no more than a month old. What is it?'

'Oh.' It was one of his riddles. 'I don't know, Larney. What is it?'

'The moon.'

'I see. Very good. Larney, tell me: do you hear that noise too?'

This elicited a strangled silence from the man, during which the *put-put-put* seemed more pronounced than ever. Larney stared at me in shrinking and blinking alarm, so I pointed towards Claremont.

'Down there. Do you hear it? That vibration.' He turned his head to follow the direction of my finger, but my question had thrown him into a paroxysm of confusion. 'It's not a riddle, Larney. It's a simple question. Do you hear that noise?'

His eyes darted back to mine. Uncertainty had distorted

his smile, flipped it upside down, but then he brightened. 'What goes round the castle and in the castle but never touches the castle?'

'Larney, please listen to me for a moment. Can you hear that noise too: yes or no?'

He kept smiling. 'The sun,' he said.

'Larney—'

'What goes round the castle—'

'*Larney*. This is important. That chugging noise: can you hear it too? Or am I losing my mind?'

Immediately I saw the error I had made. Larney processed idioms literally, and I had asked him whether he thought I was going insane. 'That's not what I meant,' I began, but there was no retracting it. Larney smiled in lockjawed panic as he backed away into the refuge of the shrubbery. 'Forget it, Larney,' I called after him, but it was too late. I'd already sentenced the poor soul to hours spent skipping over the same looped sequence like a scratched record, trying and failing to find the correct answer to the riddle I had posed. Is the young master losing his mind? He didn't like to say. I clamped my hands to my ears to shut the chugging noise out. Maybe I *was* going insane.

Ireland's Eye was a trim dun shape against the navy sea. The view my ancestors would have enjoyed was due to be bricked up again, by me. Hoarding had been erected along the boundary wall with various site notices attached. Danger. Concealed Exit. Hard Hat Area. Abandon Hope. The main road was plastered with fat tyre tracks of clay. I followed the trail to the heavy plant entrance.

Mounds of soil and rubble were heaped along the perimeter wall, waiting to be dispatched by the fleet of trucks that was parked up for the night. I stumbled in the direction of the chugging. Despite being flat, the going was heavy. Clods of clay adhered to the soles of my shoes like a snowball rolled in snow, building up only to break off again. Towards the harbour end of the site I discerned a hole, a vast one, as if a meteorite had struck. The chugging, which was now a clatter, was emanating from this crater.

I approached and peered over the lip. The earth crumbled away underfoot and I almost slithered in. It was a sharp drop. At the bottom of the pit was a whole civilisation. Machinery, lights, materials, tools. And men. There was a rake of them down there. Miniature men grubbing about in the dirt like the creatures exposed when you lifted a rock.

A man's voice behind me penetrated the clamour. I turned around. Hickey in a yellow helmet, shouting.

'I can't hear you!' I shouted back, but he couldn't hear me. He gestured at me to come away from the edge.

'Here,' he said, throwing a hard hat on my head and an arm over my shoulder. Hickey had no personal boundaries, whereas I was nothing but personal boundaries, a prickling hotchpotch. He patted my helmet. 'There y'are, Health and Safety. Good man. How do you like me hole?' There was a smell of booze on his breath.

Enthusiastic responses have never been my forte. Weak smiles are more my thing. I took the helmet off and read the safety specification printed inside the crown. 'I can't sleep,' I complained. 'The noise.'

If it wasn't in praise of his hole, Hickey didn't want to hear it. He fished a Motorola out of his high-viz jacket and marched off barking instructions into it. Judging by the dark circles under his eyes he hadn't slept much either, but for very different reasons. The man was in a fever of excitement, a child on Christmas morning.

I struggled after him but couldn't keep up, for he seemed physically adapted to the muck in a way that I was not. The boom of the crane swung overhead and lowered a cauldron into the crater. Two men at the bottom competed for it like chicks in a nest. A third man with a walkie-talkie stood back and guided the cauldron into the men's outstretched hands. 'That's it, keep her going, lads,' Hickey coached them, though they were out of earshot.

The pendulum of the cauldron seemed perilous in relation to the two men grappling for it. It could have taken them out like a demolition ball. Hickey inclined his head to me when I drew up behind him. 'The piles went in last week,' he remarked, as if I might know or care what such a statement meant. We stared into the crater's depths for a spell, seeing very different things. Everybody sees different things when looking into an abyss. I see more than most.

The men made contact with the cauldron and secured it. 'He's good,' said Hickey, 'yeah, that fella's good.' I wasn't sure whether he meant the crane driver or the man with the walkie-talkie. The other two workers tilted the vat, which was still suspended from the crane by a chain, and a grey stream of concrete came spilling out. Or maybe it was cement. I never did learn the difference.

My phone vibrated in my pocket. *Unknown*. 'Yes,' I told M. Deauville. 'Yes, I, ahm . . . Everything appears to be in order.' Like I'd know. They could have been pouring foundations of cold porridge down there. 'The foundations are going in,' I offered, and raised my eyebrows at Hickey for confirmation, but he just folded his arms and glared at me, a study in belligerence. I turned my back.

How could I have confessed my gut feeling to M. Deauville? That Hickey was digging us into a big hole. That across the country people were digging themselves into big holes, that big holes were spreading across Ireland like the pox, eating away at the heart of the island. Nobody was interested in negative sentiments. People who engaged in cribbing and moaning from the sidelines should frankly go and commit suicide, the Taoiseach had told us. My doubts were the product of a depressive mind. It was a difficult period for me but I was managing to preserve my sobriety, one day at a time.

The sun had crested the island in a peach starburst when I got off the call. I put the phone in my pocket and Hickey put his hands on his hips. 'Who was that ringing you?'

'Nobody.'

I don't know why I was being so secretive about M. Deauville. Hickey didn't know either. 'Nobody,' he repeated caustically and took a metal hip flask from his pocket. Slowly and pointedly, he unscrewed the lid. In his hands, that flask became a grenade. 'Why were you and this Nobody talking gobbledy-gook?'

I blinked at him. M. Deauville had addressed me in German, I realised. So I had responded in German. Which explained why Hickey hadn't confirmed the information about the foundations but instead just stood there radiating agro. 'That was German.'

'I don't care what it was. You better not be hiding something is all I'm saying.'

The cauldron had begun its ascent. The crane, which looked so serene from a distance, was staked at its base by metal shafts. It swung its head towards us like a lunatic in a restraining chair and the shadow of the boom came galloping across the poached ground. I shuddered when the shadow swept over me.

Hickey laughed, his breath a white plume on the chilly air. 'Is someone after walking across your grave?' He removed the pin from the grenade with a smirk and the flask started to tick. He sloshed the contents under my nose. 'Want some? Keeps the cold out.'

'You know I don't drink.'

'You were me best customer.'

'I have no idea what you're talking about.'

'Ah, sorry, forgot. That was another Tristram St Lawrence. Isn't that right?'

I held his hard hat out to him but he didn't accept it, so I set it down in the mud. Hickey surveyed me with open antagonism as he tilted his head to knock back a snifter. I caught a trace of spirit on the air. 'I have to leave,' I said, and turned for the gate.

Hickey swallowed noisily and did the post-pint sigh: *Ahhhhh*. 'Get back here, you,' he said. 'You've shopped me to the Tax Man, haven't you?'

I turned around and made a face. 'Why on earth would I shop you to the Tax Man?'

He shrugged. 'Somebody has. Why do I keep getting calls? Why do you keep getting calls?'

He was intoxicated. Like me, he had not been sleeping, but unlike me, he had been topping himself up to keep going. I knew the drill. I knew how it worked. 'Don't look at me like that,' he warned me.

'I have to leave,' I repeated for the second time, or maybe it was the third. I was turning into the incessant chugging.

Hickey pointed the mouth of the hip flask at me. 'You're his little skivvy, aren't you?' I lowered my head and smiled a hard smile. It was true. I was M. Deauville's little skivvy. Hickey pointed the hip flask at me again. 'You do everything that Nobody tells you to, don't you?'

'Yes,' I conceded with a bow. 'I do everything he tells me to. Because if I don't, I will die.'

He got a good laugh out of that. He cast his eyes around

the place in search of an audience to co-opt to his ridicule, the way he did in school. 'Die,' he repeated. '*Die*, for fuck's sake. Lookit, Tristram, nobody in this country ever died of the Tax Man. This isn't . . .' he waved the flask about in search of the correct word. 'This isn't Elizabethan England, or wherever you're from. This is *Ireland*. The Tax Man's just a big joke here.'

'Why are you so scared of him then?'

It was not a good idea to accuse Hickey of being frightened. I knew that much from school. He lobbed his grenade at my head and I ducked to avoid a Catherine wheel of spurting whiskey. The flask whizzed past and embedded itself some yards beyond in the mud.

I looked down at my jacket. An amber streak of whiskey had slashed my shoulder. I touched the stain and looked at the moisture on my fingertips as if it were my life's blood, and sometimes I think it is. Sometimes I think that whiskey is my life's blood. I levelled my eyes at Hickey in fury before turning to leave.

I stamped on the hip flask on my way to the exit. 'Ha!' Hickey shouted after me. 'Ha, ha, ha.' I left him to gouging his holes in the earth. Gouging is what gougers do best.

*

I dabbed at my shoulder every ten paces or so once I was out of his sight, still checking for blood, an animal unable to keep from licking its injury and allowing the wound to heal. The whiskey felt cool, like menthol. It felt sticky and fascinating too. The bare branches of the trees approaching the castle gates were stark against the thin winter light, accentuating the meshed ganglions of rooks' nests. I was in a black frame of mind. 'What is greater than God?' Larney demanded as I passed between the stone columns, as if the correct answer were the password required to gain admittance to the demesne. I shook my head at him: another time.

'What is greater than God?' he persisted, 'and more evil than the Devil?' The Jack Russell refrained from impeding my progress. It just stood there.

'Not now,' I said. 'Please.'

Larney practically danced in delight. 'That's not the right answer!'

'Damn your riddles.'

An expression of dismay swept across his face, a slapped child. I looked away and pressed on. I had no kindness to give him. There was no kindness in me that day.

'Nothing,' Larney called in my wake and the dog discharged a quick-fire, whip-crack volley of barks to see me off. *Ar-Ar-Ar*, rebounding against the orchard wall. The rooks exploded from the trees as if blasted at by a shotgun.

I thought that Larney had retreated to his den and I was some distance up the avenue having more or less forgotten him, being embroiled in black riddles of my own, worming seething ciphers, a stew of deformed faces, or maybe it was just one face – yes, it was just the one face, but a face that I had seen more than once, a face that had baited me throughout the days of my drunken iniquity and which had of late resurfaced in my peripheral vision – when Larney shouted the answer again: 'Nothing is greater than God, young master. And Nothing is more evil than the Devil!'

‘Where does this Larney individual fit in to all this?’

Is that a riddle? There's no straight answer. It seems very dark in here all of a sudden. Does anyone else think it's very dark in here all of a sudden? Or is it just me?

‘I’m afraid it’s just you, Mr St Lawrence.’

St Patrick's Day

NATIONAL DAY OF MOURNING

Sixth day of evidence

18 MARCH 2016

'And so, returning to the Claremont development, according to the file, it was launched in . . .'

April 2007, Friday the 13th. Hickey wanted to make a big splash. That's what I heard him blathering down the phone to the various parties involved in the launch – the publicists, the estate agents, the interior architects, the landscape technicians, the colour specialists, the fabric engineers, the carpet consultants. There were no gardeners or painters and decorators left in the country any more. You could get a degree in Lego.

Hickey was audible from outside the Portakabin, even over the racket of the construction work. He had the kind of booming voice that carries across rooms, across oceans, across the waking world into sleep. I don't need to tell you this – you've endured his garbled deposition.

'I want to make a big splash!' he'd be declaring inside the prefab while I'd be procrastinating outside, one foot on the beer crate. This stance sums up my life. 'Lookit lads, give us a big splash!' 'I'm after, like, a big splash!' As I say, he was troubled with so few ideas that he had learned to pound the living daylights out of each one.

He appointed a top London PR company, and the publicity machine had kicked in by February. The old ply hoarding was replaced by twenty-foot-high glossy boards reading *Join the jet set! Register your interest now.* Two-page-spread advertisements were placed in the national papers, and feature articles were published in the Sunday supplements. The property pages tripped over their adjectives. Profiles of Hickey appeared in various business sections, many accompanied by photographic portraits of him gazing off into the distance with Ireland's Eye in the background and a sea breeze in his hair. He had grown it long over the winter for this purpose. Long hair was required now that he was moving in different circles, or intending to. It signalled that he was a mover and shaker.

We were in the Site Office with the newspapers spread out on his desk, one headline more fatuous than the next. 'Bag Yourself a Little Piece of Paradise!' 'Live the Dream by the Marina!' 'Join the Millionaire's Circle with This Exclusive Beachfront Development! Prices starting from an unbelievable €379,000 for a one-bedroom apartment.' The prefab smelled of sour milk and rashers.

'"An unbelievable €379,000 for a one-bedroom apartment?"' I read out. 'They're right. That is unbelievable.'

Hickey swung his steel-toed, mud-caked builder's boots up onto the desk. He slurped his milky tea and did his post-pint sigh, *Ahhhhh*. 'Starting from,' he said. 'Read the small print again.'

I read the small print again. Starting from an unbelievable €379,000. 'Come on, Dessie. Who in their right mind is going to part with that for a one-bed flat?'

'There's only one apartment going on the market at that price an it's a single-aspect, ground-floor, 440-square-footer facing the bin store. The rest a the one-beds clock in at around 400 grand. The two-beds are over the half-a-million mark. An the ones with the views . . .' He winced at the price and reached for his hard hat. 'Wait'll you see,' he said, getting to his feet. 'There'll be a queue at the gate, so there will.'

He opened the door onto a furnace roar of activity. Out on the site, everything was in flux. Cranes swinging, hydraulic arms pistoning, diggers milling back and forth. It wasn't going to be finished in time for the launch. 'Doesn't have to be finished,' Hickey said without breaking his stride. Again, the problem of keeping up with him across muck. 'We'll be selling most of it off the plans. Just so long as the show apartments are ready to give the punters the general idea. Come on an have a look.'

We walked past the hulk that would one day become the landmark hotel. It was now visible from the castle, its square head gazing sadly in the window like Frankenstein's monster. *Open autumn 2007!* the brochures promised, but I didn't see how that was feasible. A digger had finished backfilling the section of trench housing a pipe. I paused to watch it pound the ground with its metal head like an animal gone berserk before realising that Hickey was shouting at me again. 'Go back an get a fucken helmet! Before we're fucken shut down!'

By the time I returned with a helmet, Hickey was laying into another patsy, a man with a suit under his high-viz jacket. The road couldn't be finished in time for the launch, the man was trying to explain to Hickey, because the pipes—

'Jesus wept, just lurry the fuckers in. That's what I'm paying you for. Nobody gives a shite if they're not perfect – the effing things are going to be *buried* – but we'll all give a major shite if there's no road on launch day an me clients have to stagger across planks in their Gucci heels.'

'Who was that?' I asked when the man had been dispatched. 'What was he saying about leaking sewage?'

'That dope?' Hickey spat on the ground. 'He's me supervising engineer. Moaning again about pipes getting broken an misaligned if they aren't encased in a protective structure before being backfilled what with the heavy construction machinery driving up an down over them while the rest a the apartments are being finished, blah blah. I don't know what that fella's problem is. Nobody gives a flying fuck about pipes an tanking an pressure tests an what have you since the Building Control Act of 1990. The Building No Control Act, more like. It's all self-certification now – you're basically correcting your own exams. Give yourself 100 per cent, I keep telling him. Who's going to check? The County Council? Ask me hoop. They're only obliged to inspect 15 per cent of all sites so they're not going to go near the big ones, are they? That'd be too much like doing a day's work. They'll inspect Missus Murphy's new granny flat instead. I'm not asking him to put his head on the block. He only has to state that the work complies with the building regulations to "a substantial extent".'

'Really? That can't be true.'

'Are you calling me a liar? That's the law in this country. That, an wearing a safety helmet.' He signalled to a roller to compact the soil over the sewage pipes, to compact the pipes themselves. I caught sight of my reflection in its approaching windscreen, just standing there in my yellow dunce's cap, letting it happen. Then M. Deauville rang. I plugged my ear with my finger and shouted to him that it was fine, it was grand, everything on site was dandy, not a bother.

'Is he coming to the launch?' Hickey wanted to know when I got off the call.

The prospect had never occurred to me.

'Bring him along,' he said, and it sounded like a challenge. 'I'd really like to meet the bloke.'

So would I. The shadow of the boom swung over my grave again and I shuddered. *Tocka tocka*. So would I.

*

'They've started queuing,' Hickey phoned to tell me not one, not two, but three days before the apartments were due to go on sale. Three whole days. I came down to see it with my own eyes.

The main road was choked with parked cars all the way back to the Burrow Road underpass. Family members were coming and going to sit it out in shifts. How did they sleep like that, with two wheels down on the road and two up on the kerb, the blood either draining from their heads or rushing to it? Ideal conditions for a killing, Hickey observed, rubbing his callused palms.

He had relegated the Site Office and its upended beer crate to a corner and installed a Sales Suite in its place with twin box balls flanking the entrance. Twin box balls were the signal. They were the wink and nod. A pair of twin box balls at a residential entrance was the telltale sign that the occupants had fallen victim to the property-lust plague.

Hickey had laid a tarmac road over the sewage pipes but it was already showing signs of buckling. I kicked at one of the ruckles. It had split in the centre like a soufflé. 'Shut up,' he warned me though I hadn't opened my mouth. The Sales Suite was a large Portakabin carpeted in tan velvet pile with black leather sofas and orange pendant lamps. On a podium was a variation on the original architectural model of the development, displayed like the Book of Kells in a glass case which Hickey clouded up with his breath.

Large-scale floor plans of the individual apartment blocks were mounted on the walls. The plans were peppered with a pox of red stickers. About a fifth of the apartments had already been sold. To whom? I looked at Hickey, who shrugged. 'A couple a the lads.' He'd done a few deals to get the ball rolling. At the far end of the suite was the door to the private salesroom where, he said, the sweet magic was going to happen.

It was Hickey's idea that we sit outside at bistro tables and keep an eye on the Sales Suite from a discreet distance. He wanted to watch his grand plan unfold. He'd had the landscape architect or the balcony dresser or the bespoke furniture designer or all three mock up a sort of afternoon-tea al-fresco vibe to give an impression of . . . He couldn't think of the word. 'What's it?' he asked me, clicking his fingers, '*genteel* living?' but genteel wasn't quite it. 'What's the word I'm looking for, Tristram? Begins with a G.' 'Dunno,' I replied. 'Anyway,' he continued, 'it's a lifestyle we're selling here is my point.'

We couldn't have asked for a better day – the first promise of summer and the show apartments glinted as they glinted in the brochures. Work had been going on around the clock under stadium floodlights which bled a spectral glow into the night sky. The crews were on double and treble pay to get the job done. A second internal wall of glossy hoarding had been erected within the site to screen the prospective buyers from the ongoing construction work. The unfinished blocks were sheathed in green netting. At the end of an avenue lined with flags stood our show block, the Lambay building. Tender new foliage shimmered at its base – the garden had been unloaded the morning before from the back of a truck. As had the Sales Suite, the bistro dining set and even the lawn. The last time I'd seen it, less than a week previously, the site had been a battlefield in Flanders. You had to hand it to D. Hickey. He had pulled off an elaborate scam.

He put on his sunglasses and sat back to contemplate the sales queue with satisfaction, watching the world go buy. The punters had been living in cars for three days by then and were dazed, dehydrated and desperate. The taxi drivers, their wives, anxious young couples, their parents, nurses and guards, all lining up to join the jet set, pressing coins into our palms like medieval supplicants. The smart money – or the slightly less stupid money – hadn't wasted time viewing the show apartments but had gone straight to the private salesroom to slap down deposits. When they came out the other side with their contracts, they headed across to get an idea of the asset they'd just acquired, calculating the resale value when they went to flip it at completion.

Those still stuck in the queue sized up the people ahead of them, worrying that they had their eye on the same apartment, and so discussing their second choice, and their third. Plan B, Plan C and Plan D. They muttered to their partners, they muttered into their phones, they muttered to their gods, anxious not to be overheard. So preoccupied were they with their quarry that they didn't register Hickey and I trained on them. They didn't register that *they* were the quarry.

Hickey leaned in. 'Is he coming?' I didn't have to ask whom he meant. I was keeping my eyes peeled for M. Deauville too.

'He says he hopes to be able to make it.' *Tocka tocka* over the phone as he had checked airline schedules last night. A nervous tingle on my part at the prospect of coming face to face. 'But he couldn't promise. Depends on flights.'

Hickey nodded. 'Busy man.'

I nodded back. 'Busy man.'

That's when Ciara, head of the sales team, emerged from the salesroom with her clipboard. I checked my watch. The apartments had been on sale for an hour and twenty minutes. Hickey lowered his sunglasses to wink at me. 'Here we are now.' He pushed the glasses back up his nose.

'Well?' he asked when she drew up. 'Are we in business?'

'We are, Mr Hickey. Just to confirm that the first fifty-eight units are now sold. A number of investors made multiple purchases. A farmer from Tipperary bought ten.'

Hickey brought his fist down hard on the bistro table: 'Yes!' His teaspoon bounced and landed on the gravel. Ciara stooped to pick it up. 'Good girl. Right. Withdraw the next sixty-five units from sale.'

I jolted upright in my chair. '*What?*' but Ciara had already *Yes-Mr-Hickey*-ed him and was marching back to the Sales Suite, bursting with self-importance. I turned to Hickey. 'Run that past me?'

He punched a number into his mobile phone and raised it to his ear before cocking an eyebrow my way. 'We decided that if trade was brisk we'd release fifty-eight apartments today an call it Phase One, then hold back the next batch, add 30 per cent to the price, an call it Phase Two. We'll launch Phase Two in six weeks. Then there's Phase Three an Phase—Ah, howaya Mr McGee, D. Hickey here. Grand job, grand job.'

I stared at him in his suit. He never looked right in a suit, same as I never looked right in jeans. A tuft of black bristles protruded from his ear, the match of the black bristles sprouting from his nose, as if something were growing inside him, forcing its way out. He was a few rungs behind on the evolutionary ladder, or perhaps a few rungs ahead on the evolutionary ladder, or on some as yet undocumented stretch of the ladder which had taken off on a tangent, so he was not a man but something hybrid, something wolfish, something that wore its pelt on the inside, because they were a new breed, weren't they, these developers. And their development was escalating. Soon they would take over. They'd enslave us. Too late: they already had. A commotion had broken out in the sales queue. An agent had placed a sign in the window:

Phase One
Sold Out

Ciara was struggling to force shut the door of the Sales

Suite. People were clamouring for entry. Tired people, thwarted people, demoralised people, panicked people, people shouting that they'd been queuing for days.

Ciara clicked her fingers over her head like a flamenco dancer and cried 'Security!' Two heavies from the former Eastern Bloc, who were built like the former Eastern Bloc, appeared and enquired if there was a problem. Fucking right there was a problem, said one man pointing at them, and a struggle ensued. The insurrection was efficiently quashed by the hired goons, as insurrections in the former Eastern Bloc tended to be.

The man who had pointed his finger rolled onto his side clutching his knee. A small child wailed in fright. Hickey clapped his phone shut and stood up to claim his winnings. '*Gracious*,' he said. 'That's the word I'm looking for. Isn't that right, Tristram? Isn't that what we're selling here? *Gracious* living.'

*

M. Deauville didn't materialise. Hickey stood between his big box balls at the close of business that evening and jingled the coins in his pockets. 'Cristal?' he offered, then winced in mock apology. He took off his sunglasses to admire them. Two grand, he remarked they'd cost him.

He turned his back and headed off, holding up a valedictory hand in that way that used to drive me mad when I had less to be driven mad by (what made him so very positive that I was looking at him?) but then he paused, dropped his head, relented, and turned around. 'Lookit,' he said, as if making a major concession, 'I'm having a barbeque next Saturday, okay? Me an the wife, up at the ranch. I might see you there. I know you're a busy man.'

'Yeah,' I said, getting up to allow two men in overalls to remove my chair and load it into the back of a truck. The rest of the bistro set had already been packed. I stood there watching the place being locked up. Checked my phone: no calls. Busy man.

I looked about for a chair but found none and in the end sat down on a kerbstone. It rocked in its moorings. Everything built by Hickey rocked in its moorings. There were no moorings.

I loitered there until the warmth went out of the sun, waiting for M. Deauville to walk through the gates and find me, the abandoned birthday boy, surrounded by burst balloons and half-eaten cake, party hats and torn gift wrapping strewn at my feet.

He didn't come and he didn't ring either but he was there in spirit. I see that now. I see it all now. Every aspect of the launch bore his hallmark. The Devil is in the detail.

‘And at what point did Dominic Dowdall enter the picture?’

I’m sorry, who?

‘The Viking.’

Oh, him. Yes. I should have mentioned. He pitched up on launch day to sniff around, sensing that juicy spoils were to be had. That's what Vikings do. They raid juicy spoils. It was only a matter of time before he stuck his whore – I mean, his oar in. We'll get to her – I mean, to that.

He rocked up with his wife and their three blond children, all of whom had ridiculous names. I realise I stand in a glasshouse in this regard, but at least my ridiculous name is hereditary. 'Leave that tree alone, Roman,' he called as the boy struggled to wrench a young Japanese maple out of the ground, but there was no conviction in the Viking's voice. Pull it if you wish, Roman, he was saying. Do what feels good. Do what feels right. Nobody is going to stop you, son, that's a valuable lesson in life. The maple snapped. Roman looked at the slender antler of branches in his hand. 'Put that down,' his father told him, and the boy cast it aside and moved on to the next target. Hickey shook his head. 'That little bollocks is going to get such a boot up the hole.'

His wife held her husband's hand and kept her counsel, smiling about herself vaguely. She was dressed for a skiing trip on a beach. Fur-lined boots on her muscular brown legs, denim shorts, a sheepskin gilet over a sun top. Hickey sized her up with interest. She had a gleaming mane of chestnut hair and a hard little nut of a face beneath it.

If the Viking noticed Hickey and me sitting at the bistro table when he came through the gates, he didn't betray it. We watched him regally making his rounds, his brown queen on his arm. He surveyed the Lambay building with a proprietorial tilt of the head before cocking a hind leg to squirt his scent on it. *Tsss*. Hickey was itching to belt over and counter-spray – I could feel him chafing beside me.

'You know he has a conviction for beating up his former partner, don't you?' he muttered.

'Yes.'

'Girlfriend partner, not business partner. He beat up a woman.'

'Yes, I heard.'

Even I knew that. We all knew that. Everyone on the hill knew that the Viking had been handed down a suspended sentence for breaking a former girlfriend's jaw. Somehow, this hadn't impacted on his social standing.

He came upon us at the bistro table when his tour was complete. 'I like what you've done here,' he told Hickey. 'I like the look you've achieved, yeah?' His great bullish head was blocking out my sun. He was a handsome man, in a coarse sort of way.

'Phase One sold out in forty-five minutes,' Hickey stated.

The Viking tossed his hair. 'Sweet. A lot of new customers for my bar.'

Hickey tossed his hair back. 'They'll be at my bar.' He nodded at the trunk of the hotel. 'Have you seen me hotel? It's going to be eleven storeys high.'

'Yeah, your hotel.' The Viking stroked his smig. 'I wouldn't mind a word in your ear about that. I have, uh . . . a proposition. You must come see my operation some evening. You know, get the tour.' He made eye contact with me to indicate that the invitation extended to us both. 'Why don't I give you a call?'

'Yeah, why don't you?'

'Excellent.' The Viking touched his temple in salute before

rounding up his feral children and sauntering off. I won't repeat what Hickey called him when his back was turned. I don't approve of that kind of language.

*

Three days later, we were summoned.

'Why are you after wearing a suit?' Hickey berated me as we made our way to the Viking's bar, 'did you have to go and wear a bloody suit?' He had never objected to my suits before. I always wear a suit, and have done ever since giving up the drink. Even on weekends. It is my Sober uniform. Every morning, I must get up and put it on.

The Viking was parading himself outside his bar on his phone in his linen and we hated him. His bar was a block of jade glass like Hickey's hotel, like McGee's bank, like the Lambay building, like everything. He lowered the phone. 'Guys, I'll be with you in a tick. Have Svetlana bring you a drink.'

He pointed to a blonde who was standing sentry inside the door. Svetlana stepped forward and held it open to welcome us into the Viking's emporium. I noted Hickey noting this – the Viking's hand command; the beautiful blonde leaping to his bidding. She was dressed in a fitted white shirt, black tie and black trousers. A long black apron was knotted around her waist. Hickey stared at her trim backside as she led us upstairs to the VIP area. He would have liked to have run a woman like that – five foot ten and slender as a runway model, her hair pinned up in a French twist. He would have liked instructing a woman like that to serve his friends.

The VIP area was empty. Nobody was Very Important that night. Svetlana guided us to a raised platform and took our drinks order. We sat looking out the window at the Viking, still strutting up and down his patch of Harbour Road. *Tsss*: he cocked his hind leg to mark the lamppost. 'I could burst that X,' Hickey remarked quietly, resorting to that word again that I find so objectionable. I nodded my agreement all the same.

He finally appeared in the VIP den. 'Gentlemen, did Svetlana take care of you?' It was not a hospitable enquiry but a power display: there would be consequences for Svetlana if she did not take care of his friends. 'She did, thank you,' I told him.

Svetlana arrived with a tray and set down our drinks. A sparkling water for me, a Carlsberg for the Viking and a double brandy for Hickey. It was the most expensive drink he could think of. He should have asked for my advice. Svetlana's nails were an inch long. Her palms were stained fake-tan orange, her lifelines and heart lines a tracery of tobacco brown. Your path in life will be a dirty one, a palmist would have told her. You will have a filthy, dirty little path.

'Jaysus,' said Hickey as he watched her arse depart, the belt of her apron tied in a smart bow at the small of her back. He swirled the contents of his brandy balloon and knocked back a mouthful: *Ahhhhh*. 'This immigration business. It's not all bad news.'

'Svetlana? Yes. The Russian girls are beautiful. Doesn't translate into the men though.'

'No,' Hickey agreed. 'Now that you say it. I hadn't looked at it that way.'

They nodded thoughtfully, two men of the world. 'The Russian men don't find Irish women attractive,' the Viking added, 'but the Russian women find Irish men extremely attractive. Did you know that?'

'Get away,' said Hickey. 'You're bullshitting me.'

'I am not. They find rich Irish men practically irresistible, in fact. They're all Roman hands and Russian fingers when you get them in a corner. Don't tell me you haven't tried one yet.'

I had never seen Hickey embarrassed before. He sniggered into his cognac glass. I glanced back at the bar to see what Svetlana was making of this. The girl stared fixedly out at the harbour lights.

The Viking signalled for another round. Svetlana collected the old drinks and replaced them with fresh ones. I looked at her tray as she removed it. The Viking's old pint was two-thirds intact. Hickey's brandy glass was empty.

The Viking nodded at me. 'I heard this fella was dead,' he said to Hickey.

'That was another Tristram St Lawrence,' Hickey told him.

I stared at them as they exploded into laughter, failing to understand the joke. 'I am dead,' I said to shut them up, but it only made them laugh harder. The Viking raised his hand for attention when Hickey had emptied his glass. Svetlana approached, exchanged Hickey's empty glass for another double, and a fresh pint for the Viking's partially consumed one. A third sparkling water was set in front of me.

Hickey didn't notice that his new best friend was sending back barely touched pints. All he noticed was my sparkling water. 'Are ya too good to drink with me?' he wanted to know. 'Is that it? Is that the problem?'

I recognised the space he was in. No drinker trusts a sober man. 'We've been over this,' I told him quietly.

The Viking looked from Hickey to me for an explanation. None was forthcoming. It was a private matter. Then my phone rang. *Tocka tocka*. Saved by the bell. I excused myself and left the table.

Hickey was red in the face by the time I returned, maybe as much as half an hour later. The call to M. Deauville had dragged out. I had raised objection after objection. 'Hickey and I . . .' I tried to explain to him, 'we have a past. He used to be my—' but M. Deauville felt that it was a necessary step in my recovery that I return to the VIP den immediately to face down my fears, so in the end I complied, having first admitted to him that I was powerless over alcohol and then accepted the things that I could not change, i.e. everything.

'Here he is,' said Hickey. 'Told you he wasn't dead.'

'Sit down,' said the Viking. 'We ordered you a fresh fizzy water.' They cracked up at that.

'It's on the house,' Hickey added and they laughed harder still. The Viking wiped a crocodile tear from the corner of his eye. He was sober. The other clown was a different story. Brandy didn't suit him. I sniffed the new glass of water. My nose detected nothing suspicious but I pushed it away to be on the safe side. That's when I spotted the nickel tray. It was the tray for delivering the bill, except there was no bill on this tray but instead a ridge of white powder to which the Viking was adding more. Hickey shoved a rolled fifty into his hairy nostril and hoovered the powder up.

'It's getting late,' I began, but the Viking cut me off.

'What have we here?' he wanted to know, looking over Hickey's shoulder. Hickey turned around and the Viking pointed at the back of his head. Svetlana duly approached. 'Show us your lovely dress, hon,' he instructed her. 'That's it. Give us a twirl.' She had by then slipped into something more uncomfortable. No more black and white. Just black, and not a whole lot of it. The Viking turned to Hickey. 'Isn't that a lovely dress?'

'Gorgeous,' said Hickey. 'Knockout.'

The Viking put a hand on the builder's shoulder. 'This is my good friend, Dessie,' he explained to Svetlana. 'My *very* good friend,' he added meaningfully. 'Why don't you sit down and join us, babe?'

Svelte Lana smiled at Hickey. 'Hi Dessie,' she said, and the way she pronounced his name lent it an almost sophisticated ring, as if there were an accent on the i. *Desì*. Hickey beamed up at her, his tusks of nasal hair frosted white. 'Howaya love!' She sat down and slid along the banquette until they were side by side. Her gold heels were five inches high and fastened around her ankles with little chains. The Viking threw me a knowing smirk. I couldn't watch. And yet I did.

Svetlana whispered something into Hickey's ear. 'Ya are not!' he exclaimed and she nodded, then leaned forward to whisper into his ear again. She sat back to see his reaction, then covered her mouth and giggled. I missed the signal whereby it was settled that he had pulled. Svetlana stood up, took Hickey's hairy hand in hers and tugged it. 'Ah no,' he objected, leaping to his feet fairly lively all the same. With the additional height of her stilettos, the girl's hips were level with Hickey's belly. Her breasts jutted out at his chin. He gazed into them and told her that she had beautiful eyes.

I checked my watch. 'That's it. I'm done.'

The Viking's hand shot out to detain me. 'Stay. I want a word.' Svetlana was leading Hickey away by the hand. 'Don't worry,' he assured me as we watched them depart, 'she's well looked after.' I stared at him. He stroked his smig as he contemplated their mismatched silhouettes disappearing through a door marked Staff Only. 'And he'll be well looked after too,' he added with the air of one who knew what lay in store for Hickey beyond that door. 'Now,' he said when Hickey was safely tucked into bed and it was just the adults, 'let's get down to business. I believe we have a mutual friend.'

'That strikes me as highly unlikely.'

'Mr Deauville?' the Viking prompted me.

'Monsieur Deauville is not your friend.'

The Viking frowned. 'Hasn't he briefed you about me yet?' The shadow of the crane swung across my grave again, though it was night and there weren't supposed to be shadows.

When I didn't answer, the Viking sat back and laughed. 'I'm running your bloody hotel. You're looking at your new business partner. And Deauville's too, and of course Hickey's. We've formed a consortium.'

'But you're a pimp. Monsieur Deauville wouldn't do business with a pimp.'

The Viking lowered his head and shook it. He shook it for a long time before picking up his mobile phone and rising from the table. 'Fuck you, St Lawrence. I amn't charging Hickey for the girl.'

*

Dark thoughts, black thoughts, dark thoughts, black thoughts, fuelling the headlong charge home, dictating the rhythm of my feet. I stumbled like a drunk in my haste to escape from him, from them, from that place, that door, Staff Only. I didn't trust the whoremonger not to spike my drink and M. Deauville had accepted him into a consortium.

I told myself over and over again that I accepted the things that I could not change, but I didn't, and I couldn't, and I wouldn't, but I had to. 'Ring,' I urged my phone, holding it out like a compass to guide me, clenching it so hard that the casing creaked. My mind howled with the need to speak to M. Deauville. Perhaps it was a test. If so, I was failing.

*

Larney didn't care or dare to show his face when I passed between the stone pillars that should have been crowned by winged dragons or hooded crows, something clawed that feasted on carrion. Instead, he chose to call out his riddle from the safety of the bushes. There is no safety, I wanted to tell him. You may as well come out of there.

'The more you have of it, the less you see,' came his voice, which was trembling with anticipation. 'What is it?'

I didn't have to give it a second's thought. It was so obvious that I almost cheered up. I had a heart and a mind and a soul that was full of it. 'That's easy, Larney. Darkness.'

'Well done,' came the response in a dry, cultivated voice that did not belong to the gatekeeper. I stopped dead, turned to the trees.

'Who's there?'

Silence.

I took a step towards the verge. A swarm of teeming shadows. I strained my eyes to discern a human form but detected only leaves. 'Show yourself,' I commanded him, but he did not. I clenched my fists. 'Show yourself!' I bellowed as loudly as I was able, and the whole demesne quaked in the night because a man's roar is amplified by darkness. Everything is amplified by darkness, particularly fear.

After an extraordinarily fraught pause, the leaves rustled and a twig snapped. Larney emerged slowly, wrists and elbows first, for his arms were raised to shield his head.

'Come here, Larney. I'm not going to hurt you.'

He inched forward in the undulating, weaving manner of a snake and came to a halt a few feet shy of me, his body crouched and averted from mine like a blackthorn growing on a cliff. Tears, snot and spittle were trickling down his face, and his eyes rolled from side to side in his head, looking up and down the avenue in search of an escape.

'Was that your idea of a joke?'

'He made me.'

'Who made you?'

'He made me,' Larney repeated, gulping air like a sobbing child.

'Who made you?'

'The man.' Larney glanced up the avenue and shuddered. I turned around. Nobody was there. 'The man,' he said again. 'He made me.'

'What man? What was his name?'

'I don't know.'

'What did he look like?' Somehow I had him by the collar of his shirt. He weighed nothing at all. When he recoiled to avoid my eye I gave his bones a shake. 'Answer me, Larney: what did the man look like?'

Larney braced in anticipation of a blow. 'He looked like you.'

I released his collar and he slunk back into the shrubbery. I wheeled around. The avenue was still empty. There was just the darkness. It was everywhere.

Seventh day of evidence

21 MARCH 2016

'To return to this barbeque at his house that Mr Hickey invited you to following the success of the Claremont launch. Other members of the Golden Circle have specified that it was at this event that the decision to bid on the Pudong site was reached. Is that your recollection?'

That would be my general understanding although I wasn't party to the actual conversation. I was late arriving at Hickey's ranch. I had assumed that he was being facetious in his use of this term until I saw the place. Hickey had built a mock-colonial ranch on the side of the East Mountain. He had cultivated the gorse and heather into lawn. A row of floodlit palm trees delineated the end of nature's dominion over the moors and the beginning of the reign of the developer.

I got out of the car when the driver could proceed no further and picked my way through a parked gridlock of executive vehicles, all of which were black. Money kills the imagination. It makes us want the same thing. Yes, of course some of the guests had arrived in helicopters. I don't know which ones. I was hardly going to ask.

Music and the smell of charred meat drifted on the early evening air. I headed up the steps to the ranch. The front door stood open. Hanging in the atrium was my grandparents' chandelier, the one stolen from Hilltop. I was staring at it when Edel appeared. She was dressed in silk the same cream as the travertine floor, which offered her pale colouring camouflage, as if this were the natural habitat of her species, just as I am stony and grey from having evolved in a castle. 'Oh,' she said when she saw me. She was carrying a foil-covered dish.

'I was just admiring your chandelier.'

Edel raised her head and looked at the chandelier as if considering it for the first time. 'Yes. It's an antique, I believe.'

'It certainly is. It's a valuable family heirloom, in fact.'

Another door swung open into the atrium and Hickey bulldozed in, catching me staring at his wife, and his wife staring at my property strung from his ceiling. 'Where are me Jaysus steaks?' he said. 'I've thirty starving people out there.' He took the dish from Edel. 'Come on,' he said to me, shouldering the door open, 'the lads are waiting.'

'You're a common thief,' I told him once Edel was out of earshot. He gave no indication that he had heard me. Such names were of no great consequence to D. Hickey. He had been called a lot worse in his time.

I followed him into a high-gloss white kitchen that looked like a science lab and through a sun room out onto a terrace. The Bills were dressed in business casual and drinking bottles of Heineken. Their wives had orange skin and yellow hair, constituting a strangely hued tribe in the pink dusk, for the sun had set on the peninsula, tinting the peaty earth of the moors a shade of purple.

'Ah, here's Lawrence!' said McGee, slapping me on the back. 'Nice bit of horse-trading you did during the week down at the beach. That, gentlemen, is what I call a tidy profit.' Absolutely, like, fair fucks, the others assented, clinking their bottles together. The Viking raised his bottle to his temple. 'How's tricks, Tristram?'

Hickey had built the barbeque with his own two hands, a selection of hot coal grills staggered at various levels like a drum kit. He stood in the middle with a set of tongs, moving from grill to grill to flip steaks, shish kebabs and gourmet sausages. 'Here, Tristram, I've the best a gear for ya. Didn't I always supply you with the best a gear? Ah relax an show us your plate.' A slab of glistening beef dangled from his tongs. 'Fillet steak from Lambay Island.'

'You know I don't eat meat.'

Hickey bared his teeth at me, the enamel gleaming through his black beard like bone exposed in a wound. 'Now how would I be expected to know a thing like that, Tristram? You've never lowered yourself to eat with me.' He threw the fillet back on the grill and fished a foil parcel from the ashes and dumped it on a plate. 'There y'are. Baked potato. Condiments an salad on the table.'

The rubber soles of a child's runners protruded from the tablecloth. A strong, briny smell was emanating from there. I lifted the edge. A boy of six or seven was down on his knees crouched over a cage. It was a lobster pot, one of several. The boy was poking at one of the lobsters through the mesh, aiming with a pencil for its eye. I took a hold of the child's wrist and prised the pencil from his fist. 'That's very bold!' I told him sharply. I don't know how to speak to children.

The child sat back on his heels and glared at me in outrage. He had no fear of adults. I thought he was about to let out a howl but instead he bit me. He seized my hand and bit me as hard as he was able. I dropped the pencil and shook him off. On the fleshy outer edge of my palm was the corrugated half-moon imprint of his teeth.

The child was purple in the face with rage. He had the unmistakable look of a Hickey – the matted black lashes dragged the eyelids down, giving him that signature dopey expression. Hickey had set aside an apartment in Claremont in each of his children's names. It's not his fault, I counselled myself, squeezing my throbbing hand. It is the way he has been reared. I picked up his pencil and confiscated it. 'Da!' he protested.

'What do you want to be when you grow up?'

'Builder,' the kid said. I dropped the tablecloth on him.

Hickey retrieved one of the lobster pots. 'I caught these lads meself this morning,' he told his guests, brandishing the pot over his head. 'Fresh from Balscadden Bay. Thought we'd give them a lash on the barbie!'

He lifted out a lobster and threw it on the grill, holding it down with his tongs when it struggled to escape. Its antennae swung around but its pincers were secured by rubber bands. Hickey looked over his shoulder and grinned.

'Shouldn't you boil it first?' one of the wives wondered. 'Aren't you supposed to boil them? I'm sure you're supposed to boil them first.'

'Here, Kyle, give us another one,' Hickey instructed his son, and the kid reached in and took out a second lobster. His father held him up so he could deposit it on the hot coals himself, followed by a third and then a fourth. Hickey set the boy down and cupped the back of his head while Kyle watched the lobsters flail.

When a lobster made it to the edge of the grill, Hickey picked it up and set it back in the middle. Then the elastic band securing one of the lobster's claws melted and its pincers sprang open. 'Da!' said Kyle in excitement. The lobster snapped at Hickey when he tried to tackle it with his tongs. 'En garde!' Hickey cried, but he couldn't access the lobster's torso and the creature made it over the edge. It landed on the sandstone paving and dragged itself towards shelter.

'It's not orange yet,' one of the wives said. 'You're supposed to cook them until the shell is orange.'

'I'm sure you're supposed to boil them first,' the other one persisted.

'Da!' the kid shouted again, pointing at the grill.

'Bollocks,' said Hickey. All the elastic bands had melted and two of the remaining lobsters were making a break for it. The other one was already dead. The second one dropped onto the paving, then the third. That's when the Viking stepped in. He stamped on each lobster with his heel then threw them back on the grill, bellies up. Their various pairs of legs extended and retracted until they finally expired.

'Who wants Dublin Lawyer?' Hickey called, holding up the first lobster to have turned orange. 'Here, Hunger – show us your plate,' and the Hunger, true to form, shoved himself to the top of the queue. Suddenly, you're all looking grossly uncomfortable. Relax, I won't divulge his name. Besides, I didn't know his name until I was summoned to this Commission and came face to face with him again all these years later. Everyone simply called him the Hunger on account of his having snaffled up every last morsel of tribunal work going back in the nineties, making a seven-figure annual income out of the State before seven-figure annual incomes became de rigueur. Hickey reckoned he was a good man to have onside. That's why he retained his services. What? Don't tell me you didn't know he was working for the other team too?

Hickey took the Hunger's plate and placed the lobster on it. He held up the plate and addressed his audience. 'Can anybody tell me why it's called Dublin Lawyer?'

'Because only Dublin lawyers can afford to eat it!' the Hunger rejoined on cue.

'Greedy X,' said Hickey, using that abhorrent word, and everybody laughed as if it were a joke and not a statement of fact. 'An there's a steak,' he added, slapping a fillet alongside the lobster. 'Surf 'n' turf. Right, who's next?'

One of the lobster's antennae twitched. 'Christ,' I said, 'it's still alive.'

Hickey came pounding over to investigate, ready to defend his handiwork to the death like any self-respecting builder, no matter how damning the evidence against it. He prodded one of the lobster's antennae with his index finger. It didn't budge. He prodded the other one. Nothing. 'He's an awful man for imagining things,' he told the Hunger. There was a gobbet of ketchup in his beard.

The Hunger ripped the lobster's claw off, cracked it open and picked out the flesh. It slipped out in a speckled orange replica of the pincer itself, ungloved like a hand. 'It's dead now,' he said, and popped the pincer into his mouth. I excused myself.

A kestrel was hovering on the midnight-blue air beyond Hickey's boundary. I watched for a while, waiting for it to swoop. Ships and aircraft were crossing the bay and sky, bodies of light travelling at varying speeds through the darkness. The beacons along the shipping lanes signalled to each other in flashes of red, white and green. They achieved synchronisation, held it for one flash, two, then eased back out again, first into syncopation and then discord, only to relent and approach harmony once more. I could have stood there for hours, willing the beacons into concord again and smiling when it happened. I should have been a lighthouse keeper.

'What happened to your hand?'

I turned around. Edel was at my side, shimmering in her silk. 'Ahm,' I said, and looked down at my hand, realising that I had been massaging it. The bite had bloomed a mottled purple. A blood vessel must have burst.

She took my hand in hers. 'Gosh,' she said, 'you're freezing. My God, is that a bite?'

'Yes.'

'Did the lobsters get you?'

The savagery that evening had been perpetrated upon the lobsters, not by them. 'Your son did it.'

'He's not my son.'

'Oh. Well, that boy.' He had called Hickey *Da*.

‘Kyle. He’s not my son. I don’t have any children.’

‘I’m sorry,’ I said in embarrassment.

‘Why are you sorry? The children are from Dessie’s first marriage. They stay with us at weekends. Or some of them do.’

‘I hadn’t realised that Dessie . . . That it . . .’ I find matters of a personal nature terribly awkward, particularly around people who are strangers to me, and there is no other type.

‘That it was a second marriage?’

‘Yes,’ I said, grateful to her for finishing the sentence.

‘Well, it isn’t a second marriage for me.’

‘Ah.’

‘What about you? Are you married?’

‘Me?’ I laughed at the prospect.

‘Why is that funny?’

‘I’m, ahm . . .’ She was right. It wasn’t funny. It was sad. ‘No, I’m not married,’ I answered, but couldn’t think of anything further to add.

‘Dessie thinks you’re gay.’

I laughed again. She was so direct. ‘Does he indeed?’

‘Yes. He says he’s scared to bend over in your company.’

‘Lovely. You can assure him he need harbour no fear in that regard.’

‘Why? Because you’re not gay or because you don’t fancy him?’

‘How could anybody in their right mind fancy Dessie?’ And then: ‘Oh, I’m sorry.’ She had married the man, after all.

Edel squeezed my fingers and turned to the sea. ‘That’s okay. We all make mistakes.’

The moon had risen and a silver path appeared on the water. A yacht scudded across it in silhouette, and then there was no other obstacle in sight, not a thing until Wales. ‘I’ve always preferred this side of the hill,’ I said, although I hadn’t known it until then. 'Dessie has done remarkably well for himself.' I didn't just mean the house.

Edel shrugged. 'I get frightened here on my own at night. It's so isolated.'

'I'm sure Dessie would throttle any intruders.'

'Yes, but he's never home since he started this project. Sometimes he even sleeps in that mangy Portakabin.'

I lowered my eyes. The mangy Portakabin was the least of her worries. The Viking's Staff Only room was her real concern. 'Yes, the project does rather seem to be taking over his life.'

'He's changed. And not for the better.'

'You mean he was once worse?'

She smiled and that was a great reward. Behind us, McGee was proclaiming that they deserved everything the Celtic Tiger had brought them because they had *balls*. 'Listen to them,' Edel said in derision. McGee's speech was met with a round of popping champagne corks, which is an acutely lonely sound when the champagne is not for you.

A light breeze stippled the sea's silver surface so it seemed a membrane had formed upon it, a membrane that might bear a man's weight. 'It looks as if you could walk on it,' Edel said. 'It looks as if you could run away. Doesn't it?'

She turned to me and I stared at her in amazement, a look she would later describe as one of withering scorn. That's exactly what I was thinking! I wanted to tell her, and I struggled to formulate that response, but in the end I couldn't quite bring myself to blurt something so unguarded and I looked back at the sea without comment.

She said she ought to be getting back to her guests, so I performed my usual pinched routine of expressing disbelief at the time on my watch, never mind that I couldn't read the tiny numerals in the dark. I watched her make her way back up to the floodlit ranch, understanding that some delicate connection had been broken, and that it had been broken by me, and then I set off home on foot across the moors.

'This is the same barbeque mentioned in both Mr McGee's and Mr Hickey's testimonies at which the proposal to purchase the farm in north County Dublin was also first mooted, is that correct?'

I wasn't present for that conversation either, but yes, they'd evidently discussed it. Hickey rang me first thing the morning after the barbeque. 'Where did you fuck off to?' he wanted to know, but instead of waiting for an answer he instructed me to be ready to be picked up at eight fifteen on Monday morning since an important meeting with McGee and the Bills was scheduled for nine. He asked me to do my best to secure M. Deauville's attendance and he apologised for the short notice. Apologised to M. Deauville, that is, not to me.

'And was it possible for M. Deauville to attend?'

No.

‘Can you confirm that these are your signatures?’
[*A sheaf of documents is passed to the witness.*]

Yes, that is my signature. And yes, that is my signature also. As is that, and that, and that. These are documents authorising the issuance of €228 million in loan notes by Castle Holdings to co-finance the Shanghai bid. Money travelled through me as freely as languages. Uncanny. That is the word they used.

The meeting began on Monday morning in the glass boardroom on the Liffey. The bank was set at the broadest point of the river where the mountain water converged with the tidal heave of the sea. Its brilliant expanse blinded my eyes so that when I turned to face the twelve men seated around the boardroom table, a murky shoal of variegations swam across their skin, and although I blinked those shadows would not be dispelled. It was the same crowd that had attended Hickey's barbeque. Yes, the Hunger was there. The Hunger was always there. The Hunger will always be with us. Look at him.

'Youse'll be able to see it from here,' Hickey remarked, standing at the window with his hands clasped behind his back. His belly was as big as a beach ball. Knock him down and he'd bounce back up.

'See what?' one of them enquired. Boyle, I think. They were all the same. Boyler, Coyler, Doyler, sitting there sharpening their knives.

'Me landmark hotel,' Hickey said proudly, but no one was interested in Hickey's landmark hotel any more. Hickey's landmark hotel was yesterday. McGee closed the venetian blinds and switched on a wall-mounted screen the size of a pool table.

A map of Leinster appeared on the screen, hatched areas indicating the zones in which development was under way. These areas corresponded to the standing army of cranes stationed across the horizon like pennants bearing regimental colours declaring which territory belonged to whom. We were more than ever a colonised nation. The Claremont site barely registered in the scale of things.

'Gentlemen,' McGee began, 'I wish to draw your attention to our next acquisition.' The screen was interactive. He reached for a substantial land bank north of the M50 and highlighted it blue. It was larger than the entire peninsula of Howth. 'We're proposing to construct a new urban quarter for Dublin here.'

Hickey folded his arms and shook his head, obstinate as a taxi driver. 'That's not Dublin.'

'It will be when we're finished with it, Dessie,' McGee said. 'It's all a question of branding.' The Bills laughed. Hickey reckoned he'd better laugh too to show that he was in on the joke.

McGee enlarged the blue site. 'What I am recommending', he continued, 'is that Mr Hickey timetables a consultation process with his pal the Minister.'

I frowned at the screen. 'But those lands are already zoned residential, according to your map. We don't need to bribe the Minister to rezone them.'

'I'm glad you raised this issue, Lawrence,' said McGee. 'Lawrence has raised an important issue: we do not need to get the lands rezoned. However, we do need to get the Metro North diverted from its present proposed course along the M1 corridor to serve these lands instead, and that's where Mr Hickey's chum Ray comes in.'

‘That’s grand,’ said Hickey. ‘I’ll have a word with Ray. Ray will take care a that.’

‘Can I leave it with you, Dessie?’

‘You can a course, Mr McGee.’

‘Excellent. Get a good price off the fucker. These ministers are taking the piss.’

McGee closed that window and opened another. It was a map of a city built on a river, the distinctively serpentine Thames. ‘Right, gentlemen: London. The profits being generated by the Irish property boom are being reinvested across the water.’ He tapped the toolbar and a rash of flags sprang up across the city. ‘The tricolour is already flying here,’ he said, tapping one of the flags. A photograph of Claridge’s appeared on the screen. ‘And here.’ Hamley’s toy shop on Regent Street. ‘And here.’ Versace’s flagship store on New Bond Street. ‘And here, and here, and here,’ he went on, navigating from one flag to the next. Tiffany & Co. on Old Bond Street. The Savoy, the Connaught, the Berkeley hotels. The Unilever building on Blackfriars Bridge. Goldman Sachs and the Daily Mail building on Fleet Street. Rothschild’s HQ in the City, the Citibank tower in Canary Wharf. ‘Plus we’re steadily buying up the Docklands. We’re invading London not with armies but with hard currency. This is our next project.’ A photograph of a whole block stretching from Harvey Nichols to Harrods. ‘This will set us back the princely sum of 530 million. We’ve outbid the Abu Dhabi royal family.’

‘Nice one,’ said Hickey.

‘Is that sterling or euro?’ Boyler or Coyler or Doyler asked.

‘Who gives a shit?’ said the Duffer. ‘We’ll make that on the farmland alone. Once we get the Metro diverted and hyperinflate the price.’

‘And London is just the start,’ said McGee. ‘Questions?’

There were none.

After the motion to annex London had been passed, it was time for lunch. It was served in an adjoining room. I left the building to take a call from M. Deauville. 'They're talking about making a load more trophy purchases in London,' I told him. 'They're all draped in the green jersey up there.' I kept my voice to an urgent whisper, wary of being overheard, for the plaza was crawling with investment bankers. I could be shot for desertion.

'I see.'

Tocka tocka in the background, always the *tocka tocka*, so that I felt I was vying with a thousand others for his attention. 'They're planning on purchasing the Battersea power station.'

'Mmmm?' He sounded interested, but only mildly. Did he appreciate the scale of the acquisition?

'It's a prime redevelopment site. Thirty-eight acres in Central London. Seven million square feet of mixed-use residential, retail and office space. And £150 million of the £400 million purchase price will be funded by issuing loan notes.' I hissed those last two words as if they were contraband, a hard-drugs consignment. *Loan notes*. IOUs.

I waited for M. Deauville to plead caution – to plead reason – to point out that this whole thing was getting out of hand, that it was one matter when we were talking about the site across the road from the castle gates where I could keep an eye on things, keep an eye on Hickey, but that we now appeared to be entering a realm of fantasy. *Tocka tocka* on the other end of the phone until even that petered out and I was listening to silence. Was he still on the line? I looked at the screen. The call-duration counter was running. I put the phone back to my ear.

'They're buying it with *debt*, M. Deauville,' I said at the risk of repeating myself. 'That's what they're talking about up there. They're paying for £150 million of the Battersea site with *debt*.'

'How can you buy something with *debt*?' I persisted when he passed no comment. 'I don't understand what's happening any more.' I glanced up at the penthouse suite to make sure they weren't spying, but the glass reflected the sky. Office workers were striding about checking themselves out in the many mirrored surfaces. They spoke in a contorted nasal accent that hadn't existed in Dublin in my day. I didn't like this hard new elite. They made me feel that my day was over. 'I'd better go back upstairs,' I eventually conceded when it became evident that I was only taking up M. Deauville's time.

There was an acrid smell of sweat in the boardroom, or maybe it was the smell of money. 'Can't we open a window?' I asked, tugging at my shirt collar, 'isn't there a window we can open?' but nobody was listening to me. McGee stood up and I sat down.

He touched his giant screen to reveal a satellite photograph of an archipelago.

'What the fuck is that?' said Hickey, eager to display his hunger to learn. Top of the class was not a role in which he was well versed.

McGee eyed him over his glasses. 'Are you seriously telling me, Mr Hickey, that you don't recognise The World in Dubai?'

A confused hesitation and then Hickey laughed. A course he recognised The World in Dubai! Any developer worth his salt recognised The World in Dubai, and D. Hickey had been monitoring property prices there for months, ready to swoop and make a killing. It was all a question a timing, wasn't that right, lads? He looked around the table.

McGee zoomed in on one of the islands. 'Last month, we purchased the Ireland Island for €28 million and we're developing it into an Irish-themed resort, to include a large internal marina,' a computer-generated image of a marina on the screen, 'apartments and villas,' accompanying artwork, 'a gym, hotel and an Irish-themed pub. To distinguish it from the other islands, the Ireland Island will feature a recreation of the Giant's Causeway. And so, going forward.' He enlarged a grey blob in a navy ocean. 'What we're here to do today, gentlemen, is purchase Britain.'

'Why?' I asked.

Laughter. They thought I was joking.

'Now,' McGee continued, 'given how much property we've added to our portfolio this quarter, we'll have to issue commercial bonds to cover it.'

Commercial bonds. More debt. McGee didn't have any money left and yet he refused to fold. I recognised the compulsive behaviour of an addict. This wasn't a boardroom. This was a betting shop. McGee needed to join the programme. They all needed to join the programme. But first they had to hit rock bottom. You couldn't help them. They had to help themselves. I put down my pen and folded my arms.

My mouth was sour with the taste of coffee. The girl in the pinstripe suit brought in a fresh pot on the hour and the men obediently contemplated her backside, for this ritual was a duty, it was being part of the team.

I took the opportunity to catch Hickey's eye. 'I think we should leave now,' I told him quietly, and he threw me this imploring, panicked look: don't ruin this for me, *please*. It wasn't the wealth that Hickey was after, I saw then, or not only the wealth, but also the opportunity to sit at the big boys' table, to be on the other side of the fence for once in his life. *Can I leave the Minister with you, Dessie? You can a course, Mr McGee!*

McGee summoned another map onto the screen and slid his glasses down his nose to peer at us over them, nodding gravely as if yes, it was true: he was divulging the blueprint of a top-secret military base. 'This, gentlemen, is the real target. We're onto the hard stuff now.'

Shanghai.

More food appeared when darkness fell, as well as a brace of bottles of Brunello di Montalcino. McGee made a show of blowing the dust off the labels to demonstrate their vintage. He had tried to fill my glass and I had covered it with a demurring hand. 'You'll take a drop,' the man insisted, and Hickey had shot him a warning look, shaking his head as if I were a volatile animal to be handled with caution. McGee had backed off. The wine was rich in tannin and it blackened their lips. I could smell it on their blackened breaths, their blackened hearts, their blackened souls. All of them laughing in a medieval display of mettle and Hickey laughing loudest of them all, having discovered the dark art of the calculator. What I cannot remember is anything being funny.

'My colleagues inform me that you've placed a bid on a site on the Pudong skyline,' M. Deauville commented some hours later when I left the boardroom to accept his call. *Tocka tocka, tocka tocka*: messages were criss-crossing the World Wide Web like shooting stars. The news had travelled fast. This was big. I had known it was big. M. Deauville had known it too. Perhaps he had been testing me earlier. Seeing what I was made of. Seeing if I would go all the way.

It was maybe two or three in the morning by then and my eyes hurt. McGee had suggested a ten-minute break, so I had located an unlocked office at the end of the corridor in which to take the call. I closed the door and slid down its length to the floor, grateful for the respite of the darkness. There were twelve men drinking around that table. I wanted bitterly to make it thirteen.

'It's hard,' I told M. Deauville, struggling to control my voice.

'I know.'

I gazed at the workers scattered throughout the floors of the building opposite. So many of them although it was the middle of the night, their faces gaunt in the glare of the computer terminals at which they stared so intently that they barely registered the cleaning staff working around their sedentary forms, servicing them like drones in a beehive. *Tocka tocka* they pattered into their keyboards, for all of us were wired into a universal network, monitoring each other's activities across the globe. 'I know,' M. Deauville repeated. 'I know it's hard.' He sounded more alert than when we had spoken at lunchtime. It must have been a new day in his part of the world. Son of the morning.

'Regarding the Pudong site,' I said, wrenching my faculties back to business matters, 'we are presently waiting to hear whether our bid has been accepted.'

Tocka tocka: the ivory ball skipping along the spinning roulette wheel. It settled in a pocket of black.

'*Bona fortuna*, Tristram,' M. Deauville said and rung off. Only then did I register that our brief conversation had been conducted in Latin. *Bona fortuna*. M. Deauville had given me his blessing. And that, looking back on things, was the turning point.

*

The earth rotated and returned the sun to us, bringing with it a startling revelation. The men were padding around the boardroom in an exhausted delirium by then, the mark of the plague still staining their lips. Calls had been made across the world. Contracts were being drawn up in various international financial institutions. Things had started to happen. We had already flipped one of the hotels in London and shifted a shopping mall in Dubai, extracting value of over €100 million from those two transactions alone, every cent of which we moved like a stack of poker chips onto the Pudong site, stationing our army at the mouth of this most strategic of ports.

And then what? Then we waited. Close of business in Shanghai wasn't for another half hour yet. A call had been promised. The phone was set out in state by McGee's right hand. We could do no more.

It had been such a busy night that we did not know what to do with this idleness. We kept an ear out for the phone, trying not to. We kept an eye on the row of clocks, trying not to. Dublin, Dubai, Shanghai; not London, New York, Tokyo as of old. The axis of world power had shifted. I lifted a slat in the blinds to squint out at the shimmering river. It was another beautiful day and everyone had a headache.

Hickey and I had by that point thrown all our projected profits from the Claremont site, combined with an additional €128 million in loan notes issued by Castle Holdings, into the centre of the boardroom table, forming one of those columns in the cluster of poker chips that had been placed on the square marked 'Shanghai' and I was praying for us to win, I was pleading for us to win. Every fibre of my being was focused on that outcome. *Bona fortuna.* That's when I experienced the startling revelation: that maybe McGee was right. Maybe wealth could be created out of debt and fortunes amassed overnight. Hickey sat with his hairy forearms on the table, his shirtsleeves rolled up past his elbows, his tie tossed over his shoulder in a manner he possibly considered debonair and sweat stains as big as dinner plates under his armpits. If this worked, he would become an extremely wealthy man. Wealthy enough to buy the Castle and Environs out from under my father several times over, to buy any castle he wanted. A millennium-old order would be overturned in a matter of months.

And if it didn't work?

The telephone rang. Silence in the boardroom, twelve grown men pretending they weren't there while the thirteenth listened carefully. 'Thank you, Mr Guo,' said McGee. He replaced the receiver in its cradle and held it there like the throttle lever of a jet engine, forcing his will down the line all the way to Shanghai.

'Gentlemen,' he finally addressed us, 'I have kept you very late. Go home to your wives and apologise on my behalf. Tell them that while they slept you earned tens of millions each overnight.'

Hickey got to his feet and I got to mine. Everyone gravitated towards the head of the table, towards McGee. Laughter again only altogether different in quality. This was the shrill, unguarded laughter of disbelief.

'So you signed a contract to purchase the north County Dublin farm that morning?'

Yes. First we signed the contracts, then we went to see what we had bought.

Hickey dropped me home to get some rest before setting back out again. I slept until the afternoon then stumbled outside into blazing sunshine, unsteady on my legs, as if I had been bedridden for many years, for all of my life in fact, but was now for the first time bearing my own weight, a man on whom a miracle had been performed. *Bona fortuna, Tristram.* My luck had turned. M. Deauville hadn't called since the deal, but then, he didn't need to. For once, I wasn't dying for a drink. I raised my face to the sun and my eyelids glowed pink. Maybe the dark days were over.

I wandered up the avenue past Father's ski lodge of an hotel to the wild rhododendron gardens. May is their month. I have missed their famous display on more occasions than I have caught it because that is the kind of man I am, or was; the kind who let himself lose out on the best part of things.

I found her there, or she found me. Edel. Hickey's wife.

'Oh,' she said, because that's how all our early conversations began – with an expression of surprise. 'I came down to see the rhododendrons. They're at their best at this time of the year.'

'Is that a fact?' I said in mock amazement, for I was feeling playful and capricious and expansive all of a sudden, traits I had never experienced while sober. I felt drunk, in fact, now that I think of it. Drunk as a lord.

She lowered her head. 'You already knew that.'

'Yes, I already knew that.'

We were walking then, deeper into the gardens. She was leading and I was following. I don't know how we arrived at this arrangement, just that we did and that I was very happy. Edel was wearing a white sundress. Her blonde hair was tied in a high ponytail and her bare shoulders—

Forgive me. One moment.

*

Thank you, Fergus. You will appreciate that I find the subject difficult. I was the king of the castle and she was my difficult subject. The heat was almost tropical at the base of the bluff; we might have been wandering through a jungle in Borneo. The blossoms were staggered up the jagged incline in hues of red, pink, purple, peach and white until the bank gave way to sheer rock face, and the rock face to blue sky.

The path grew lush and overgrown. Edel kept her head down as she picked her way along it, and those shoulders looked so delicate that I ached to protect them from all the badness in this world, though she seemed untroubled by it. 'I'll have to get these paths cut back,' I blustered in an effort to assert my authority, and she threw me this look over those shoulders before disappearing behind a screen of leaves, leaving me wondering whether it could possibly have meant what I hoped it did. Such a difficult, difficult subject.

A halter-neck. That is the type of dress she wore. A white cotton bow was knotted at the nape, but that is by the by. Or maybe it isn't. I suspect that various undocumented forces were at work upon me during that period – of which the white cotton bow knotted at the nape of Edel's neck was one – but that I'll spend the rest of my life trying and failing to get to the bottom of the other agencies that invisibly and inexorably exerted their pull, and that, furthermore, the rest of my life *should* be spent this way, that all of us who were implicated *should* spend the rest of our lives this way, examining the aftermath for clues, sifting through the rubble, though I appear to be alone in this endeavour.

We almost collided when I pushed through the leaves to find her waiting on the other side in a drift of wild garlic. It felt natural to place my hands on her waist. Her waist seemed their natural resting place. She reached up and plucked a leaf from my hair before initiating the kiss that initiated everything, but that is beside the point. I had never touched another man's wife before, but that is also beside the point. I no longer understand the point. I no longer know why I'm here. Just that I am here but she is not and that is the end of that.

*

The forest looked more than ever like a jungle when we emerged some time later from our dell. Edel took the path that forked up the hill and I took the one winding down, but instead of going home I stood watching her ascend through the rhododendrons, the little bow knotted at her nape, a butterfly that had alighted on her neck. I had tied that bow myself. No trail of footprints betrayed our bower. There was no sign that we had been there at all. I was not sure whether I could even find my way back to that place again, and at the same time, by the same token, I'm not sure I ever found my way out of it. I'm still there, or part of me is, my choked morsel of a heart.

She reached the point where the castle lands ended and the real world began. As I turned to leave something caught my eye. A familiar shape was crouched beneath the gunnera. I pounded over and pushed back the giant leaves to expose

Larney squirming on the forest floor, the serpent in paradise. I cursed him, I cursed the filthy little goblin. 'I didn't see her!' he whimpered up at me. 'I didn't see her diddies!'

*

Down at the castle, a shiny new monster truck was parked in the courtyard. Hickey jumped out. 'Where the fuck were you?'

'What business is it of yours?'

'Have you seen the shagging time?'

I nodded at the truck. 'What the hell is that?'

'Why aren't you answering your phone?'

We were both full of questions that neither party was prepared to answer. Hickey jerked a thumb at the passenger door. 'Go on, get in. Better late than never.'

This wasn't about Edel. Were it about Edel, I would already have been burst. 'Late for what?'

'Are you for the birds? Late for viewing the farm, a course.' He hauled his weight into the cabin and the contraption bobbed like a raft on its tractor tyres. Those tyres were as disproportionate as football-sized breast implants. 'What are you waiting for?' he shouted out the sunroof.

I opened the passenger door. A cream leather interior in a utility vehicle struck me as a poor call. 'Does Edel approve of this monstrosity?' I was desperate to talk about her.

'The wife?' Hickey pulled a face without looking at me. He was punching letters into the keypad of the satellite navigation system and it all looked a bit implausible, his hairy hand trying to operate technology. 'What's it to her? Ah, for fuck's sake. It says it doesn't recognise the place.'

'That's because it isn't a place.'

'It will be soon.' Hickey started the ignition and did his post-pint sigh. '*Ahhhhh*, listen to her.'

He barely gave the Claremont site a second glance as we passed, which was most out of character, considering he'd been pretty much living down there according to Edel, though I reckoned he'd been spending his nights behind the Viking's Staff Only door. He pressed a button in the console and my seat tilted back. He pressed another and the sunroof sealed shut. A third and the leather steering wheel rose in his hands. 'Height adjustment,' he noted with satisfaction, then produced a folded page from his shirt pocket. 'Here. McGee's office emailed that.' It was the site map.

Hickey had already lobbied the Minister for Bribes. Ray had concluded that diverting the Metro would be an expensive and time-consuming business but he saw no reason why it couldn't be rolled out were enough money invested at the pre-planning stage.

'How much?' I asked.

'A quarter of a million.'

'Jesus.' Greedy X.

The architect had similarly agreed that Hickey's proposal to build a new urban quarter on the site to accommodate Dublin's burgeoning workforce was achievable, but then, Morgan was paid to design whatever he was told to design. Hickey was so fired up with his plans for the farm that I wondered whether he had even partially grasped the magnitude of the international property portfolio that we had acquired overnight.

We took a right onto the M1. After travelling for a distance that I considered sufficient to establish that this farm could never function as part of the commuter belt, Hickey turned off and we found ourselves, or lost ourselves, in flat, featureless farmland. No rivers, no mountains, no coastline, no inhabitants, and not a whole lot of farming either.

I frowned out at the ragged hedgerows with their mud-spattered leaves. 'How much did we pay for this again?' but Hickey couldn't remember either. We were searching for a rusty green gate. That's what the directions said, scrawled in his potato-print hand on the back of the site map. *M1, fourth exit, left, rusty green gate.* The map itself didn't extend to encompass the motorway. There was no reference point from which to navigate. A crazy-paving pattern of local boundaries, but no *X marks the spot* to reveal the chest of gold. If this was what they had managed to sell us in our own backyard, God knows what we had purchased around the globe in our delirium. I went to toss the useless page into the back seat but there was no back seat in the truck. I sat with the map on my lap.

We were travelling along a tertiary road with no white line down the middle. The sun was shining through Hickey's window, and then it was shining through mine, and then it was shining through Hickey's window again. We were going around in circles. 'Ask for directions,' I said to annoy him – we hadn't seen another soul for miles. The few old farmhouses that we passed looked neglected and sad. There wasn't what you'd call evidence of a local housing need. 'The Celtic Tiger didn't bother venturing this far north,' I noted.

'We are the Celtic Tiger,' said Hickey. 'We're here now.'

More byways, more barbed-wire fences snagged with silage bags. I could already see the newspaper graphics in the property supplements: a dot indicating Malahide and our new urban quarter next to it as if the two were side by side. And the punters would believe it because they wanted it to be true, and lately in this country, wanting something to be true made it true. Wanting something to be worth a hundred million made it worth a hundred million. I checked my phone. No word from M. Deauville.

The satellite navigation system indicated that our vessel was adrift in a sea of black. The sun was low in the sky. Soon it was going to get dark. Country dark, that is, real dark; there was no street lighting. Hickey and I weren't used to country dark. 'I think it might be time to turn back,' I told him. 'We'll come out again in the morning.'

An old black Audi A6 came booting up from the rear and overshot us on a blind bend, its registration plates mud-caked to illegibility. Three clipped male heads juddered about in the back seat and one of them turned to eye us. Whatever he said made the others turn to look too and then they were gone. 'Fucken Eastern Europeans,' Hickey muttered. The Audi was a left-hand drive. Plus the Irish no longer drove cars as old as that.

The road narrowed into a lane and the lane narrowed into a cart-track with a mohawk of grass running down the centre. A very bad feeling was brewing inside me. 'This can't be right, Dessie,' I said, but what I meant was: Dessie, this is wrong.

Finally, a rusty green gate. For Sale by Public Tender read the sign erected on stilts like a prison watchtower, Sale Agreed nailed across it. Hickey killed the ignition and jumped out to empty his bladder into the ditch before wrenching the gate out of the long grass and shouldering it back into the field like the turning arm of a mill. I sat peering out at Dublin's new urban quarter – fields of scutch grass and clumps of gorse. The sky was a dusky wash of blue and the first of the evening's stars had appeared. The heavens, I remember thinking as I gazed up at them. And down here, the hell.

Hickey was delighted to get an opportunity to see what

the truck could do, so we reared over hillocks and plunged into troughs, the white scuts of rabbits bounding out of the headlamp beams as he gunned the throttle. Then we hit something. He slammed on the brakes and whipped around in his seat to peer out the back window. 'What the fuck was that?'

I hadn't seen anything either. The impact had been loud but dull. We had collided with something soft and heavy. 'Don't get out,' I warned Hickey because the bad feeling was even stronger in the field, but he jumped out to inspect the front of the truck, running his palm along the bull bars. 'Doesn't seem to be any damage.'

I lowered my window. 'It sounded like an animal. Maybe it was a badger?'

He shook his head. 'This is a raised chassis. It has a clearance of over three feet. A badger would've fitted underneath. It was something bigger than that. I don't understand how we didn't see it in the lights.' He spat into the grass. 'It's dead now in anyways.'

Then we heard the animal howl.

'We can't leave it like that,' I said. 'We should go back and find it. Have you got a torch?'

'It's a hammer we need. I left me tools in the old truck so that's the end a that.' He was hauling himself back up into the driver's seat when the thing wailed again, a blood-curdling sound. 'Ah fuck it. I suppose we'd better put it out of its misery.'

So we both got out and went combing through the long grass in the violet twilight. I came upon a snowdrift of feathers where a killing had taken place. The strong brown wing feathers yielded to the downy white ones as layers of the bird were stripped away. When the feathers ran out, I encountered what looked like a fox's brush. I got down on my hunkers to illuminate it with the screen of my phone. It was indeed a severed fox's brush. The nub of the tailbone was the leathery black of a gorilla's palm. No blood – this wasn't a fresh wound. The blue light attracted Hickey's eye. 'Have you found it?'

'No.'

We moved on.

Hickey disturbed a pheasant then. It exploded out of the grass, a clatter of whip-cracking wings, and he flinched backwards with a *whuuh!* 'The size a tha!' he grinned over at me, keen to laugh it off because it did not sit well on him, having his fright witnessed by another man, even if it was only a man like me. Then we heard a whimper. It was coming from a mound of gorse. Hickey picked up a rock and we approached.

It was woody old gorse, left to grow unchecked for so long that you could walk between the trunks propping up its prickly canopy. The closer we got, the higher the mound loomed, and then we saw the glowing eyes. And the glowing eyes saw us. They had been watching us all along.

Neither of us said a word, just about-turned and legged it straight back to the truck. When we were both in, Hickey hit the central locking button and the accelerator pedal. He didn't stop to shut the rusty gate when we finally found our way out. 'But what if it escapes?' I said and immediately regretted voicing the question, because in referring to it I had confirmed that there was an It. Hickey didn't answer.

'Do you believe in God?' he asked me some miles down the road. Night had fallen by then. Real dark, country dark.

'No.'

'Do you believe in the Devil?'

'Don't be absurd.' The quality of his silence made me turn to him. 'Why, do you?'

His face was lit electronic blue by the screen of the GPS, which indicated that we were still stranded in a void. 'Yes.'

'You believe there's an actual man called the Devil who walks amongst us?'

'I do,' Hickey asserted with vehemence, keeping his eyes on the road. 'I seen him. Down at the Steak one night. The lot of us were standing around a bonfire outside the cave when suddenly there was this face on the other side a the flames, standing right across from me an looking at me mate Shane. Staring at him, like. Boring holes into his head. He was black. An I don't mean African black. He was a white man but his skin was black, an shiny an greasy, so I elbowed Shane an says, 'Who's your man? Who brought him? Fucker seems to know you.' But Shane couldn't see him. 'Where?' he says, an I nodded across the bonfire but your man had already went. But I *seen* the prick. I *seen* him there that night. A few hours later, Shane was dead. Drowned. Fisherman's son. Never learned to swim. You remember Shane.'

'I'm sorry, Dessie, I don't.'

'You do. He was in the little school with us. Did you know he was dead?'

'No, I hadn't heard. I must have been away.'

'They said you were dead too.'

'That was another Tristram St Lawrence.'

'That's right. Another Tristram St Lawrence. Common name.'

I lowered my head. 'Yes, it is a remarkable coincidence.'

We journeyed for another mile or so without speaking. Hickey turned the heat on full. 'Perishing in here,' he complained, though it wasn't. Moths blundered into the beams of the headlamps, and a frog made a break for the other side of the road, getting its timing spectacularly wrong. The amount of vehicles that passed that way – maybe one or two each night, and maybe none at all – why did it have to wait until then?

'Have you ever seen the Devil?'

'No, Dessie, I haven't.'

'I think you have seen him. I think you just didn't know it was the Devil. Or that you just didn't admit it was the Devil. That's what I think.'

'Is it?'

'It is. Do you think he'd talk with an English accent?'

'Please, Dessie.'

'Or would he be one a them mad fuckers from Kerry? You know where they hold the Puck Fair? The Puck is another word for the Devil, isn't it? Isn't that right, Tristram? Isn't the Puck another name for the Devil?'

'I don't know, Dessie.' So don't keep asking me. We were going around in circles again but there was no sun to orient-ate us this time. No moon either, that I could see. And no St Christopher, the patron saint of travellers. The dashboard of the new truck was bare.

'I'd say he'd be English. Like you.'

'I'm not English, Dessie.'

'You know what I mean. I'd say he'd talk posh like you.' Hickey pondered the Devil's accent as we raced along the country lanes. The blackness of the surrounding fields facilitated this strain of thought. There could have been anything out there. 'Yeah,' Hickey concluded, 'the fucker at the bonfire with the coal-black skin didn't look like a Kerryman to me. He didn't look human. I'd say he was English. A posh English toff.'

The lane was steadily tapering and the hedgerows crowded in, a scrawny rabble clamouring at the windows to get a look at us, convicts in a prison van. They dragged their claws along Hickey's new paintwork. 'Jesus,' he whispered. I glanced at the GPS. It was still reading a blank.

'Tell us this, Tristram: why don't you drink any more?' The heat in the truck was overpowering.

'Because it'll kill me, Dessie,' I told him, although it was none of his business.

'Why, what were you drinking, strychnine?'

Trying to make light of it. There was no light to be made of it. Addiction was a dark road. 'Alcohol, Dessie. If I drink alcohol again, I'll die.'

Hickey couldn't get his head around this. 'Is that what they tell you in the AA? That if you take a drink you'll die?'

'Not immediately, but yes, I'll die.'

Hickey laughed. 'An you believe that shite?'

'Yes, Dessie, I believe that shite. I believe that if I started drinking again, I would keep drinking until I drank myself into the grave.'

'An you laugh at me for believin in the Devil?'

'I didn't laugh at you, Dessie. We all have our private conceptualisations of Hell.'

'Private conceptualisations of Hell,' he repeated dubiously, giving the words his full consideration. '*Private conceptualisations of Hell.* So what you're saying is, it's in me head?'

'The Devil was invented by man, Dessie.' And like the nuclear bomb, once we invented him, we could not uninvent him.

Hickey shook his head. 'I know what I seen that night. I know the Devil was standing at that bonfire. An I know that two hours later me mate Shane was dead.'

Why had I denied knowing Shane? I remembered Shane well enough. I hadn't heard that he was dead. 'Where's your St Christopher?'

'In the old truck.'

‘Oh.’ Silence. Miles of silence ensued. There was much to weigh up. ‘I don’t think we should go ahead with this project,’ I finally said.

‘Too late,’ said Hickey. ‘We already signed.’

Of course. Last night, or was it the night before? During the night of delirium, we had signed every contract put in front of us. *pp M. Deauville*, I had inscribed beneath my signature; *per pro.*, *per procurationem*, through the agency of. By the power delegated to me as his procurator, his steward, his proxy.

‘Here, Tristram?’

‘What?’

‘Do you ever feel he’s in the back seat?’

‘Who?’

‘The Devil.’

‘Stop it, Dessie.’

‘Jesus, Mary and Joseph, you sounded exactly like him just there!’

‘I mean it. Enough.’

‘When you’re driving around, I mean. Like now, for example. Do you ever feel he’s sitting right behind you just out of range of the rear-view mirror?’

‘No,’ I said firmly, ‘I don’t.’

‘Or maybe he doesn’t have a reflection. Maybe that’s why I can’t see him.’

‘Or maybe you can’t see him because he isn’t actually there.’

‘Nah,’ said Hickey. ‘He’s there, all right. I can feel him. Breathing down the back a me neck.’

*

The relief when the first street light appeared on the horizon was immense, a glimpse of dry land to a shipwrecked man. A sign for the motorway soon followed and we hurtled towards the orange glow of civilisation. The navigation system started tracking our position again. I didn't care that Hickey was speeding. I could not get out of that black hole fast enough.

'I do right now, Tristram,' Hickey said out of nowhere. We were stopped at a red light at Sutton Cross by then. At least forty minutes had passed between us in silence, Hickey blessing himself every time we passed a church, and sometimes when we didn't. The Cross was deserted at that hour of the night.

I was frankly surprised when Hickey had slowed to a halt at the empty junction. I had expected him to bulldoze through the way he bulldozed through everything. Why, having broken all the other rules, had he chosen to obey this one? The rules of logic, of business, of matrimony, the rules of the Irish State – a trail of broken rules lay scattered in his wake as if a tornado had passed through town, and then he decides to stop at a red light after midnight? I looked at him. 'You do what right now?'

'Feel him in the back seat.'

'Who?'

'The Devil.'

I turned away to look out at the crossroads. The two of us stared dead ahead like a pair of mannequins. The skin on the back of my neck crawled like the pelt of a cat because as soon as Hickey said it, I felt it too. Felt him. Breathing on me.

The lights changed to green. We pushed on. Motion somehow alleviated it, that sense of the Devil bearing down on us, contracting his tensile spine.

'Why do you think I bought the truck, Tristram?' Hickey asked me at Corr Bridge. He was over-enunciating his words.

'I don't know, Dessie. Why did you buy the truck?' I was

over-enunciating my words too. We were under observation now. We were speaking before an audience.

'Because it has no back seat.'

'I see.' We trundled on.

'Nowhere for him to sit.'

'I got that.'

He rolled down the electric window after dropping me off. The castle hovered in darkness, a damp slab of stone. 'I still feel him breathing behind me though,' Hickey stated grimly, inclining his head to indicate the space to his rear, the non-existent back seat that we were both afraid to look at. The window glided up again, sealing Hickey in with his cargo, and no St Christopher to protect him.

Eighth day of evidence

22 MARCH 2016

‘Mr St Lawrence, these lands you describe as your proposed new urban quarter for Dublin: would this be the farm in Oldcastle?’

That would be correct. 'The most expensive scrubland in Ireland,' as the *Irish Times* dubbed it when news of the deal was officially released a couple of months later. A profile of Hickey was published in the business section, with a picture of his shaggy head in a football jersey, describing him as a small-time builder with little formal education who had started out with garage conversions and renting prefabs to schools and graduated to developing the prominent coastal Claremont site and acquiring an international property portfolio within the space of ten years. Currently on to his second marriage to a marketing executive also from Howth, father to nine – nine! – children with his first wife. Then the article made reference to a powerful publicity-shy business partner, considered to be the mastermind of the operation but about whom little was known other than that he was connected at the highest level to the world of international investment banking.

I dropped the paper and stood at the window with a racing heart and mind. Mastermind of the operation. Powerful publicity-shy business partner. So Hickey had a puppet master too. Background figures were yanking his strings just as surely as they were yanking mine. He hadn't the wit to pull it off, and, frankly, neither did I. We had bought properties in countries we couldn't locate on a map.

I checked my phone. M. Deauville hadn't called. He would already have seen the morning's papers. His information service would have drawn the extract to his attention. This silence was a bad omen. I phoned Hickey.

'I was about to ring you,' he shouted at me over the racket – he was on site. On the old site, that is. The original one. The one we should have stuck with.

I eyed the man in the tower crane as if eyeing Hickey. I hated that he had a peephole into my privacy. I resented his vantage point. 'I just saw the *Irish Times*.'

The background noise fell away and I heard the drum of footsteps across a raised floor. He had retreated into the Portakabin. 'Yeah.'

'Who is this "powerful silent partner" that they're talking about, Dessie? Your "shady business associate"?'

'You, ya fucken eejit. You're me shady associate. Listen, get your arse down here now.'

'I can't. I have a board meeting. The legal team is arriving as I speak.' A black Mercedes S class was crunching across the gravel, reflecting warped silhouettes in its polished flanks.

'Well, come down the minute it's over. We could be bollixed.'

*

The barrister and his assistant shook my hand in front of the Castle Holdings plaque at the top of the terrace steps. I led them inside to the steward's room.

Once we were seated, the assistant, a young man who was devilling for the barrister in the Law Library, took a laptop from his briefcase and powered it up. The barrister produced a mobile phone. He dialled a number and set the device on speakerphone before placing it in the centre of the table. The three of us listened to the foreign ringtone.

Click. 'Yes?' M. Deauville. My heart sat up in recognition,

a dog responding to his master's voice. How strange to hear him in an official context. How strange to hear M. Deauville answering a phone, in fact. I was the one who answered to him. Those were the terms of engagement.

The barrister listed the names of the three persons present and the young devil took notes. *Tocka tocka* on his laptop. The barrister read out the minutes from the previous board meeting: a list of properties acquired and the amounts paid for them, the extent of the loan notes issued to date – millions. M. Deauville proposed the adoption of the minutes and I seconded him. 'Any Other Business?' the barrister enquired, turning to me.

'None,' I dutifully responded as the statutory Irish resident of Castle Holdings Ltd. A spider was suspended from a gossamer thread directly in front of my face. It was a small specimen, brown with yellow flecks, and its legs were bunched so tightly that it formed a sphere. It plunged further down its thread until it hovered just above the tooled leather surface of the desk. I don't know why I mention the spider. Other than to remark that I wished it wasn't there, but it was there, and I lived with it, along with a number of other monstrosities that made their home in mine. The devil hit *print* and his portable printer fired out the minutes. It was most efficient. His master checked them for errata before placing them in front of me. He proffered a lacquered pen with which to sign. The spider scuttled back up its thread. I uncapped the pen and couldn't help but pause to admire its craftsmanship.

'You know, you should never share a good fountain pen,' I said by way of making conversation now that the dirty work was done. 'The nib has adapted to your hand.'

'Don't worry about the pen, Mr St Lawrence,' the barrister advised me, indicating where my signature should be inserted. 'This pen has adapted to many hands over the centuries.'

I scratched my name on the dotted line and returned the endorsed minutes and the pen. The barrister witnessed my signature with his, then handed the document to the devil, who stowed it in his briefcase. M. Deauville rang off at that point. I gave the barrister the unopened stack of post that had arrived addressed to Castle Holdings Ltd. Harps from the Irish taxman and block capitals from the North Americans: 'IMPORTANT TAX RETURN DOCUMENT INSIDE.' M. Deauville's counsel accepted the correspondence and thanked me for my time. I saw the two of them back out to their car.

Didn't I find this arrangement odd? No, Fergus, not in the least. It is what my family has done for centuries, I suppose. Managed our estate. That's what passes for work amongst the landed gentry: authorising others to undertake it on our behalf.

'By the way,' I said to the barrister as he was lowering himself into the back seat, 'could I get M. Deauville's number from you?' I took out my mobile phone. 'I appear to have, ahm, deleted it from my contacts folder.'

The barrister glared up at me in outrage. I had deviated from the script. 'I'm afraid that won't be possible,' he muttered tightly before pulling the door of the Mercedes shut as hard as he could manage.

*

'Have you gone up thirteen floors on that hotel?' I asked Hickey when I found him in the Portakabin. I needn't have bothered pitching it as a question. Hickey had gone up thirteen floors on the hotel. Any fool with an eye in his head could see that.

'Don't mind that now. We're in trouble here.'

'For the love of God, you can't just go up two extra storeys.'

Hickey pointed at the paint-spattered plastic chair in front of his desk and raised his voice. 'For fuck's sake, Tristram, this is serious. Shut the fuck up and sit down.' I shut the fuck up and sat down.

He turned his back on me and flicked a switch. 'Useless piece of shit.'

I jumped to my feet. He had found out about Edel. How? Because someone knew about our affair. *I didn't see her diddies!*

'Cheapo fucken crap. Jesus Christ, who designs this shite?'

The kettle. He was referring to the yellowing plastic jug kettle, trying to manhandle it onto its base. The thing eventually connected with the power supply and the orange switch lit up. He looked over his shoulder.

'What are you standing there for?'

'I . . . Can I help?'

'You? Help? With a faulty appliance? Stop the lights.'

I sat back down on the paint-spattered chair and watched him make a cup of tea. He made only one, so I presumed it was for him until he placed the mug in front of me. 'There,' he said as if setting me a challenge. Which he was. Curds of sour milk floated on the surface. 'Thanks, Dessie.' I adjusted the position of the mug but did not raise it from the table.

He sat down on the other side of the desk, put his head in his hands and shook his great mane slowly. Oh Lord God, I realised, he knows. He knows that I am in love with his wife, and that his wife is in love with me. How could he not know? The birds were singing about it in the trees. The sun was shining about it in the sky. Yes, we had been seeing each other all summer, Edel and I, but that is a private matter.

I sat there awaiting my punishment like a schoolboy. A girly calendar was tacked to the wall behind Hickey's head.

Miss September's breasts were as hyper-inflated as the tyres on his truck. Finally, he raised his face. 'The Viking,' he told me darkly.

'Oh,' I said in relief. 'Why, what of him?'

Hickey averted his face, as if he couldn't yet bring himself to speak of such things, and it was insensitive of me to ask.

'What? Has he ratted you out with Svetlana?' That would explain why Edel had come to me in the first place. The spurned wife.

'The Russian one? No, she's grand. It's her pimp that's giving me a pain in the hole.' He resumed his slow, sour head-shake, and his mouth performed a series of expressions of revulsion, as if nauseating words were teeming inside it, filling it with bile until he could hold them in no longer. He sprang to his feet and threw open the door. I thought he was going to puke but instead he hawked a gullier into the yard where it sizzled in the sun, glutinous with agro.

He shut the door and returned to his seat. 'The Viking's after getting to Ray.'

'Getting to him?'

'Yeah. He wants the Metro North diverted to service his land.'

I was missing something. 'What does the Viking want with the Metro North? The Dart's already servicing Howth.'

'Not his land in Howth. His land in some kip I never heard of on the other side a the M1. An he gazumped us on diverting the Metro this morning. It's going to terminate in his farm, not ours.'

'But our farm is worthless without the Metro.'

'Correct. We'll be down ninety-eight million.'

Ninety-eight million. Could we really have paid that? I lowered my eyes to the curdled milk. 'Well, we're just going to have to cough up even more to the Minister then, aren't we? How much is he extorting from the Viking?'

'€300,000.'

'Bloody hell. So we need to come up with €310,000.'

'Nope. We need to come up with half a mil.'

'That's not how bidding works. You go in with your lowest offer.'

'This isn't bidding. This is bribing. The Minister says it'll cost half a mil in "professional fees" to get the Metro North diverted to service our farm. He read in the *Irish* fucken *Times* this morning that we're going to make a profit of over a hundred million on the new urban quarter so he wants a slice. Fair's fair, is what he told me. Otherwise, the Metro North goes east to the Viking's field. An oh yeah, he wants this "professional fee" to be delivered as a package.'

'What, in a big brown envelope?'

'No, a financial package. He wants a certain amount a the apartments from the farm – he hasn't said how many yet – to be placed in various offshore trusts that can't be traced back to him. He's had a spot a bother in this regard in the past, as we all know. Plus we've to throw in the redevelopment of his gaff to include a 3,000-square-foot extension to the side an rear with swimming pool and gym. I mean, we can't just hand the man half a million lids in cash, obviously.'

'Obviously.'

'Except that he wants half a million lids in cash to be handed to him first.'

'What?'

'This is it. He wants half a million lids lodged as a "planning bond" an when he gets his apartments and extension he'll give us our cash back.'

'I've heard it all.'

A knock on the door then. Hickey threw his head back as

if this were the final straw. 'Oh Jesus Christ *what*!' he shouted at the ceiling.

A labourer in a helmet inserted his head. 'There's a man here from Iarnród Éireann, boss. Says the railway owns the north-west corner of the site.'

'Tell him to go and shite.'

'Fair play,' said the labourer and shut the door.

'The Viking,' Hickey said bitterly, stoking his rage. 'Because a that ponce, we need an extra quarter mil. I'm already at the pin a me collar. Where am I going to find that sort a money?'

'The country is awash with money. Ask McGee. I mean, he's throwing cash around.'

'Not any more, he isn't. He says he has a liquidity issue, not a solvency one.'

'What's that supposed to mean?'

'Dunno. He just came out with it. I rang him an says, Ulick, be a good man an loan us some extra money there for the Minister; an he says, Dessie, we have a liquidity issue, not a solvency one, but the fundamentals are sound. Then he says we said *we'd* take care a the Minister.'

'No, you said *you'd* take care of the Minister.'

'Yeah, but you're me shady associate. So when I says I'll take care a something, that means *we'll* take care of it.'

The top buttons of his shirt had come undone, revealing a lewd tangle of chest hair. I didn't like to gawp so I focused on Miss September's cleavage instead. 'The writing's on the wall, Dessie. It's time to pull the plug.'

'We can't pull the plug. The contracts have been exchanged. We have to get that shagging Metro redirected or else we're down ninety-eight million for a farm that isn't even any good of a farm, according to the *Irish Times*, although all farms are dumps if you ask me. So go talk to your money man about spotting us the extra quarter mil. Dickville. Give him a bell.'

pp M. Deauville. I had exchanged contracts on his behalf for scrubland that didn't even register on a GPS. 'It's not that simple, Dessie. I can't just call him.'

'Why not?'

'I just can't.'

'Let me talk to him then.'

'You can't either.'

'A course I can. It's his investment too. He'll thank you in the long run, believe you me.' Hickey took out his mobile phone. 'What's his number? Call it out to me there.'

'Trust me, Dessie. I can't tell you his number.'

'Give us your phone.'

'No. Hey!'

He grabbed my phone because that's how he had operated in school – by simply appropriating the things he wanted. And that's how I had operated too – by simply letting him.

He was prodding away at it with his hairy digits when he sat back and frowned. 'Here, why did me wife call you this morning?'

This may come as a surprise to those assembled in this chamber but I am a dreadful liar. I gaped at Hickey and Hickey gaped at me and it seemed that we were building up to something – something big, something explosive, something that would splatter all over the ceiling – when my phone rang in his hand.

'It says *Unknown*. Is that him?'

I nodded.

Hickey pressed the green button and raised my phone to his ear. 'Hello?' He lowered it again and looked at the screen. 'Prick hung up on me.'

'Oh.' Your wife called me this morning because she . . . because I . . . because we . . . Because what?

My phone rang again. Hickey reluctantly returned it. I checked the screen. *Unknown.*

'Hello? Yes, it's me this time, M. Deauville. That was, ahm, Mr Hickey. Indeed. The board meeting went very well, thank you. Everything is in order. Ahm, on another matter, something has cropped up here. We've encountered an unanticipated expense pertaining to the farm in Oldcastle. One of the planning bonds has just doubled. No, not the County Council's bond, it's an additional bond concerning the ahm . . . the construction of the Metro. Ah. Is it? I see. Yes. I fully understand. Indeed, most unfortunate. Of course. The First Step was that we admitted that we were powerless over alcohol,' M. Deauville and I chanted together, 'that our lives had become unmanageable, and we came to believe that a Power greater than ourselves could restore us to sanity.'

I put the phone back in my pocket after we had completed a quick run-through of the Steps. Because she is worried about you. Your wife called me this morning because she is worried about you. She thinks you're working too hard so she called me to ask after your welfare. Which is why her number showed up on my phone. That's what I would tell him.

'What'd he say?'

'He says he can't do it.'

'He has to do it.'

'Well, he says he can't. He says the Market is nervous.'

'About what?'

'About a credit event.'

'What's a credit event?'

'I don't know.'

Hickey narrowed his eyes. 'Something's going on. Why is

everyone pulling out? Why is McGee pulling out? Why is your lad pulling out?'

'I don't know.'

'You do know.'

'I don't know.'

'You knew everything in school.'

'This isn't school.'

He brought his fist down on the desk. 'Fuck,' he shouted, then conjugated the verb in the imperative. Fuck this, fuck that, fuck the other. Fuck you, fuck him, fuck the Viking. I looked down at the curdled milk and waited for the storm to pass.

The Portakabin door burst open behind me, as if some critical level of air pressure had been reached and we'd blown a gasket. I looked up and turned around. Hickey was gone, shot from a cannon. I sat back and looked at his calendar. Miss September had no hair other than on her head, which struck me as connected to some pathology of Hickey's, what with his being so hirsute and Miss September being so—

Engine roar. I turned around in my seat again. The monster truck was revving at the door. 'Are ya coming or wha?' Hickey shouted from the driver's seat. 'Because someone needs to sort this gee-bag out.'

Which gee-bag? Didn't matter. Any gee-bag would do. I pocketed my phone and followed him out.

'This would be the day that the assault on Mr Dowdall took place?'

Who?

'The Viking.'

Oh, him. The alleged assault. No, that took place the following morning. Hickey drove the few hundred metres down the road to the Viking's green gin palace and parked in his loading bay. St Christopher was back on the dashboard, a dribble of glue oozing from his base. Hickey rammed the heel of his hand against his big horn and kept it there until Svetlana appeared at his window.

'Yes, Mr Hickey?'

That turned my stomach – a woman with whom he'd had sexual relations calling him Mister. 'Get your boss out here, love.'

'He isn't in the bar at the moment.'

'When will he be back?'

'He didn't say.'

Hickey folded his arms over his belly. 'Well, we'll just have to wait for him then, won't we?'

Svetlana nodded and returned to the bar. Hickey contemplated her arse, giftwrapped in the apron bow.

I checked my watch. 'Are we just going to sit here?'

'Yep. We're just going to sit here til that cockhead comes out.'

'Svetlana just told us he isn't in there.'

'See that?' Hickey indicated the Range Rover Sport parked up ahead. 'That's his pathetic shitbox. He's in there.'

A text arrived. I took out my phone and the screen screamed Edel's name. Hickey turned his head. I hit delete without reading the message and returned the phone to my pocket.

'Was that your man?'

'No,' I said, and then realised that I should have said yes. Yes, that was your man. It certainly wasn't a text from your wife.

'Here, what was all that earlier about a Power greater than yourselves?'

'It's one of the Twelve Steps, Dessie. "We came to believe that a Power greater than ourselves could restore us to sanity." '

Hickey kept his arms folded and addressed himself to the invisible listener standing at his window. 'Sounds like a cult to me.'

'AA is not a cult. It's a recovery programme.'

'An is the French fuck in this recovery programme too?'

'I don't think M. Deauville is French.'

'Why do you call him Monsieur then?'

'French is spoken in many parts of the world, Dessie.'

'So where's he from?'

I had first encountered him in Brussels. 'He's Belgian, I think.'

Hickey had no insight to offer on the topic of Belgians. He had no racially insensitive observations or random associations to submit. 'Tell us again how you know this fella?'

'He's my sponsor.'

'In the AA?'

'Yes.' Where else?

'What's a sponsor?'

I quoted the literature. '"Our leaders are but trusted servants; they do not govern."'

'An that doesn't sound like a cult to you?'

He had me there. I conceded him his point.

'So, would Fuckville be the one who told you that you'd die if you took another drink?'

'M. Deauville didn't have to tell me. I could see that for myself.'

'But he did tell you?'

'As it happens, yes.'

'He's brainwashing you.'

'No, he's supporting me.'

'An everyone in the AA has one a these sponsors?'

'Yes.'

'So there's, like, one geezer at the top? One big head-the-ball who knows everyone's secrets because all the individual cells are reporting back to him, like in the IRA?'

'It doesn't work like that.'

'How does it work?'

'Not like that. It isn't a military organisation. And it isn't a hierarchical structure. "Each group should be autonomous except in matters affecting other groups or AA as a whole."' I was quoting again.

'Sounds dodgy to me.'

I nodded at Svetlana through the window to change the subject. 'Are you still consorting with that girl?'

'Who, the Russian bird? Ah sure, you know yourself.'

'What does that mean?'

Hickey shrugged. 'It means: ah sure, you know yourself.'

'What about Edel?'

'Edel?' He smirked mirthlessly. 'Don't talk to me about Edel.'

Silence as my mind worried this nugget of information into shreds. What did *Don't talk to me* mean? Was it the same as *Ah sure, you know yourself*? I pressed my eye against this peephole into their marriage but I was on the wrong side of the door. The lens was distorted and offered conflicting views depending on where you stood. *Don't talk to me* as in: Edel doesn't love me any more, the marriage is gone, or *Don't talk to me* as in: I suspect she's having it off with another man an I'm going to kill him with my bare hands when I find out who he is.

He cleared his throat.'Have you noticed anything funny going on lately?'

Here it comes. Why did my wife call you this morning? Why is she never around? 'Funny?'

'Yeah, funny as in men standing around.'

'It's a building site, Dessie. Men stand around.'

'No, men in suits. I had to call me foreman over today. I says to him, "Who's your man?" because this fella in a suit had appeared on site, but when me foreman looked over, your man was gone.'

'So?'

'So something funny's going on.'

'Like what?'

He addressed himself to the driver's window again. 'Might be the Tax Man.'

The phone chirruped in my pocket. Another text. I didn't move. Hickey looked at me. 'Are you going to open that or wha?'

'I'll open it later.'

'Why? Is it your man again?'

'No. It's your wife.'

He laughed at that. He thought it was a joke.

*

At a quarter past one in the morning the last customer staggered out and Svetlana switched off the lights. I deleted the latest in Edel's chain of texts and stashed the phone before elbowing Hickey awake. 'Whuh?' he said, sliding back up in his seat. 'Where is he?'

'He hasn't come out yet.'

He shivered. 'Jesus Christ, it's bleedin perishing in here.'

Svetlana emerged and locked the double doors behind her. No sign of the Viking. Hickey looked up the road. The Range Rover Sport hadn't budged. 'Are you sure he didn't come out?'

'Positive. I've been watching all night.'

Svetlana pulled the shutters down and clipped them into place. She waved goodnight to us and then activated the key fob in her hand. The Range Rover flashed its hazard lights in response. In she got and drove away, just like that. We sat outside the empty bar on the empty street looking at the empty parking space, then Hickey exploded and punched the steering wheel which detonated the horn. The Viking was out there sniggering at us. We hated him. And he hated us.

Hickey started the engine. 'Right. That's it. I've had it.'

'Where are we going?'

'For a little drive.'

He turned right onto the West Pier and drove down the wrong side of the road. The pier was deserted. He could drive wherever he liked, I reasoned, trying to quell a flurry of alarm.

'Beautiful moon out tonight,' he noted. Although this was a perfectly valid observation – the moon was especially pure that night, and the sky especially clear – it was not the class of remark that might be expected from Hickey and it alarmed me further still. 'Sometimes,' he added, 'I come down here to think.'

'You wouldn't come down here that often, then,' I said, to get us back on track.

'That's funny, Tristram. You're a funny man. Yeah.' He nodded. 'That's what everyone's been saying about you lately. He's a bit funny, isn't he, that fella? Something funny about him.'

It didn't sound quite like Hickey's voice. I was afraid to turn my head to check. 'Who's everyone, Dessie?'

'Oh, you know. Everyone.'

We trundled past shuttered restaurants and fishmongers, the ship's chandler and the ice factory, piles of ropes and nets. No sign of life on the quayside. The fishing boats had already departed for the night.

'Do us a favour an pop open the glove compartment for me there.'

I leaned forward and clicked it open. A metal curve glinted amongst the truck's manuals. I whipped my eyes away in shock. A gun.

'Give us me flask there like a good man.'

I looked back into the glove compartment. A hip flask. It was only a hip flask. I took it out. It was full.

He glanced at the flask. 'Be a star an take the lid off for me, would ya? I'd do it meself only I'm driving.'

I unscrewed the cap and held the flask out. Hickey swallowed a mouthful and did the post-pint sigh: *Ahhhhh*. The smell of whiskey filled the cabin. He handed the flask back.

'Tanks a million. You'll have a drop yourself.'

'No thank you.'

'Go on. Warm yourself up. It's bleedin freezing in here.'

'I'd rather not, thanks.' A blatant lie.

'Ah, sorry. Forgot.'

'Not to worry.' I put the cap back on.

'I wouldn't bother doing that,' he smirked. 'You're only wasting your energy.' I twisted the cap as hard as I was able.

We crawled along the centre of the pier. You would think we were leading a funeral procession. You would think there was a coffin in the back. Then Hickey took the truck out of gear and let it roll to a halt. He pulled up the handbrake but did not cut the engine. This is an odd spot to stop, I thought. Neither here nor there.

'Is that a seal?' he said suddenly, sitting up and craning his neck to get a better look.

'Where?' There were no seals in the harbour, as far as I could see.

Hickey pointed at the moonlit water. 'A little black head popped up over there and looked right at me. It must of been a seal.' He jumped in his seat. 'There he is! It *was* a seal. Jaysus, me heart. For a minute there, I thought I seen the Devil again. Ah for fuck's sake, Tristram, are you blind or what? Follow the line a me finger.'

I wasn't looking at the water. I was looking at Hickey.

'Look at the little fecker,' he said, shaking his head in disapproval. 'His skin all black and slimy like the Devil's. The holes instead a ears, as if his real ears got burnt off in a fire. The sneaky little bollockses duck out a sight before you can get a proper look at them. Seals are disgustin if you think about them for too long.' He turned to me. 'D'ya know what I mean, Tristram?'

I said nothing. I didn't know what he meant but I knew he meant something. The pilot light at the top of the beacon on the East Pier was pulsing behind his head. It seemed quite close but a deep channel of water divided us. Deep enough and broad enough for trawlers to pass.

'God knows what you'd find if you dredged Howth Harbour,' Hickey remarked. 'God knows *who* you'd find, more like. I used to think when I was a kiddie that there was this big plug you could pull an the whole thing'd go whirling down the drain. All the boats'd be left sitting on the bottom, keeled over on their sides. The fish'd be flipping about in the mud. They'd find the skeletons. An the seals. Yeah, the seals'd be snared rapid. Here, give us that.' He grabbed the hip flask as if I'd been hogging it. 'Ah, ya sly bastard,' he said with a wink when he discovered the tightly screwed cap. He wrenched the thing open and knocked back another mouthful, making a face as if the contents burned: *Ahhhhh.* I closed my eyes and inhaled the fumes.

'You're very pale, Tristram. That's another thing everyone keeps saying about you. They say: he's very pale, isn't he? Hasn't he gone very pale? He wasn't always that pale, sure he wasn't? Death warmed up. That's what they call you behind your back. Did ya know that? Death warmed up. Something funny there. Jaysus, it's fucken freezing in here.' He ratcheted up the heating dial.

I didn't rise to it. Accept the things you cannot change.

'Good to be alone though, isn't it, all the same? Just you an me on our own beside the sea having a nice friendly little chat. No one to interrupt us. Bit a peace and quiet from the wife. I always felt that this was my turf down here. You rich kids had the hill, the run a the mountains an that. The coves an the rock pools on the other side, the sunny side. South-facing. Isn't the Dublin Bay side south-facing? Isn't that right, Tristram? Some dickwad grows grapes up there, I heard. But we had down here.' He lightly depressed and released the accelerator for emphasis. The engine revved but it was disengaged. The truck was going nowhere.

Hickey gestured with the flask at the boulders buttressing the end of the pier. They formed a staggered descent to the sea. 'That's where we'd go fishing, me an the lads, down on the rocks. Mackerel an herring. Smoked cod. We'd be sitting there casting lines an drinking tins for hours. These inner-city heads would come out on the Dart an the lot of us'd be talking absolute shite, total fucken rubbage. They thought we were posh! They were in bad shape, them lads. On the gear, ya know yourself. Not the gear you were on. I took care a you, Tristram. I made sure you got nothing but the best. But these poor fuckers. They were on the dirty stuff. The night'd usually end in a punch-up. Then we'd shake hands. They were good lads. Best days a me life. But there'd be these rats crawling around between the rocks.' The engine note rose and fell. 'Sea rats. Have ya ever seen a sea rat, Castler?' I blinked. No one had called me by that name in years. I had almost forgotten that I had been that person. 'They're black with this greasy, spiky fur, like them young fellas with the gel in their hair. You'd see them scuttling around between the cracks. The rats, not the young fellas, ha ha. It's like the seals. The rats an the seals. This place is literally crawling with them. This place is coming down.' He shook his head and took another swig from the flask. *Ahhhhh*. That smell. Lord, that smell.

The surface of the sea was ruckled black and silver. Like life, I remember thinking, for in my heated state of mind everything reflected my predicament. The surface of the sea was like life: an overwhelming, unending onslaught of peaks and troughs, but silence and darkness if you let yourself go under. As I had gone under once before. And must never go under again. 'It's late,' I said, looking at my watch.

'Ah get a life, Castler, it's not that late. Plenty a time for sleeping when you're dead. You're not in the grave yet. Though we all heard ya were. I suppose it was kinda odd that there was no funeral. If you had of been dead, you'd of had a funeral. I only just thought a that now. I'd of went along. Signed me name in the buke an that.'

'You're too kind.'

'Ah fuck off ya smart arse. You always were such a smart arse. Sit back and chillax there for a minute. Sure, in the good old days we'd of been down here all night. Drinking until dawn. Best days a me life.'

Engine rise, engine fall, engine rise, engine fall as Hickey turned memories over in his head. He swilled back another snifter and smiled at some recollection. *Ahhhhh.* He had entered the first stage of inebriation, which is perfect, just perfect; it is heaven. That mellow, impeccable stage when nothing can harm you. The log fire is crackling away on the inside and you are safe in your warm little snug. I'd have given my right arm to feel that way again. But I couldn't give my life.

Engine rise, engine fall, rise, fall. 'Mad when you think that if they hadn't built the pier, we'd of been in the sea right now. We'd of been sitting at the bottom a the ocean like a right pair a fucken eejits. Isn't that mad, Castler?'

I stared ahead. Why had he dragged me out here to listen to this nonsense? Halfway down the pier where no one could see us except the fish heads. The fish heads, the crab claws, the lobster shells and all the other gutted creatures. I suppose I fitted right in. A hollow man, a human shell. Why did my wife call you this morning? Because she's worried sick, and so am I.

I released the catch of the seat belt. 'It's been a long night, Dessie. I'll make my own way home, thanks.'

He gunned the engine. 'You're going nowhere.'

Hickey had already left the perfect stage of inebriation behind and entered the phase of anger and paranoia. I knew that stage well. I was familiar with the spec. I reached for the handle of the door but he activated the central locking. Trapped.

'Let me out of the truck.'

'No.'

Engine rise, engine fall, engine rise, engine fall, as he deliberated over the fate of his prey. 'You've changed,' he finally remarked. 'D'ya know that?'

'Yes, I know that.'

'You used to be such a mad fucker.'

I lowered my head in shame.

'What happened ya, Castler?'

'I wasn't well then, Dessie.'

'What was wrong with ya? Were ya sick?'

'In a manner of speaking.'

'Ya seemed fine to me.'

'I was troubled, Dessie. I wasn't myself.'

'So who were ya?'

'I just wasn't myself.'

'And who are ya now?'

'I'm myself now.'

'You're an arsehole is who ya are now.'

'Yes, well,' I said. 'I have to accept the things I cannot change.'

He jammed his foot down on the accelerator and the engine gave an almighty roar. 'Stop coming out with that mental shite!' he shouted over the din. 'I'm sick of it. Sick to me back teeth!' He released the pedal. The roar died down. 'I preferred ya the way ya were an I didn't even like ya then. But there's something funny about ya now.'

'So you keep insisting.'

'What was all that muck you were shiteing on about earlier on the phone? Something about a Higher Power?'

'My Higher Power is there to restore me.'

He snorted. 'D'ya hear yourself?'

'Yes, Dessie, I do.'

'And tell us again: who exactly is this fella ya yammer away to about your Higher Power?'

'Monsieur Deauville. He is my sponsor, Dessie.' We'd been over this.

'Are ya sure about that, Castler?'

'Of course I'm sure.'

'Are ya though, Castler? Are ya really sure?'

'Yes, Dessie, I'm really sure.' Though I wasn't sure I understood the question.

'Because I'm not sure, Castler. I'm not one bit sure about that fella, an that's being honest with ya now. Who is this joker he does be mutterin away to half the time, I have to ask meself. The one who says jump an he says how high. Have ya noticed that ya always whisper when you're on the phone to him, Castler? Whisper whisper whisper, as if youse are up to no good.'

'Monsieur Deauville keeps me sane, Dessie. He is the voice of sanity.'

'Sanity? Mother divine. I'd like to hear what the voice a sanity sounds like. Can I have a listen, Castler? Can I earwig in on youse the next time he calls? Here, I know: put him on speakerphone. Yeah. I'd like to listen to the voice a sanity. I haven't heard it in a while.'

'You have to be in the programme, Dessie.'

'I have to be in the programme?'

'Yes, Dessie.' That's what I just said.

He burped. 'Can I join, so?'

'Anybody can join. The only requirement for joining Alcoholics Anonymous is a desire to stop drinking.'

'Sound. Where do I sign?' He knocked back another mouthful. *Ahhhhh.*

'You have to be committed to your sobriety, Dessie.'

Hickey looked at the flask. 'But sure, how will they know I'm still on the batter? They've no way of telling, not unless someone rats me out. Now who would rat me out, Castler? Who would do a thing like that?'

Silence. He sloshed the contents of the flask.

'Ya were a very secretive kid,' he continued. 'We never

really got to know ya, did we? That's what the lads said when we heard ya were dead. We couldn't really miss ya because we never really knew ya even though we'd been in school with ya all them years.'

'I could say the same about you, Dessie. I never really knew you either.'

'I don't think ya could say the same about me, though, Castler, strictly speaking. I think ya had the measure a me fairly early on because ya were one a them kids that was always watching. D'ya remember the way ya used to shop us to the teacher? The way he'd give ya the sheet a paper if he had to pop out, an you'd write down the names a the kids who were messin while he was gone. D'ya remember that, Castler?'

'No, Dessie.'

'*No, Dessie*,' he said in his version of my accent. 'A course you don't, but that's all right because I remember. I can remember for the both of us. The teacher put you in charge because he knew you'd rat us out. An ya did. An my name was always at the top a the list a messers. That's why I hated ya. That's why we all hated ya.'

'Is that why, Dessie? And me thinking it was on foot of my superior intellect and elevated social standing.'

Hickey examined the flask. 'D'ya know wha, Castler? I feel we're finally getting somewhere here. Do you feel that too?'

I shrugged.

'What was that, Castler? I didn't hear ya.'

'I'm not sure I care any more, Dessie, to be honest.'

'*To be honest?* Suffering Heart a Jaysus, has it come to that? Are we going to be *honest* with each other now?' My phone started ringing. 'Answer it,' he instructed me, as if I were his hostage.

Unknown read the screen. Thank Christ it isn't Edel, I thought in my innocence.

'Oh,' was all I could say when I heard what M. Deauville had to tell me.

Hickey revved the engine in search of attention. 'Is that the voice a sanity? Put him on to me there. Tell him I want a word.'

'I'm sorry, Monsieur Deauville, could you repeat that please?'

'It's over, Tristram. The money is gone.' Which is what I thought he had said.

'Tell him about the planning bond,' Hickey badgered me. 'Tell him we need more money for the planning bond,' but this was serious. I blocked my free ear the better to hear Deauville, or the worse, because I could barely grasp the gravity of what he was telling me.

Hickey wrested the phone from my hand. 'Lookit, bud,' he told Deauville, 'it's like this: without that money, we're wanked,' and then '*Fuck*. He's after hanging up on me again.' He threw down the phone. 'What was he saying?'

I couldn't speak for a moment. My mind was racing. My thoughts were skipping grooves. 'He said.' I swallowed and started again. 'He said that a bank has gone under in New York.'

Hickey shrugged. 'Big swinging mickey.'

I covered my eyes with my hands to try to focus on the information. 'He said it's not just any bank. It's one of the largest investment banks in the US.' How had Deauville phrased it? Terms were ricocheting inside my skull. *International banking crisis. Global financial collapse. Drastic losses*. I tried to string them into a sentence. 'It's an instrumental bank,' was all I managed. That wasn't even the word Deauville had used.

Endemic or systemic, something like that. 'He says the money is gone.'

'What money?'

'All of it. All of the money. My money, your money, McGee's money, Castle Holdings' money. The country's money. He says it's gone.' I laughed in horror. Not a pleasant sound.

'Gone where?'

'I don't know. Just gone. Deauville rang and said that all of the money is gone. That credit event he was saying the Market was nervous about? It just happened.'

'Is our money gone?'

'Christ, it's worse than gone,' I realised, thinking out loud. Pennies were dropping like anvils. 'We still have to pay it back.'

Hickey hadn't yet gotten his head around *gone*. 'It's very simple,' he said, bulldozing aside the facts as though matters could still be resolved by the brute force of his will. 'Frenchie or Kraut or whatever the fuck he is will lose his investment if he doesn't stump up the cash. Get back on to him an spell it out.' As if we were in a position to issue demands.

'Deauville will lose nothing. He says he's a senior bondholder.'

'What does that mean?'

'He says it means he's immune. He says it means we take the hit.' All of the money in the world was gone, and already, within a few minutes of it having evaporated, it seemed implausible that there had been so much of it in the first place.

'We'll flip the international portfolio. Make a profit.'

'Profit? Oh Dessie.' I actually felt sorry for him then. 'Deauville says the markets are in collapse. He says the world economy has begun to implode and that our assets have junk status. He says no one is going to want to buy them. And we paid for them with borrowed money. We paid for them with credit. Which in fact means debt. We owe more money than we can possibly count.' I laughed again. In horror. I couldn't help myself. Nor could Hickey. He started ranting. I kept laughing. The two of us making all this hysterical noise. I thought the cabin might explode. Either the cabin or my head.

'It can't just be gone,' he shouted over and over, as if saying it would make it true like in the old days, but the old days were gone. Everything was gone. The money in particular. 'Money doesn't just disappear into thin air. Someone has to have it. Some fucker has our money. That foreign prick has our money. Where does he live?'

'I don't know.'

'You do know.'

'I don't know.'

'You do know.'

'I don't know.'

Hickey raised his fist to me. 'Don't,' I warned him. I tried the door again. Still locked.

A strangled gurgle of frustration and he punched the steering wheel instead. Then he shoved the engine into gear. The truck shot forward, throwing us back in our seats. He hit the brakes and we collided with the dashboard. 'Why are ya protecting him?' Hickey screamed. 'He controls everything you do. You do everything he says. Here.' He grabbed the hip flask and thrust it into my face. 'Have a drink.' I pushed the flask away.

He twisted out of his seat and jabbed the flask at me again, gouging it into my gums. His foot was back on the accelerator and the unsteered truck hurtled along. The neck of the flask smashed against my teeth like the barrel of a gun. I did my best to fight him off, but . . . you've seen him. He was too strong. And I was too weak. I was too weak.

Hickey braked hard and the whiskey backwashed into my mouth. I could taste it and it could taste me. It latched onto the scent of my blood. Off we shot again. 'Have a fucken drink, Castler,' Hickey bayed at me, gripping a hank of my hair. I glimpsed the end of the pier over his shoulder and then the truck was launched.

A fleeting airborne moment between this life and the next. This is it, I thought, to hell with it. I gulped the whiskey down. 'That's the man!' Hickey encouraged me before we were both hurled against his door. The truck landed with a crunch not a splash. We had hit the rocks. The tide must be out, I thought inanely. Yes, the tide must be out.

The whiskey seeped into my bloodstream along with the dire consequences. Hickey had me in a headlock. I didn't struggle but instead huddled against the wall of his chest, the warm and hairy wall. The worst possible thing had just happened. I cowered there.

'Are we dead?' Hickey wondered in a muffled voice. 'What d'ya reckon, Castler? Are we dead or wha? Ah here, sure you already are.'

'That was another Tristram St Lawrence.' My voice was muffled too. The headlock had turned into an embrace. I was nestled in his arms.

'Get off me, ya puff.' He pushed me away but I slumped right back. The cheery contagion of the whiskey had turned my limbs to rubber.

'I'm not a puff. I've been riding your wife.'

He laughed at that and gave me a clap on the back, followed by a harder one to let me know that he meant it: get off me now, ya puff. I laughed too, at the shock he had in store when Edel told him the news. Not my problem. I was in the cosy room with the crackling log fire.

Hickey manhandled me back into the passenger seat, my head lolling like a corpse. I saw the lapping waves, the moon, the sleek black shape of the island, the world before electric light. I could have been looking through the eyes of the original Sir Tristram. His blood ran in mine, along with all the bad stuff, which was steadily rising.

The truck was cast up on the boulders like a shipwreck. Hickey tried to start the engine but the ignition refused to catch. He wrinkled his nose. 'Do you smell diesel?' He sniffed his armpits. 'Am I smelling diesel?' He thumped the horn. 'They told me this yoke could drive over *anything*.'

The cosy room started to recede. I was reversing towards a cold and draughty corridor. I had to stay in the cosy room, whatever the price. I gave the flask a shake. Empty. I had polished it off. It had polished off me. I let it drop to the floor. We both lay there drained.

'Don't worry,' Hickey reassured me, 'there's plenty more where that came from.' He reached beneath his seat and produced two bottles of Bushmills. 'One for you and one for me.'

I grasped a bottle. 'Good man,' I said, although he was a bad one. I broke the gold foil seal and glugged a treble down.

'Look at you,' Hickey sneered, the beard smothering his face like ivy.

I tried the door. It was still locked. And so was I. 'I'm frightened,' I think I may have admitted in a small voice. I cannot guarantee that I managed to get the words out although I know that I certainly tried. You'll have to ask Hickey for confirmation. You'll have to ask him for confirmation on a lot of things from here on in. 'I am frightened of the dark, Dessie,' my few surviving sober cells tried to confess before they too succumbed to the influence and slipped under. The vault I carried around in my chest opened then. It plunged down and connected me to the bowels of Hell. It plugged me in. And that is where the night stops. Except that it didn't stop. It never stops. Something else takes over. Your body carries on without you. There is no you.

*

Lemony sunlight and raucous screeching. I flinched at the commotion. A trawler was on its way back in with the night's catch, a flock of seagulls scavenging above it. I could have reached out and touched its salty metal flank, the boat seemed so close. All those primary colours.

I raised my head carefully. It had changed in constitution and was too heavy for my neck. I was lying on the flat of my back looking at my feet. No shoes and one sock. We were no longer where I'd last seen us, although I had no idea where we had last been seen. And there was no us; that was the other thing. I was prostrate on a boulder on my own.

I propped myself up on my elbows. A slash of seagull shit spanned the length of my thigh. It was white with a cock-eyed olive-green pupil. I brushed it off to discover that it was still wet. I looked at my smeared fingers in disgust. They were trembling.

A whiskey bottle was lodged between the boulders. I rolled onto my belly and prised it out. Where had it come from? More importantly, where had the contents gone? Then I remembered. I dropped the bottle and vomited. I won't go into that.

I stood up and the world stood up with me. Together we jerked upright but the backwash knocked us down. I crouched with both hands on the sun-warmed boulder, a sprinter on the starting block. Suffering Jesus, my head.

Another trawler chugged past. I could hear the bastards onboard laughing at me. The state of your man.

Hickey's truck was up ahead, pitched at a jaunty angle. I picked my way across the boulders like a crab, keeping my head as level as was possible. I tried the handle of the passenger door. Still locked. I shuffled around to the other side.

The driver's door was ajar, the cabin empty. 'Dessie,' I called but got no answer. I sniffed the air. Diesel.

St Christopher was on the floor and so was my phone. I crawled in carefully to retrieve it. No texts and no missed calls. Edel hadn't phoned. Nor had Deauville. I spotted the hip flask wedged by the handbrake and gagged but kept it down, although I should have let rip all over Hickey's seat. If you ask me whether I have any regrets, yes I do and that is one.

I climbed back out but he wasn't to be seen. There were only two ways he could have gone: into the sea or up the pier. 'Dessie,' I called, clinging to the door for balance. I checked my watch. It was missing. I judged it to be about 7 a.m. It was a spectacular morning but there was no getting away from the darkness. The darkness had been poured back in, the guts of a whiskey bottle. I leaned over to vomit between the rocks.

I didn't find Hickey up on the pier but I did find my shoes. They were neatly set out at the edge. Abandoned shoes on the end of a pier are never a good omen. I stooped to reach for them and a cannon ball collided with the inside of my skull.

I groped about for my shoes while keeping my eyes on the beacon. The trick was to focus on a distant point. Yes, that was the trick. It was all coming back to me. Like riding a bike. I located the shoes and slotted my feet into them. The foot that was minus a sock encountered an obstruction. I tipped the shoe's contents onto my palm. My watch. That was another bad omen. I never removed my watch.

I got the shoes on but the laces were beyond me. I saw a pole and latched onto it. The pier revolved around this pole as if it were the axis of the earth. It supported a bright yellow life-ring holder from which the life ring had been removed. The life rang ring a bell. I tried again: the life ring rang a bell. Despite its absence, I had a distinct mental image of it – it was new and tomato red. I had a distinct physical sense of it too – surprisingly hard and surprisingly light. I had held the life ring in my hands. But why had I needed such an object? Who was I trying to save?

An orange nylon cord extended from the holder, the fuse cable to a stick of dynamite. I clung onto the pole and considered this cord with mounting dread. It snaked across to the pier wall and disappeared around the corner, a link to the chaos of last night. I did not feel able for what lay in wait on the other end of the cord. 'Dessie!' I called.

I followed the cord around the corner. On the far side of the sea wall, down by the lapping waves, tethered to the end of the orange string like a tramp's mongrel, was Hickey's prone body, the life ring around his neck.

I clambered down the rocks. His body was sprawled across two boulders as if he had fallen out of a plane. I had woken to terrible sights in the past. Terrible, terrible. Can't bear to think of them. That was another Tristram St Lawrence. I could never go back there. And yet I just had.

I got down on my knees and took Hickey by the shirt collar. His right arm was twisted above his head like the wing of a crashed bird. The yellow letterbox of face between his beard and his hairline revealed two bloodshot eyeball crescents.

'Dessie,' I begged him. 'Can you hear me, Dessie? Can you open your eyes? Answer me, for the love of God!'

His mouth was hanging open. I lowered my ear to it. He was breathing, and his breath was rank.

I slapped his face and he grunted in protest. I don't know why I kept slapping him – well, I do, and so did he. His head rolled from side to side in the life ring to evade my hand and then he seized my wrist. It took him a few goes to blink his pupils into alignment – they had rolled into the back of his head but to differing degrees. He cried out in pain when he tried to lower his twisted arm. I had to help him guide it down.

'Get off me,' he said, and got to his feet. 'State a ya. You're covered in bird shite.'

The life ring sat upon his shoulders like an Elizabethan ruff. He lifted it off and tossed it into the water. 'Jaysus,' he said, rotating the twisted arm in a backstroke, 'I'm getting too old for this.' He tucked his shirt into his trousers and off he went, across the boulders up to the pier, not a bother on him.

I crawled after him up the rocks on all fours. He was standing at the end of the pier looking down at his beached truck. He turned to shake his head at me. 'Extreme terrain, them thieving bastards told me. Said it was built to navigate extreme terrain.' He held up his mobile phone and took a picture. 'They can come an winch it up themselves, so they can.' He hawked a gullier down on it. 'D. Hickey ain't paying for that.'

But D. Hickey would pay for it. And so would I, and so would everyone on the island. That's what Deauville had said. But pay with what? We had purchased everything with debt.

Another trawler passed. Hickey raised a hand in greeting and a hand was raised back. He checked his watch. 'Right, the Evora will be open. We'll get a swiftie in before work. Hair a the dog.' I leaned over and vomited, or tried to. Nothing left. 'Mind your shoes,' he advised me. 'Good man. Are ya right?'

We set off for Harbour Road. Gulls were watching us from every available ledge, a thousand yellow eyes. Halfway down the pier we noticed the brand-new Porsche Cayenne Turbo S parked in the repair-yard lane. A vehicle like that is designed to be noticed. That is its primary function. The Viking's Range Rover Sport was parked beside it. 'The early bird catches the worm,' said Hickey, and changed course.

The Viking was sitting behind the wheel of the Porsche, his head thrown back and his eyes screwed shut. I tried to hate him but my hatred was weak by then, which meant it wasn't hatred any more. The Viking would pay for it too. All of us would pay for it, many times over and for the rest of our lives.

Hickey marched up and rapped on the driver's seat window. Svetlana's pretty head popped up in surprise. 'Mr Hickey,' you could see her pronounce behind the glass. The Viking dived for his flies while his bargirl wiped her mouth and scrambled for her belongings.

Hickey yanked the door open and tore in there like a terrier. He reefed all 200 pounds of the Viking out of his seat by the scruff. I had never seen strength like it. I stepped out of his way to watch. The man was still struggling with his Armani zipper when Hickey flung him across the dusty laneway as if he weighed no more than an old coat.

'Ya dirty bollocks!' he was shouting when Svetlana screeched past in the Range Rover, swerving to avoid the sparring pair. Would she pay for it, I wondered as she veered around the corner – never to be seen again as it turned out. Neither she nor the Viking's SUV. But she already had paid for it, I realised. Paid a disgusting price.

I turned to the men. Hickey had the Viking up against the wall. Yes, that is when the alleged assault on Mr Dowdall took place, although there was insufficient evidence to prosecute. Me? No, sorry, can't help you there, Fergus. I didn't see a thing.

Ninth day of evidence

23 MARCH 2016

‘To return to the issue of the—’

Fergus, Fergus, Fergus, Fergus, I know you feel obliged to occasionally butt in, as well you might considering your outrageous salary (which is a whole other crime against the Irish State, but that's another day's work); however, would it not be best for all concerned at this stage if you simply let me bash on? I'm getting to the really good bit, which is the really bad bit, the bit that still makes me shiver.

Hickey and I took up position on the barstools of the Evora, our arses lined up in a row with the arses of the fishermen. My arse was born to be there. It had assumed its rightful seat. I did my post-pint sigh: *Ahhhhh.* Hickey's stranded truck was the talk of the town. There was heated speculation surrounding the upcoming spring tide: how high would it go – as high as the truck? – and whether the truck's enormous tractor tyres would set it afloat. 'Not my problem,' Hickey stated, basking in the attention. 'D. Hickey ain't paying for that.' But he was. We would all pay for it, many times over and for the rest of our lives.

When the fishermen climbed down from the stools to go home to their beds, we took our business around the corner to the Cock, which was just unbolting its doors to the late-morning trade. It was good to be out and about.

'Howaya Gick. Who've you got there?'

'Lads, it's Tristram. You remember Tristram. Tristram St Lawrence, from the little school.'

'Castler? I thought he was dead.'

'Nah, he's just gee-eyed. Look at the cut of him. Stocious, so he is.'

It was all about pacing so I stuck to the pints. I drank until I was sober again. Sober enough to take myself into the jacks to scrub the hardened gullshit off my trousers. My ribs were killing me. I pulled up my shirt to discover a purple bruise. I came out looking like I'd pissed myself, they said, but at least I wasn't covered in shite. Another round of pints and a good laugh, both at my expense. Put it on my tab, I told the barman. I never carry cash. Hickey didn't wash the Viking's blood from his shirt, which darkened as the day progressed from a valorous scarlet to a tarnished brown.

On the television set mounted over the bar, chief executives were being perp-walked out of the bank in New York that had collapsed the day before, taking all the money with it. Hickey kept disappearing to answer his phone. 'Tell us if you notice any dodgy Xs standing around,' he confided in my ear when he returned from one of these calls.

'Dessie, the Tax Man is not an individual person, per se. And he isn't even necessarily a man these days. Could be the Tax Woman. Have you ever considered that?' Hickey just looked at me and shook his head as if I could never begin to understand.

In the late afternoon we took off down the hill again to survey our interests, two men of the world. The foreman was waiting for us outside the Portakabin. 'What the fuck is this?' Hickey demanded, gesturing at the deserted site. The machinery was frozen mid-manoeuvre – loads suspended in the air, the arms of diggers reaching out – as if a spell to arrest time had been cast.

'It's the men,' the foreman explained, but it wasn't the men: it was the money. It had stopped flowing and so had everything else. The site had ground to a halt. The money hadn't appeared in the men's accounts that morning, and it hadn't appeared the week before either, which was the first I'd heard. Deliveries were no longer arriving through the gate. Creditors were banging at the door. The men had walked off the site, taking with them as much equipment as they could carry in lieu of two weeks' wages.

The foreman removed his helmet and held it out to Hickey, upturned like a begging bowl. 'Really sorry boss,' he said, and seemed to mean it. He paused on his way to the gate and glanced back. 'Oh, and em . . . the Gardaí were looking for you.'

He allowed his eyes to drop to the bloodstains on Hickey's shirt before hurrying away muttering apologies. And that was the end of him. He vacated the premises with his hands in his pockets and his chin on his chest. Would he pay for it? No two ways about it. Him and all the other workers in the country, many times over and for the rest of their lives.

'That's great,' said Hickey when he was gone. 'That's just fucken brilliant.' He placed the foreman's helmet on the ground, jogged back to get a run at it and kicked it with his builder's boot. The impact was crisp and hollow, a sound that in normal circumstances would have been swallowed by the general racket. Now that the general racket had ceased I found I missed it. I could hear myself think, which was the last thing I needed. The helmet smashed into Block 7 and dropped onto a stack of bricks. A half-unwrapped toilet stood next to the bricks, the lid up.

What then? What next? There was no next. I stood there assessing the damage. The greater part of me still is and always will be. Hickey's hotel had two illegal storeys. Only one of the apartment blocks was complete. The other seven stood shelled with gaping window openings. It had fallen apart so quickly. As quickly as it had begun, I suppose, and with as little warning. Building site to bomb site overnight. We were witnessing the remnants of a dead civilisation, one that had left nothing but wreckage in its wake, the Vandals or the Goths. Except that it had not been civilised at all. Civilisation was the wrong word.

'We'll have a cup a tea,' Hickey pronounced. I assumed this was sarcasm but followed him into the Portakabin just the same. I took my place in the paint-spattered chair, and, sure enough, he set about making two cups of tea, manhandling the yellowing jug kettle onto its plastic base as he had a mere twenty-four hours earlier before our world had crashed. It gave him something to do with his hands. He was still having trouble connecting with the power supply.

'Can I help?'

'You? Help? With a faulty appliance? Stop the lights.'

There was comfort in the routine.

The orange switch finally lit up and he shovelled four spoons of sugar into his cup – no, five. Six in total. I suppose it was good for the shock. The peaty brown tea was similar in colour to the dried blood on his shirt. He added milk and curdled floaters rose to the top. The milk was still sour. 'Ah dear,' he said with unexpected stoicism, then opened the window and horsed the carton out.

His mobile phone rang. He smirked when he saw the name on the screen and showed it to me. *Ray Lawless*. Hickey shook his head. 'At least that greedy prick will take a hit. Every cloud.'

Yes, every cloud. Every rainy Ray cloud. Speaking of which. I turned to the window. A downpour was coming. And then the downpour came.

*

We sat out the torrent sipping endless cups of black sugary tea. It got so dark that Hickey had to switch on the lights. We listened to the rain and, when the rain had stopped, we listened to droplets falling from the scaffolding.

'Did you hear Gerry Coyle died?' Hickey asked me. Night had fallen by then. We hadn't moved in hours.

'No. Which one was he?' I thought back to the faces in the jade glass boardroom. Boyler, Coyler, Doyler. Not one of them was over fifty.

Hickey shrugged. 'Dunno. He's dead now in anyways. Hung himself off the banister this morning. Poor wife. Young family.'

'Hanged,' I whispered to myself.

Hickey was frowning. 'Who were those people anyway? In the Golden Circle. Who were they all?'

'I thought you knew them.'

'No, I thought you did.'

'We were those people, Dessie,' I realised and he looked at me in puzzlement. He didn't see it in those terms and I doubt he ever will, but there was no way around it. We were those people.

I winced. My ribs. I placed my palm on the pain and held it there. A flashback from the night before. Me lying on the rocks and Hickey's steel-capped boot taking aim.

*

My stomach was rumbling. Hickey opened a drawer, but instead of producing another naggin of whiskey to help us forget the whole mess, he took out two king-sized Mars bars, one of which he tossed my way. It was the most thoughtful thing he'd ever done for me. The Mars bar and the black tea.

'Now what?' he asked.

'Now we pay.'

'With what?'

Good question. All the money was gone. 'With our personal assets, I suppose.' Some developers gave personal guarantees and some were limited companies. We were the former kind. We were sole traders. We had traded our souls.

'You mean, like, me truck?'

'Yes, and your family home.'

That got a rise out of him. 'They will on their holes get their filthy hands on D. Hickey's gaff. I'm not having it. I'll get it put into the wife's name.'

'That would probably be a wise move. I'd make an appointment with my family solicitor, were I you.'

'Yeah, the Hunger will know what to do.' He settled back into his seat and chewed his Mars bar. Then he had a thought. 'Here, will youse lose the castle?'

'No. The castle belongs to Father. The banks have no recourse against him.'

'Thank fuck for that.'

'I'll lose Hilltop though,' I realised. Jesus. Not that Hilltop would even begin to cover it.

'Ah lads. Marry some internet bride an put it in her name.'

'I'd rather not, thank you.'

'Any other bird whose hand you'd consider?'

'Your wife's.'

He laughed at that. He thought it was a joke. And maybe it was. Maybe it was all a big joke. She hadn't called me. She hadn't answered calls of mine. 'I suppose it's difficult,' Hickey conceded, 'for the gays.'

I was about to disabuse him when something else recurred to me. 'Remind me again where you got the keys to Hilltop?'

'Off the cleaners.'

'What cleaners?'

'I don't know. One a them. All the cleaners in the village have keys.'

'To what?'

'To your homes.'

I was appalled. 'Is that true?'

'A course. An here, remember the gummy oul pony we found in the garden? The one what could barely walk? It's Edel's. From when she was a kid. Isn't that mad?'

'I don't believe you. Edel would never neglect a defenceless animal like that.'

Hickey pursed his lips. 'I'd put nothing past that woman. Biggest mistake a me life, leaving me first wife for her. Poor Bernie. Heart a gold.'

He shot upright in his seat and froze. 'Did you hear that?'

I froze too and listened. 'No.'

There came a battering on the door then, so loud that we both leapt to our feet. 'Don't answer,' I heard Hickey warning me as I flung open the door to see what could possibly be so urgent. A menacing X was standing on the other side.

Although he stood in the yard, putting him at a disadvantage of several inches to me, his frying pan of a face was level with mine, and I am a tall man, as you can see. I could tell before he even opened his mouth that he was not Irish. We simply do not breed men of this stature.

'Yes?'

'Desmond Hickey,' he stated, uttering the syllables as discrete units, four separate sentences. Dess. Mond. Hick. Eee.

'What of him?'

'Dess. Mond. Hick. Eee,' the menacing X repeated in his glottal accent. It occurred to me that this was the only English he possessed. That it was the only English he required to accomplish his mission.

'He is presently engaged, I'm afraid. Thank you for calling.'

I closed the door in the giant's face and turned to Hickey, who stared at me beseechingly as if there were something I could do to shield him. Me. I was his line of defence. It had come to that.

'That's who you mean by the Tax Man, isn't it?'

Hickey nodded.

'He's one of your creditors, isn't he? He's been sent by one of them?'

Hickey nodded again. 'Yeah.'

I was getting the hang of this game, now that it was over.

There was another clatter on the door and Hickey shot past me and lashed the bolt across, as if that would prevent the giant X from gaining entry. It was the grade of bolt typically found on the back of a toilet cubicle door, that is to say, it provided no protection whatsoever.

He looked wildly around the four walls but there was no escape hatch. 'Fuck it,' he said, 'we're fucked.'

There came a pattering on the roof as hailstones fell. At least, we hoped they were hailstones. It sounded like a handful of earth being sprinkled on the lid of a coffin. The focal point in the Portakabin shifted upwards. We both looked at the panelled ceiling, and then we looked at each other, two men on the edge of an abandoned building site, trapped in a container of sour air, and a giant X on the rampage outside. A giant X who could see us, but whom we couldn't see, since the windowpane revealed only our stark reflections.

'We should get curtains,' I whispered.

'Yeah,' Hickey sneered. 'That's exactly what we should get right now. Curtains.' He kicked my paint-spattered chair and it back-flipped against the wall. Then the lights went out.

'What's happening?' I asked him. The blackness was welling up inside. I tried to swallow it down.

'We've been disconnected from the generator. He's disconnected us.'

'Why? What's he up to out there? What's he going to do to us?' Bury us, was my guess. Bury us or burn us. Light a fire under us. That's what I'd have done. I listened for the sound of petrol being doused about.

Instead, an engine started up. It was one of the machines, a digger or a dumper. They all sounded the same in the dark, or they did to me. I discerned Hickey's form watching at the window. The engine was getting louder. His head dipped in a double-take, then he raced for the door.

'Get out!' he shouted, 'he's coming at us!'

We scrabbled at the door but couldn't locate the bolt in the darkness. The claw of the machine punctured the ceiling and we flung ourselves against the wall. It plunged through the centre of the Portakabin and gouged out a section of floor, taking my paint-spattered chair with it.

'X!' Hickey was screaming, 'you fucken X!' and I wasn't screaming anything at all, as such; I was just screaming.

The claw stabbed at the Portakabin a number of times in search of its prey, then it jerked upward and out of sight. We remained flattened there, braced for a second onslaught, but instead the machine reversed. We tracked its progress with our ears. It was heading for the gate. I closed my eyes in relief. Night air was flooding through the hole.

'He's repossessing it,' Hickey realised, and took off clambering over the debris to jump out the broken window. I listened as he started up another machine and went booting after the repossessed one, and you'll have read in the papers how that particular confrontation panned out. He was a brave man, Hickey, I'll give him that. A braver man than me, which is not to say much for him. I could be dead, I realised with a flutter of vertigo when they were both gone and silence had returned to the empty site. I clutched my aching ribs and rocked. Dead, I could be dead. I could be just as dead as the other Tristram St Lawrence. The lucky one.

*

Larney was waiting at the castle gates when I rounded the corner, standing bolt upright against the ribbed column like a Coldstream Guard. I had never seen his body unfurled before, for he had always been the crooked man who walked the crooked mile. As a child, I had believed that the nursery rhyme was about him. I would not have imagined that he could be so tall.

'Good evening, Larney,' I said, the lie tripping off my tongue. It was not a good evening. It was a bad one. And it was going to get worse.

'The young master didn't come home last night.'

I paused between the gateposts. The Gardaí must have come knocking. 'No, I—'

'The young master didn't come home last night,' he repeated, cutting me dead.

I looked him over. Something wrong there. More wrong than usual, that is. Stroke? 'Indeed, Larney, you are quite right,' I said carefully. 'I didn't come home last night. That is most observant of you.'

He squirmed with pleasure, he positively writhed, and I regretted my harsh tongue in the past. All he needed was to be thrown the odd word of praise. He was just a big child, like the rest of us.

He straightened into his sentry's stance. Remarkable. I had presumed his twisted spine was a birth deformity.

'There were five men going to church,' he began, 'and it

started to rain. The four that ran got wet and the one that stood still stayed dry. Why?'

'I don't know, Larney: why?'

'He was in a coffin!'

'Ah, very good. Well, goodnight, Larney.' I set off up the avenue. He shot forward to detain me and cleared his throat.

> 'The one who makes it, sells it,
> The one who buys it, never uses it,
> The one that uses it never knows that he's using it.

What is it?'

'I don't know, Larney. What?'

But instead of revealing the answer, he went back to the beginning and recited the riddle again in full. I gazed at the stars while I heard him out. Being civil had only encouraged him. This could go on all night.

When he had finished, I still didn't know the answer.

'A coffin!' he said.

'Another coffin. Excellent.' I sidestepped him, but he planted himself in my path a second time because suddenly he had grown uncharacteristically nimble. Uncharacteristically nimble and uncharacteristically bold.

'There is a coffin,' he began. 'The mother of the person in the coffin—'

'That's quite enough, Larney. Let me pass.' I was on a short tether where he was concerned. It took no time at all to reach the end of it.

He sighed as if I were trying his patience and began again. 'There is a coffin. The mother of the person in the coffin is the sister-in-law of your father's aunt. Who is the corpse in the coffin?'

'I'll say it one last time, Larney.'

'And so will I,' he rejoined firmly, looking me square in the eye. I caught my breath at his daring and took a step back. He reached out and placed his index finger on my sternum to stay me, to literally stay me, for I could not move. That crooked finger arrested my progress. 'Who is the corpse in the coffin, young master?'

'Take your hands off me.'

'Who is the corpse in the coffin?' he repeated very slowly, as if I were the simple one, not he. I looked down at my chest. His fingertip had started to burn.

'I don't know, Larney. Who is the corpse in the coffin?'

He left me hanging on his reply, an insect mounted on a pin, before retracting his hand. Once contact was broken, I crumpled into a coughing heap, clutching my ribs although my sternum hurt more. Look. [*Witness unbuttons his shirt to reveal a small oval scar.*] He branded me. The Devil's fingerprint.

'Get back,' I gasped when I was able. 'Get back into your little hovel!' Larney shrivelled into a twisted form once more and retreated to the gate lodge as fast as his limp permitted, followed by the Jack Russell, which I only noticed then, it had remained so subdued throughout this encounter.

*

I glanced up as I was racing away from him up the avenue to see the castle burning brightly through the trees. At first I thought it was on fire. Every light shone, every door was thrown open. Even the cellar had been breached – lights glimmered up through the grates. A search party had stampeded through each wing and floor. What could they be looking for? Me, I realised. 'The young master didn't come home last night.' 'The Gardaí were looking for you.'

There was no patrol car parked on the gravel, just Father's old Polo, but I stopped dead in shock when I crossed the threshold and found what was waiting for me inside. 'Oh thank God,' said Mrs Reid, jumping to her feet. 'I've been looking for you everywhere.'

Mounted on trestle legs in the centre of the great hall was a coffin. Candlesticks stood on either side of it, twin flames burning. Mrs Reid had been keeping vigil at the head of this coffin. And she had been crying. Her plump cheeks glistened with tears. She opened her arms to embrace me. A set of rosary beads was woven through her outstretched fingers. I held my post by the door.

The lid of the coffin was open. I could not see the corpse inside, not from my post by the door. I did not abandon my post. I looked at Mrs Reid. 'Who is the corpse in the coffin?' I demanded of her, as Larney had demanded of me.

'Pet,' said Mrs Reid. 'I am afraid I have some terrible news. Your father . . .' She blessed herself. 'Last night. God rest his soul.'

I was unable to piece these clues together. I looked at the coffin, and then back at her. 'Who is the corpse in the coffin?' I demanded again.

'Come here to me, pet,' she said, after a brief hesitation. 'You're in shock. I have him laid out. Why don't you come over and see him?'

I gestured at the pillar candles, the row of empty chairs, her rosary beads, the paraphernalia of Catholic mourning. 'What do you call this?' I sounded for all the world like Father. Or maybe she spoke first. Yes, I think that Mrs Reid may have spoken first, although I cannot swear to it. I cannot swear to anything, for normality had slipped out of sync.

The details tumbled out of her mouth in no particular order, for she was as disorientated as I was. Mrs Reid and I had fallen into the same pocket of chaos. We were at sixes and sevens in there. 'I went looking for you as soon as I found him,' she was saying. 'I didn't know what to do. Your bed was unslept in. I couldn't bring him to a funeral home – he'd have hated a place like that. Dr Chapman said it was his heart. I've had the Guards out looking for you all day. I knew something was wrong when he didn't come down for breakfast in the morning. You know your father – he never slept in. The military past. That's why I laid him out in his uniform. Right as rain the day before, not a bother on him. It was how he would have wanted to go. I couldn't have left him in a funeral home. He was born upstairs. So I laid him out myself. At least here he's with his people.'

Meaning the portraits, I had to assume. The stark truth of the matter was that Father had no people left. The row of vacant chairs only drew attention to the absence of mourners.

The candles flickered and Mrs Reid blessed herself again. I glanced at the ceiling. The wind was whistling through the empty passages upstairs, droning in chords like an aeolian harp. I had not known that it could do that. I had never heard that sound. I realised how little I knew about the castle, but that with Father deceased I was now at the helm. Perhaps it was protocol that all doors be thrown open upon the death of the head of the St Lawrence family so that the wind could sweep through and allow the castle itself to keen. For the Castle was dead. The Castle was in the coffin. Long live the Castle.

'Sometime during the night, love, in his sleep. It was very peaceful,' Mrs Reid was reassuring me, although even Mrs Reid, who never failed to give me the benefit of the doubt, must have registered that I had not enquired after his suffering.

'Where are the dogs?' I wanted to know instead. I fully understood that I was getting it wrong, that even in death I was getting my relationship with Father irredeemably, irremediably, irrevocably wrong.

Mrs Reid clapped her hand to her mouth. 'The dogs. I forgot to feed the dogs.'

Father fed the dogs.

'The gate lodge is to be vacated in the morning,' I announced. This was my first edict as the Lord of Howth.

Mrs Reid hurried to my side. 'Sit down, love. You've had a terrible shock. God almighty, your hands are freezing.' She tried to steer me into one of the mourner's chairs but I was having none of it.

'Larney has to go,' I decreed. 'That's the end of it. We bury Father tomorrow and then we throw Larney out.'

Mrs Reid stopped trying to warm my hands with hers. 'Larney?'

'Yes, Larney. Furthermore, he is not welcome at the funeral. On no account is he to show his face. I want him gone.'

'Larney *is* gone, love. He has been dead for years.'

'Years,' she repeated to reinforce her point when I just stared at her. 'Sure, didn't I lay his poor crooked body out myself?'

‘*What?*’

Fergus, it gets worse. 'Tristram!' Mrs Reid cried after me when I broke free of her and fled the castle, but the poor soul was too terrorised to venture past the threshold, not after what I had told her – that I had seen a dead man. *Who is the corpse in the coffin?* You are, Larney! You're the corpse.

My brain had slipped into its default groove and was chanting the usual repetitive guff – admitting that I was powerless over alcohol, humbly asking my Higher Power to restore me to sanity, accepting the things that I could not change and all the rest of it, when it struck me that it was nonsense. That I was chanting pure nonsense and had been for some time. 'Do you hear yourself?' Hickey had asked me, and suddenly I did. I did not accept the things I could not change. I would change the things I could not accept. Starting with Edel.

I set off uphill towards the rhododendron gardens. I could hear Mrs Reid beseeching me to come back until her voice faded along with the lights of the castle. It was dark and quiet then. I was at large.

I climbed the jungle bluff and emerged onto the open slopes of the West Mountain. The city lights glittered below. Edel had made this journey first, across the two mountains from her home to mine, wearing that dress I'd been so afraid of getting dirt on, that white sundress knotted at the nape with a butterfly.

I crossed over to the East Mountain. The lighthouses flashed messages to each other along the length of the coastline – *Here! I'm over here! Where are you?* I threaded my way along the bridle tracks. It was September and the heather was in flower. *And we'll all go together, to pick wild mountain thyme, all along the blooming heather. Will you go, lassie, go?*

Although it was late, maybe one or two in the morning by my reckoning, the lights burned in the house on the edge of the moors. Edel was having a sleepless night too. I saw as I approached that a JCB was parked on the driveway. As well as a digger, a cherry picker, a steamroller and one of the gennys. But not the clawed thing that had almost killed us. The giant X had successfully made off with that. Hickey had stashed the remaining machinery where he could keep an eye on it. He was circling the wagons. Edel's two-seater Merc looked tiny and fragile against their primitive bulk.

I made my way around the side of the house, peering in at each window until I found her. She was perched on a high stool at the breakfast bar in her science lab of a kitchen, sheaves of documents spread out around her on the polished granite worktop. I hadn't known that she wore glasses. I was about to tap on the windowpane when I spotted her mobile phone on the counter. I took out mine.

Will you go, lassie, go? I texted.

Her phone lit up but she did not. She read the text and returned to her paperwork without so much as a smile. It wasn't quite the reaction I'd anticipated. There was a calculator on the countertop too, one of those office models that printed its results onto a roll of paper. It seemed unlikely that Edel should possess such a device. It must have belonged to Hickey. Though that seemed unlikelier still.

She tapped in digits, inputting them without raising her eyes from the stacks of paper, for hers were fingers that knew their way by touch around a numeric keypad, it turned out. She frowned at the result that the calculator churned out, tore off the strip of paper and started again. The numbers were not adding up. They never would add up, no matter how she finessed them. All of the money was gone.

I'm outside, I texted. *Please meet me at your front door.*

She sat up and took notice when she opened that text, and deliberated for a few seconds before removing her glasses and slipping off the stool. I ran back around the side of the house, narrowly reaching the front step before she did.

'Are you out of your mind showing up here?' she whispered through a fractionally opened door – Hickey must have been inside. She took in the cut of me: the dirty clothes, the unshaven chin, the bloodshot eyes. And the smell. Not forgetting the smell. The fumes of stale booze on an empty stomach were enough to fell a donkey.

'*Will you go, lassie, go?*' I sang gently to her, thinking that . . . well, it's difficult to know precisely what I was thinking, except that I was thinking it very strongly at the time. Thinking it so strongly that I could see it. Us. A future together. Life.

'Oh my God, are you drunk?'

'No, darling. Not any more.'

'Look, it's a bad time, Tristram,' she said. 'I don't need this right now. There's . . . well, you know the situation yourself. He's lost everything. We're trying to see what we can salvage.'

'If you've lost everything, then you have nothing left to lose. Hickey has nothing left to offer you. So come with me.'

'For God's sake, how can I go with you?'

'It's very simple. Pack a bag. Or don't pack a bag. Come as you are.' I held out my hand, but she just looked at it.

'Listen, Tristram, all this – us? It has to stop. I'm sorry. You should go home. You look like you haven't slept in a week.'

She tried to close the door but I held it open. I was stronger than her. Or so I thought. 'My father died.'

She lowered her head. 'Yes, I heard. I am sorry for your loss.'

'The castle is mine now. Come with me across the moors. It's a soft night. You won't need a coat. Make that same journey you made at the beginning of summer in your white sundress. You always wanted to see inside the castle. Now you may. You are its princess. You shall have your own wing.'

'Tristram,' she began carefully, and joined her palms together as if praying for the right words to come, and I couldn't help but admire the gesture, as I had admired all her gestures, all the flourishes her hands had performed, although the solemnity of this one warned me to be afraid of what she was about to impart. She took a deep breath to fortify herself, and so did I. 'Tristram,' she said again, 'I realise that this isn't the best time for you to hear this, in light of your father's sudden passing, but they're going to come after your assets now, and some assets can't be hidden. Some assets can't be stashed. JCBs and diggers and all that junk parked on the driveway can be made to disappear, as can sums of money, but assets like a castle, assets like your grounds? There's no place to hide assets like that. There's no way of sheltering them. It's unlikely they'll remain yours for much longer, I'm afraid. All I can suggest is that you go down and strip the place of valuables while you still have a chance.'

Hickey's voice butted in behind her. 'Where are the Hobnobs, love?' At a time like this.

She turned and I caught sight of him over her shoulder, standing with his back to us in the kitchen, barefoot in his jocks. Not that hairy after all. 'They're in the cupboard, Des.' Wearily, as if they'd been over this a million times.

Hickey contemplated the wall of identical white high-gloss units. 'Where's the cupboard, love?'

'Oh for God's sake, I'm coming.' She turned to me. 'I have

to go. Let's be fair about this: we all partied. But now the party's over. Go home, Tristram.' She closed the door in my face.

The last thing I saw was the chandelier that Hickey had stolen from Hilltop. But why would Hickey want my chandelier? A chandelier was just a big light bulb to a man like him. It was her. She had spotted it. It had caught her eye, so she had instructed him to take it down. *Strip the place of valuables while you still have a chance.* 'Keep it,' I said to the shut door. 'Keep the chandelier. It's made of glass, just like you.'

I reeled down the driveway, turned to gape at the ranch in disbelief, reeled down the driveway some more, turned to gape in disbelief some more. I reached the row of palm trees and planted myself there like one of them, still hoping that she'd relent, as if a woman like her had the capacity to relent. A woman as hard as her, a woman as brittle as her, a woman made of glass. I could see that now. I could see right through her now. Transparent as glass.

The journey back all along the blooming heather was a series of random footholds that either rose up to meet my step or pulled sharply away. It was wild mountain time. I tripped on tussocks and plunged into ruts, checking continuously over my shoulder for her slight figure, walking backwards for whole stretches, still praying that she'd come after me, that it was a test, or a trick or, well, anything. Anything other than what it had been. Go home, she had said, knowing that there was no home. That with Father dead the castle had passed to me, and through me, the perfect conduit, and was already gone, gambled away. She had worked it out before I did. She had done her sums. Hickey hadn't been doing the sums. She had been doing them for him all along.

Where are you? the Baily lighthouse flashed, majestic upon its rock.

I'm down here, the lighthouse at the tip of the East Pier flashed back. *Come get me.*

I'm trying, the Baily signalled. *I'm stuck.*

I stopped and crouched over at Michael Collins's rock. The pain was a fist clenching my heart. 'Please stop,' I asked it, 'please let go,' but pain doesn't listen, pain doesn't obey. My mind was grubbing about in tiny circles. It was digging little holes. The sheer fall of mountain into the sea might have demarcated the end of the world and the end of mine. If I hurled myself into the black depths in full view of her home, she would never look out her picture window again without seeing the precipice over which she had driven me.

Don't think I didn't give it serious consideration.

May I have a glass of water, please?

Thank you, Fergus. That's better. But not much.

And my father lying dead in his coffin with only his housekeeper to mourn him. His name was Amory but I always called him Father. He never called me Son.

And Larney not lying dead in his coffin. That was the other thing. Dead, and yet out and about.

The lighthouse beam swept the bay. *Here! I'm down here. Please come.*

Oh Jesus, I can't, I'm stuck.

I felt the tremble of an incipient mental decline, a twinge on the gossamer threads of my troubled mind, alerting me that something nasty had alighted on my web, a black and ugly article. The signal was gaining strength. Rail tracks tingle before the train comes down the line and something big was coming down mine. Then my phone started fizzling. I took it out of my pocket and stared at it. The thing was fizzling like a shorting fuse. I turned around, I don't know why. I do know why: I sensed a presence. The moors were deserted. I needed a drink. Oh God, oh Jesus, oh anyone who would listen, I needed a drink. I needed one then, and I need one now.

*

Larney was lying in wait for me in the rhododendrons. Larney had been lying in wait for me all my life. Larney is lying in wait for us all. We know not the hour. He had an absolute corker ready for me; game, set and match. He chose not to reveal his face, but instead called it out from the cover of the glossy shrubs.

'What walks upright and yet has no spine?'

I kept moving and my phone kept fizzling and the train tracks kept tingling away. Something big was coming down the line, something nasty.

He shuffled out and the whole forest shook, down to the last leaf. 'Are you not playing?' he taunted my retreating form. 'Are you not playing with the rough boys any more?'

I started to run and he limped after me, the two of us threshing through the dark. He knew those trails as well as I did. Like the backs of our hands.

'Answer me, young master: what walks upright and yet has no spine?' I could feel him wheezing down the back of my neck.

'You!' he answered when I did not. 'You have no spine.'

That wasn't the corker. He still had the corker up his sleeve.

'Wait, wait, *wait*,' he called after me, demolishing the undergrowth in his path. 'I've got a better one for you. Are you ready?'

This was the corker. And no, I wasn't ready.

'Who is Monsieur Deauville?'

I stopped dead in surprise. Larney stopped too and so did the racket. 'Where did you hear that name?'

'Every soul in Christendom knows that name. I'll make you a deal: answer the riddle and I'll let you go free.'

I took off down the hill again, listening to him, despite myself. Considering his offer. He was hard up behind me again in no time.

'But there's a catch, young master. You have to answer the riddle correctly. So here we go: who is Monsieur Deauville?'

M. Deauville is my sponsor.

I didn't speak the answer. I merely thought it. But Larney contrived to hear it all the same.

'Wrong answer, young master,' he declared with glee. 'Monsieur Deauville is not your sponsor. Now, as I said, there's a catch.'

We emerged from the gardens onto the top of the avenue. And that's when I heard it. *Tocka tocka*. The catch. I turned around. Larney was trotting across the tarmac. My eyes dropped to the source of the sound.

'Larney,' I said, and pointed. 'Your feet.'

Larney looked down at his feet. His teeny tiny little feet, not much bigger than champagne corks. He broke into a mocking jig to showcase them. *Tocka tocka, tocka tocka*. Not fingertips flying across a keyboard but the sound of hooves.

'Oh God,' I said, 'oh Jesus.'

'*Deh*,' said Larney, 'not *doh*.'

That cultured tone. He was speaking in M. Deauville's voice.

'*Deh*,' he said again, 'not *doh*.'

'What?'

'*Deh*,' he repeated, 'not *doh*.'

'I don't understand you.'

'*Deh* not *doh*, *deh* not *doh*, *deh* not *doh*.'

At that, I turned and made a run for it. No spine. He followed in close pursuit. We lashed down the hill together, going at it hell for leather, an Armageddon of noise on the dark still avenue. *Deh*-not-*doh*, *deh*-not-*doh*, *deh*-not-*doh* – his infernal chant was charged with the rhythm and momentum of a runaway train. Something big had come down the line, something huge.

The man – if he was a man – was fastened to my side, his limp now a thing of the past. The faster I ran, the faster he ran with me, the two of us belting neck and neck, a race to the bottom, until I realised that I wasn't running at all, that I was being carried, swept along, coupled to his locomotive, our limbs pistoning in sync. I screamed in the wind, screamed my head off. But he screamed louder:

'*Deh*-not-*doh*, *deh*-not-*doh*, *deh*-not-*doh*.'

The chant accelerated as we gathered velocity. We swerved around the sharp bend in the avenue, our shoulders skimming the row of tree trunks that Father had slathered in white paint as a preventative measure against traffic collisions, and this detail struck me as unspeakably piteous. White paint, God above. We were so hopelessly ill equipped, so tragically unprepared, for the calamity that lay in store for us. Then the lights of the castle appeared through the trees. I flung out both arms to steer myself towards their safety, a drowning man flailing for the shore, but to no avail. It wasn't up to me any more. I was just a passenger. We were going to shoot right past it. Larney was taking me down to the gate lodge, down to his lair.

But no. He clapped on the anchors when the avenue of whitewashed trees opened out into the courtyard. The staccato *deh*-not-*doh* expanded into a sentence, a life sentence, you might call it: 'It's not *doh*-ville, you duh head,' he said in scorn before jettisoning his load, sending me vaulting headlong across the pebbles. 'It's not *doh*-ville, you duh head, it's *deh*-ville.'

What?

I just thought the question. I couldn't speak. I couldn't breathe.

'It's not *doh*-ville,' he repeated wearily to his feeble-minded ward. He now stood directly in front of me for he could spring from one coordinate to the next like a flea. 'It's *deh*-ville. *Deh*-ville, not *doh*-ville, yes?' He sighed in exasperation at my benightedness when I failed to respond. 'Do I really need to spell it out to you?'

And then he did. He really spelled it out to me.

'Dee. Eee. Vee. Eye. El.'

The castle was droning, the lights were shining, the heavens were spinning, and the hells. I shook my head. *The Devil is my sponsor?* Again, I did not succeed in saying this. My participation in the diabolical lesson was wholly silent.

Larney clapped his black hands together. 'The penny drops.'

I crawled away across the gravel, down on all fours by then. He alighted in front of me once more. Hooves. I scrambled in the other direction. Hooves. No matter which way I turned: hooves. I looked at the hooves, and then up at his glowing eyes. He now towered sixty feet high.

You said your name was Deauville.

'Don't give me that. You heard what you wanted to hear. And look at the state of you now.'

He executed a courtly bow and I bolted past him up the terrace steps. Mrs Reid and her rosary beads were inside. When I made it to the threshold, in disbelief that this had been permitted, that I was being allowed to go home, M. Deauville – now half the size of a man – trotted forward and performed a goatish dance. *Tocka tocka, tocka tocka*. 'And you know what time it is now, young master?' he asked when the dance was complete. 'It is time to give the Devil his due.'

Final day of evidence

24 MARCH 2016

‘Mr St Lawrence, during this period, would you describe your mental state as delusional?’

Oh absolutely, Fergus. No doubt about it. Show me an Irishman who wasn't delusional during the boom. And by that same token, show me an Irishman who still is.

Priests must have been smaller in the sixteenth century. That is all that I can say. They seem so portly and plodding now, lumbering from one familiar haunt to the next in search of a little human contact, the battle having been lost and won, but they must have been smaller in the bad old days when holy war still raged. I took myself under the castle, along the winding subterranean passages to the priest hole. The last place anyone would look for a priest was in the bowels of a Protestant fortress.

The first time I had been down there – the only time I had been down there – was as a boy of nine or ten accidentally coming upon it; beneath a dresser, through a trapdoor, down some steps, then down some more steps, along a passage, around a corner, up a spur that split from the main passage, and behind a wooden panel. A boy of nine or ten could slip into the priest hole, but it barely accommodated a fully grown man. I could not stand up – the ceiling was no more than five feet high. So I sat. I slid the wooden panel shut and sat in the crumbling matter that had accumulated over the centuries on the cold stone floor. Desiccated mouse droppings and insect legs; woodlouse shells and the bristles of rats. That was my best guess, anyway. That's how I pictured my den. I had no idea what I was sitting in – I couldn't see a thing and it had no smell, not any more, other than the smell of damp stone. I clasped my knees and buried my face and I hid, Fergus, I hid.

I hid actively. It demanded intense concentration to sit tight. I actively willed myself into invisibility, erecting a force field with my mind, because the moment I stopped effacing my particles was the moment I would be found. By him. Deauville. He was on the prowl. Priests in the sixteenth century were small hunted men doing the job of a Hercules. No wonder the other team won.

There was no lighting since the sub-cellar level of the castle – including the dungeon that Hickey had so desperately wanted to see, the dungeon that all the kids had so desperately wanted to see – is not wired for power. There was no running water either unless you counted the dripping wall. The priest hole was excavated into the bedrock. What would happen, I caught myself idly wondering at one point, in the event of torrential rain? I slammed the door shut on that prospect and resumed my active hiding again. And no mobile-phone signal, it goes without saying, not through all that stone, but although I switched the phone off, it kept fizzling away. So I removed the battery. No joy. Eventually I smashed the device into smithereens and scattered the shards amongst the rest of the detritus on the floor of the hole, which was not a hole, strictly speaking. It just felt like one.

The phone contrived to somehow continue sizzling, and it quite possibly sizzles still, and may sizzle for all eternity. Frankly, that wouldn't surprise me, but frankly, nothing could. The fraud squad swept its remnants into a bag as evidence in the ongoing effort to trace M. Deauville. Best of luck with that, lads. For the record: I do not want the phone returned when your investigation comes to an end, which I believe won't be long off now.

I lasted, they tell me, three days in the priest hole. This I find hard to believe. Harder to believe than the literally unbelievable things which I know to be true. As far as I was concerned, I was banged up in there a fortnight, licking the dripping wall for sustenance. I heard Deauville's footsteps from time to time. *Tocka tocka, tocka tocka.* I can tell you a thing or two about mortal fear. My blood pounded so thickly it felt like muscle, a mass of muscle lodged in my neck pumping like a heart. *Doom, doom,* it went. I didn't move an inch. There wasn't an inch in which to move. The priest hole had no back door, no escape hatch. It was a very good place to do away with a priest. Maybe the crumbling matter on the floor was priest – another thought to slam the door on. I huddled there with my jaw locked open in panic, waiting for a *knock knock knock* on the wooden panel.

Who is the corpse in the coffin, young master?

Sweet Jesus, it's me.

For an extended portion of my confinement – and each portion was an extended one, and each one was confined – I grew convinced that Deauville was in that cell with me, as indeed he possibly was. When I moved, he moved fluidly around me to ensure we never collided. Sometimes I swiped the air to catch him out, but there is no catching the Devil out. And for one dire passage of time, one truly diabolical interlude, I became convinced that I was not under the castle hiding from Deauville, but already in Hell, and that this was it for eternity. Imagine. A stone cell too dark to see in, too small to stand in, too cold to sleep in, and not another soul to speak to ever again. The fear almost paralysed me. The recollection of it still does. *Doom, doom.* Hell.

This is where the crucifix came in. There was a crucifix nailed to the wall. It seemed when my hands first discovered it that the sheer force of my terror had caused it to materialise. I channelled many feverish thoughts into this crucifix during that period, thoughts I would never have suspected a rational mind like mine capable of producing. I have since seen the cross in the cold light of day. I requested it from my hospital bed, but when the garda took it out of the bag, I told him that he had brought the wrong one.

It was made of wood all right, a grainy greyish oak, but the face of Jesus didn't hold a candle to the one I had seen in the dark. That face had even fleetingly alchemised into that of my mother and we were together again. The face on the cross that the garda produced was rudimentary, and yet when I closed my eyes and ran my fingertips over the notches, the sweet countenance appeared once more. It just goes to show. What precisely it goes to show – what precisely the whole sorry mess goes to show – I cannot yet say, none of us can yet say, other than that it demonstrates the power of two interrelated and potentially disastrous variables regarding the impossibility of certitude on the one hand and the infinite pliability of the human imagination on the other. One can never truly know where one stands, and yet one can be adamant about that position.

I put the crucifix into the drawer of the nightstand and pushed it shut. The garda looked disappointed. I should perhaps have given the relic its day in the sun after centuries spent nailed to an underground wall, but I was done with all that Higher Power stuff. A piece of wood wasn't going to save me.

*

I woke one . . . I was going to say one morning, but there was no telling whether it was day or night in the priest hole. I thought my eyes would acclimatise, but there was nothing to acclimatise to. I couldn't see my own hand. It is terrifying to wake in true darkness. I woke because something had crashed to the ground out in the passage. This was followed by a curse, a big mucker curse – Ah fer Jaysus' sake – and then a second object clattered to the stones, betraying a level of incompetence and general clumsiness uncharacteristic of M. Deauville. Evil incarnate did not accidentally knock things over. Evil incarnate was deft.

I jumped to my feet and got a hammer blow to the crown of my head from the low ceiling. I managed to slide the wooden panel across before slumping through it and passing out.

I came around to a blaze of light. The garda flicked the torch beam at the mouth of the priest hole to establish that it was empty before speaking into his lapel. 'Lads,' he began in a high-pitched voice, then cleared his throat and started again, an octave lower: 'Lads, I think I have him.'

The torch returned to my face. 'How are you getting on there, sir?'

All authoritative now, doing his best to sound professional because he was just a big schoolboy underneath the uniform, jubilant at being the one to have found the fugitive. They're all big children, essentially, the Gardaí, and although that may sound like a criticism, I intend it as praise of the highest order. It is the greatest compliment I can pay my fellow man. The ones who were never childlike are the ones you have to watch out for. The ones who have mastered their emotional impulses. The ones who are cold. *Strip the place of valuables while you still have a chance.* The garda's face lit up at having found me and it was a heartening thing to see, and then it was a disheartening thing, because I realised that my own life was to be empty of such innocent triumphs, empty of clear-cut achievements, empty in general. No *I found him!* moments for me, because I never found things, I only lost them. Anyway. Back to the question.

'How are you getting on there, sir?'

Stunned, was the answer. Too stunned to recognise that I was stunned. I was lying on my side unable to raise my head from the stone floor. Grand, Garda, I tried to respond, but nothing came out, so I blinked up in friendship at him, wagging my tail like one of the setters to say, Boy am I glad to see you! Or at least I lay there thinking that I was wagging my tail because I was seriously confused by the wallop to the skull. But that is by the by. Now that this whole protracted palaver is coming to an end, I find that I can't keep from blurting random incidental stuff, like the bore at the cocktail party who, sensing that he is losing you, takes a firm hold of your sleeve and keeps talking, only faster.

'Are you Tristram St Lawrence?' the garda enquired for the record.

I wagged up an affirmative.

'Aidan,' he said into his lapel, 'we're going to need an ambulance.'

He helped sit me up against the wall – 'Jesus, your hands are freezing' – and unbuttoned his jacket and draped it over my shoulders. It is the moments of kindness that stand out. Perhaps because there have been so few of them. I am not asking for sympathy. I am not asking for anything. I am just saying that it is the moments of kindness that stand out.

The garda shone his torch into the priest hole. We both watched in fascination as the beam of light excavated its dimensions. So that's what it looked like. A coal bunker.

'Were you on your own down here the whole time, sir?'

'Yes,' I said, and then, 'no.' I lowered my head in embarrassment. 'Actually, I'm not entirely certain.' Tears sprang from my eyes, forming pale channels in the centuries-old grime that coated my face, as I was to discover some hours later when I met my reflection over a metal hospital sink, although it wasn't the grime that made me recoil. The grime could be washed off.

The guard patted my shoulder. 'Not to worry. We'll have you out of here in no time.' I suppose he thought I had lost my mind. And I suppose I had.

The sound of other voices reached our ears. I managed to master my tears, which was a relief to us both. The intimacy had been awkward. I have no talent for it. Neither did the guard. 'Help is on its way,' he repeated more than once, reassuring himself as much as me. Help was blundering down the passage, bumping into the objects the guard had already knocked to the floor, sending them scudding across the flagstones until they came to rest, whereupon Help tripped over them again. The garda winced. 'We're up ahead, lads,' he bawled. 'And would ye in the name of God take it handy! Those are priceless antiques.'

Back to me. 'Do you think you could get to your feet?'

I nodded.

The garda hooked my arm over his shoulder and raised me up, but the legs were dead under me so he lowered me back down. It's frightening how quickly muscles wither. It's frightening how quickly everything withers; your mind, your world, your life. 'Just relax there, Mr St Lawrence. They'll be here any second.'

'Tristram,' I offered, a name which inevitably sounds more formal to an Irish ear than *mister*. Castler, I should have told him. Me name is Castler, how's the form? A saucepan lid or shield or some such thing hit the floor spinning, a shimmering metallic crescendo at which the garda apologetically shook his head. We looked into the darkness in anticipation. I was expecting a whole SWAT team to come bursting around the corner, the amount of noise they made, securing the exits, flinging me to the ground, barking at me to keep my hands where they could see them, but in the end it was just a straggle of rank-and-file officers, cobwebs snagged on the peaks of their caps.

*

I think you probably have the rest of the details on record from here, Fergus – the ins and outs, the ups and downs, the twists and turns. There is not much more I can add. Carted out on a stretcher, squirming at the sun, bruised, ragged and shivering, smeared in grime. I've been found in worse states. It used to be the order of the day. And then M. Deauville rescued me and I owed him my life. The ambulance was waiting in the courtyard. So was Mrs Reid. I heard her before I saw her. All I could see was the sky.

'Is he alive, Guard? Oh God, tell me he's alive!'

Her face projected above me as if peering into my pram. Her eyes shot to the top of my head and she covered her mouth with her hand. The rosary beads were still threaded through her fingers. 'Sacred Heart of Jesus,' she whispered.

'What?' I touched my head but found nothing amiss – no dent, no blood, no crack. 'What is it, Mrs Reid? What's wrong with my head?'

Mrs Reid lowered her eyes to look into mine. 'Nothing, pet,' she reassured me, and squeezed my freezing hand for emphasis. 'There's nothing wrong with your head. There is not a thing in the world wrong with your head, do you hear me?' Then she started to cry.

'I'm sorry, Mrs Reid.'

'I thought you were dead, love.'

'That was another Tristram St Lawrence.'

She looked up at the garda through her tears. 'He's not a bad boy,' she petitioned him, still clutching my hand. 'He's not a bad boy. He's just . . . well, look at him, Guard. Sure you can see yourself. He's very troubled.'

*

Some hours later, I met my reflection in a mirror over a metal hospital sink. It wasn't the sight of my chimney-sweep face that made me recoil. It was my hair. It had turned white, and not a gleaming helmet of silver like Father's, but chalky white. Just like that, in a matter of days. Look at me. I'm an old man. All washed up. Barely forty.

The garda had coffee waiting for me in a polystyrene cup. 'Not the standard you're used to, I'm afraid,' he apologised as he handed it over. I smiled. Nobody knows what I'm used to.

'So what are the charges?' I finally asked when he began making noises about taking his leave. The doctors wanted to keep me in overnight for observation. The guard could hardly slap on the cuffs there and then.

He had been about to place his hat on his head but he lowered it and frowned. 'The charges?'

'Yes. What have I been arrested for?'

'You haven't been arrested, Mr St Lawrence. Your housekeeper reported you as a missing person. And now you're found.'

'I see. So when am I going to be charged?'

'With what?'

'I don't know yet. That's why I'm asking you. Economic treason?'

'That isn't a crime.'

'Isn't it?'

The garda put his hat on. 'I don't think so. But I can check?'

'Would you mind?'

He left the room and I waited for him to get back to me. I'm still waiting. Everyone is still waiting. That was eight years ago now.

‘Thank you for your time, Mr St Lawrence. That concludes matters.’

Do you think? Not for me it doesn't. Nothing can conclude matters for me. I figured that while I'm here, Fergus – while I am back in the country for this brief spell to answer your questions – I might as well pay a visit to the castle before departing these shores again. See what became of it sort of thing. It could be decades before I return again, if I ever return at all. I have no idea who even owns it any more, or whether anyone even owns it. It may languish still in that holding pen created by the Irish State for all I know, that portfolio of unsaleable property generated by the doom – I mean, the boom; impounded like a stray in the dogs' home begging passers-by to take pity on it. Good home wanted for a good home. One careless owner. I am afraid to ask. I am afraid to ask what became of my castle. Why am I smiling? Because I'm sad. Because it's sad. Because I don't know what else to do with my big stupid mouth.

It was a dry, brisk, bright afternoon when I finished giving my evidence. I recounted the exchange with the garda in the hospital ('Pray charge you with what, noble sir?' 'Why, you jackanapes, with economic treason!') and that was the end of that. The stage hook appeared to haul me off. A clerk led me out and a cavity opened within. I was yesterday's man.

I did not immediately leave the court building but instead sat brooding on the headmaster's bench in the public area. There was a clue I must have neglected to impart, a damning detail to nail the case once and for all and finally make someone pay, but no matter how I wracked my brains I could not put my finger on what that incriminating particular might be.

I took out my phone and searched for the next available flight back to Mumbai. There was nothing until the following evening. It was Easter and the airlines were booked out. A whole afternoon to kill and no notion of how to kill it. The Devil makes work for idle hands. For trembling ones too, for hands with the DTs. I booked a room in an airport hotel.

I set off on foot up the Quays along the silver Liffey. *riverrun, past Eve and Adam's, from swerve of shore to bend of bay, brings us by a commodius vicus of recirculation back to Howth Castle and Environs.* Do you remember? It used to be written on the tenner back when we still had our own currency.

On O'Connell Street preparations were afoot outside the GPO for the celebration of the Centenary of the Easter Rising. One hundred years since the Proclamation of the Irish Republic and our sovereignty had been hocked. It was Holy Thursday and the panic-drinking was already under way, what with the pubs shutting to mark Good Friday. It would get messy on the streets of Dublin that night.

I caught a northbound train. In case you haven't already rumbled me, I am unable to drive. I've gotten through my whole life making that admission to no one. I may as well get everything off my chest while I'm on a roll. The Dart passed Hickey's construction graveyard before pulling into the station. I could hardly believe my eyes. It was all still there: the tombstone blocks with their gaping doorways, the building rubble, even the forlorn tower crane, untouched except by vandals and the elements. The Claremont site had been neither levelled nor completed but simply abandoned, stranded as it had stood the day all the money ran out, a war memorial. The show apartments were occupied but already betraying symptoms of their slipshod construction: cracks running the length of the façade, mossy stains weeping from the gutters, the bloom of rust beneath each balcony. In place of the Maserati carrying a surfboard was a neon Dyno-Rod van, its crew rodding the sewers.

Access was still via the construction gate, the grand entrance depicted on the sales brochures having failed, like everything else, to materialise. Hickey's Portakabin was still there, crushed like a can of Coke, and my paint-spattered chair was no doubt in the vicinity had I the heart to look; I did not. The thirteen storeys of his eleven-storey hotel were draped in tattered netting like a famine refugee. I keep saying it was Hickey's hotel, but it was mine too. I was equally responsible, equally irresponsible. *Scum* was spray-painted at periodic intervals along the perimeter hoarding.

I crossed the road to the ribbed columns of the castle entrance. *Sir Tristram has passencore rearrived.*

The iron gates were open. That threw me. I had presumed I'd find them chained shut, that I'd have to scramble over the orchard wall. I passed between the pillars and braced myself for the trip-trap crabwalk of Larney. My blood fizzed like anaphylaxis. It ionised in my veins.

Nothing. Still as a rock pool. As chilly and silent too. I pushed my way through the glossy shrubbery to the glade in which the gate lodge stood. Windows were broken and roof slates missing. A buddleia sprouted from the chimney stack and the garden was a poisonous ragwort thatch. I hadn't laid eyes on the place since my childhood, about a thousand years before, and although I had been dragging my weary carcass around ever since, I did not think I could find the strength to drag it much further. The gatekeeper's cottage was a derelict wreck and so was I.

Something was coming over me. It was taking hold. I had never known exhaustion like it. I laboured up the avenue in search of Mrs Reid. I had no right to expect to find her sitting at her kitchen table as if nothing had changed, but I did, and on some level I still do. For a full eight years, the figure of Mrs Reid had been sitting at her kitchen table in my mind's eye, a refuge for my thoughts when a refuge was needed, which was often, a night light during the many bad dreams. The mind needs to preserve chambers of sanctuary and she was mine. But her net curtains were torn and the padlock clamping her door shut had streaked the paintwork with rust. I am ashamed to say that I have no idea what became of Mrs Reid. It did not occur to me that she would be evicted upon the seizure of my assets. Never thinking of others; that was me all over then. All of me, all over then.

Equally, and oppositely, I did not expect to find M. Deauville's brass plaque, his tarnished calling card, still on display by the front door, but then, who was left to remove it? Not a soul. The castle was gaunt and deserted. They say it has a ghost now. I would like to join him. At times I think I already have.

My key did not fit in the lock. That was a kick in the teeth.

I went around the back. The castle was boarded up like the rest of the country. A carpet of bindweed had smothered the sunken gardens. I paused at the tradesman's entrance but continued around to the vandal's entrance and climbed through that instead, seeing as I was the biggest vandal of them all. They had pulled off the plywood boards and broken the catch on a sash window. Cider cans littered the parquet floor like autumn leaves.

The interior was suspended in gloom. I flicked a light switch. The power had been disconnected. It hardly mattered. I didn't need lights. There was nothing left to bump into. The furniture had been removed. I made my way along the corridor, throwing open door after door. The silverware, the china, the paintings, the books in the library, the bookcases themselves: gone. The marble fireplace bearing the family motto had been prised from the great hall, exposing an aghast and toothless mouth. I gaped at it and it gaped back. *Qui Panse*. Not any more. Strip the place of valuables, Edel had warned me. Why am I still banging on about her? No one is listening any more.

In the rhododendron gardens, the invasive common species had prevailed. Father had culled the ponticums annually, identifying them by marking their barks with a slather from his pot of white paint while they were in flower, but the collection had been left unattended for so many years that the specimen varieties had been choked. I closed my eyes and raised my face. Spring sunlight shimmered down on me through a canopy of translucent new leaves. It was on a sunshot day in early summer that I had found Edel here, or she had found me, and all these years later I could still see her picking her way through the showy blossoms like a woodland fawn. The garden path up which she led me had long since been swallowed by briars. I would never find that dell of bliss again, if I ever really found it in the first place. She is up in the house on the edge of the moors, I am told, still trying to make the sums add up. Hickey signed it over to her and then she threw him out. The last I heard he was driving a taxi.

I was thinking of them both when the rambler joined me. 'Nice old pile, isn't it?' he remarked. I turned to him but he kept his gaze on the castle, which, when I contemplated it through his eyes, framed by the boughs of spring blossom, could have been an illustration from a child's storybook, a fairytale with a prince and a princess and a wicked elf. 'Desperately sad, really, when you think about it,' the rambler continued. 'The first St Lawrence, Sir Amoricus, was a descendant of Sir Tristram, a knight of the Round Table, or so it is alleged. And now it has all come to such an undignified end . . .'

Ah, a local historian. God preserve me from local historians. The things they have written about our family. My door is open to real historians, but a local historian is merely a nosy local by another name. This one carried with him an upturned golf club, and he leaned his weight on its moulded head, a man who was not yet ready to admit to the world that he required a walking stick to get about. 'Continuous succession to the Barony of Howth remained in the direct male line from 1177. But the final son was a bit . . .' The local historian spun his finger by the side of his head to indicate a churning brain. 'A bit funny. You know yourself.'

I did.

'A tragedy, really. He died recently.'

'Did he?'

'Yes. Overdosed in an airport hotel.'

'When?'

'Soon. Tonight.' The historian checked his watch. 'It is happening as we speak.'

It took me an age to absorb this information. An age, an age. I am still grappling with it. I am floundering to this day. I looked to the historian. 'Can't anyone save him?'

'Like who? There is no one. He has no one left. The hotel cleaners will find his body in the morning.'

'But he's not in the hotel room. He's here. He's with us.'

The historian shook his head. 'He couldn't bring himself to make the journey home when it came down to it. Couldn't face up to witnessing the damage he'd done, so he went straight to the hotel instead. Locked himself into the room, switched off his phone, knocked back a jar of sleeping pills with the contents of the minibar. A coward right to the bitter end.'

The historian reached forward and used the vulcanised

handle of the golf club to raise the shoot of bramble that strayed across our path and hook it back on itself. I marvelled at the offhandedness of this gesture under the circumstances. A man was dying, a young one, barely forty. 'The benighted fool had squandered everything, you see. Every last farthing and more besides. What past generations had laboured to create, destroyed just like that.' The historian clicked his fingers. 'A whole way of life gone. He racked up a debt that can never be settled. But a debt must be settled, mustn't it? Isn't that the nature of a debt?'

I lowered my head in shame and noticed that the historian had etched an eye in the earth with the handle of the club. I took a step back. 'He had notions, the young master. Thought he could make millions overnight. They all thought they could make millions overnight. But that's the problem with setting yourself up as a little god. You invite the other fella in. Don't you?'

'Don't you?' the historian persisted when I failed to answer.

'Yes,' I admitted.

'Desperate, the devastation they wreaked. It is nothing short of diabolic.'

At this word, the birds stopped. The secret creatures in the undergrowth stopped. The very air, I tell you, stopped. I looked up. The historian and I stood alone on a spotlit stage, waiting to say our lines. We had been waiting to say them for years.

'I know who you are,' he said softly.

'That was another Tristram St Lawrence.'

'No. That was you.'

'I thought I was dead.'

'You are now. The family line has come to an end.'

Down the hill, where the whitewashed trees opened onto the expanse of gravel, the castle had begun to keen. The historian lowered his head as a mark of respect. Bearing this news had afforded him no pleasure. If one thing stands out about my miserable tale, it is this: that it has no winners.

The historian squinted at the setting sun. I was stricken by an overwhelming sense of things coming to an end, of the torch being passed on, or not passed on, just extinguished. 'It's getting late,' he told me, barely telling me at all. 'It is time to leave the garden.'

I found myself at a loss and looked about frantically. Quite what I was searching for, exactly, I still do not know, and I possibly never will know, but I felt certain that I was forgetting something, that I was leaving some critical belonging behind, some vital possession without which everything, everything, everything would go awry. I appealed to the historian. 'Now, you mean?' I asked him, panic surging up my throat. *Doom, doom* went my heart. 'Do you mean we're leaving now?'

'Yes, now, I'm afraid.'

I was afraid too. Afraid and unprepared. I glanced up. The sky was rapidly dimming.

He guided me to the exit – or was it the entrance, and if so, the entrance to what? – and he extended a crooked hand when we reached the crooked stile. 'After you,' he said, but I refused to move, just dug in like a petrified animal. *Doom, doom.* 'What about my mother?' it occurred to me in a wild flash of hope. 'Does this mean I'll see my mother again? Will my mother be waiting for me there?'

'Your *mother*?' The historian rolled his eyes in derision. 'No, you fool, of course not.' Whereupon my back buckled into a crooked spine and I was propelled by force through the stile. When we were both on the other side I heard it, heard them.

Tocka tocka.

Deauville had come to collect. A debt must be settled. That

is the nature of a debt. The Devil linked my arm and we began the descent. I closed my eyes but my eyes would not close. They would not close. I tried and tried. I'll keep trying. I must keep trying. I can only keep trying. I am afraid of what I will see.

I wish to thank the Arts Council of Ireland, An Chomhairle Ealaíon, for their generous financial support during the writing of this novel.